"Breier serves up a sweet and sour and ultimately redemptive delight of a mystery, redolent of '80s Florida and adolescence in all its sinister glory. I devoured it."
—**Kelly Link, author of** *Magic for Beginners* **and** *Get in Trouble*

"*Sinkhole* is a thought-provoking, highly atmospheric, and immensely readable debut about growing pains and facing the truths we'd rather run from. Breier summons both the '80s and Central Florida to great effect."
—**Jonathan Evison, New York Times Bestselling Author of** *Small World*

"Surprising and affecting, it's a terrifically entertaining exploration of emotional abuse and the cost of leaving your problems behind."
—**Jeff Somers, author of** *The Electric Church*

"Equal parts *Freaks and Geeks*, *The Bad Seed* and *Welcome to the Dollhouse*. I declined invitations to go out while I downed it in big gulps because I had to know what happened next."
—**Liz Mason, manager of Quimby's Bookstore (Chicago)**

"...sticky, pre-digital, late 20th-century teenage attachments will suck you into a Central Florida liberally seasoned with '80s deep cuts."
—**Ayun Halliday, author of** *No Touch Monkey!*

"Lies open up like sinkholes in Davida G. Breier's compelling and nostalgic debut. Little fibs widen into gaping manipulations that swallow entire lives and turn the pages. Filled with spot-on nods to '80s culture, which rekindle the teen angst in us all, the truth could be a lifeline if these characters are able to climb out of what they lost in their youth."
—**Gregg Wilhelm, Director, Mason Creative Writing, George Mason University**

"...delivers an astounding addition to coming-of-age stories. This riveting homage to the '80s features a love letter to Wild Florida, a part of the state very few tourists and residents experience. Told with the same passionate love of the land that captivates fans of James Lee Burke, *Sinkhole* transports readers to the noisy, humid, bug-ridden, and wondrously beautiful inland Florida."
—Meredith Morris-Babb, former Director,
University Press of Florida

"Both haunting and haunted, *Sinkhole* exposes a universal truth that childhood is complicated and high school can be both formative and devastating. Those experiences have lasting, powerful, and profound ramifications. What Breier reveals so masterfully in her debut novel is a narrative filled with self-doubt, unseen possibilities, and the hope and freedom of recognizing, finally, the face looking back at you in the mirror."
—Brad Bertelli, author of
The Florida Keys Skunk Ape Files
and *A Local's Guide to Bloodline*

"Sentence by sentence, the ground begins to give way in this marvelous tale."
—Rafael Alvarez, author of the *Orlo & Leini* stories
and *The Wire: Truth Be Told*, and screenwriter
for HBO-TV's *The Wire*

"*Sinkhole* sucked me in and swirled me through page after page of guilty pleasures and hard-won insights from intimately relatable characters. A mature first work—more, please!"
—Susan Gore, PhD, Board President,
LGBTQ Resource Center, Gulfport Public Library

"I was riveted by every page and the plot twists kept me guessing. The characters are authentic and the dialog real. A brilliant debut novel with a perfect alchemy of people, plot, and place."
—Marianne C. Bohr, author of *Gap Year Girl*

Cover photograph: "Lake Istokpoga" by Davida G. Breier.
Cover and book design by Alex Dimeff.

Library of Congress Cataloging-in-Publication Data

Names: Breier, Davida Gypsy, author.
Title: Sinkhole : a novel / Davida G. Breier.
Description: New Orleans, Louisiana : University of New Orleans Press,
     [2022]
Identifiers: LCCN 2021031083 (print) | LCCN 2021031084 (ebook) | ISBN
     9781608012305 (paperback ; acid-free paper) | ISBN 9781608012312 (ebook)

Subjects: GSAFD: Suspense fiction. | LCGFT: Thrillers (Fiction)
Classification: LCC PS3602.R4455 S56 2022 (print) | LCC PS3602.R4455
     (ebook) | DDC 813/.6--dc23
LC record available at https://lccn.loc.gov/2021031083
LC ebook record available at https://lccn.loc.gov/2021031084

Printed in the United States of America on acid-free paper.

UNIVERSITY OF NEW ORLEANS PRESS
2000 Lakeshore Drive
New Orleans, Louisiana 70148
unopress.org

SINKHOLE

A NOVEL

DAVIDA G. BREIER

UNIVERSITY OF NEW ORLEANS PRESS

For Jan, Earl, Patrick, and Garnet

"The companions of our childhood always possess a certain power over our minds which hardly any later friend can obtain."
—Mary Wollstonecraft Shelley, *Frankenstein*

"Perhaps the rare and simple pleasure of being seen for what one is compensates for the misery of being it."
—Margaret Drabble, *A Summer Bird-Cage*

CHAPTER I

PRESENT - JUNE 2001

When I was eighteen, I killed my best friend.

It's all I can think about as I start my car. I should be thinking about my mother, who is lying in a hospital bed. I should be a better person. A good person wouldn't be fumbling for justifications, trying to hide.

My brother Michael called last night. We barely speak. He said I should probably come home. He probably didn't mean to use the word "probably" because his meaning was absolute. I could hear the accusations without him making them. His civility was cutting. When he said my name, the "M" in "Michelle" was so crisp and formal.

I considered making another excuse about why I couldn't be there and living with the consequences. My whole life has been spent living with the consequences.

Instead, I'm wiping the dew off my car windows and throwing a grocery bag onto the backseat. I'm buzzing inside, the snap-crackle of a night spent trying to drown out the shouting in my head. Voices telling me what I should and shouldn't do and what I should have done. I know I must have slept at some point, but it wasn't enough to face driving to fucking Florida. To face going home.

I've avoided Central Florida for fifteen years. That's not true. I can't even state simple facts without lying. I've avoided who I was—who I am—for fifteen years. Florida got all mixed up in the blame. I left and never went back. I couldn't go back. I got what I wanted and left everyone behind. My escape became a prison.

Home. I think of that word and feel a piece of newspaper rasping against my fingertips, fluttering to the ground. I hear a phone receiver slamming down. I see "I'm scared" scrawled against the inside of my eyelids when I close them. I hear, "...out of our lives forever." I've blocked those thoughts, those words, for years. My only peace has been oblivion. I want to stay there. In my head, home isn't a safe place.

Holidays and birthdays came and went. It started with the small lie of, "I can't miss school," and that lie bloomed into "I can't get anyone to cover my shift" and "my boss won't give me the time off." The tried-and-true lies of familial avoidance. After a while, they quit asking. My mother still calls, and sometimes I can't bring myself to answer. When we do talk, we never *say* anything. We pretend. We stay on script. My job, her job, my brother's job, who died, and the weather. My brother stopped calling years ago. They both know I am lying.

I don't know why Michael asked me to come home. I know he doesn't really want me there. They are better off without me. But then I think of Gladys A. Anderson.

I'm probably too late anyway.

My name is Michelle A. Miller. The *A* is for Ann, but I've never been told why. Maybe they thought the *M*s needed something in the middle, like the pivot in a seesaw. Like it would balance me. My name should be an immutable part of who I am, but it isn't. At work, I call myself Anne.

Ann Miller, the actress, was born Johnnie Lucille Collier. When people are called something else, it is usually to hide from who they were. I work in the medical records department at a hospital in suburban Atlanta. I'm single. I live by myself. No children and no family history of cancer. I am not pregnant or on any medications. My pain level is between one and two, physically speaking. My emergency contact is a TV character with a fake phone number.

These are the kinds of personal history questions I stare at all day long. Furthermore, I don't have a cat, and I drive an anonymous-looking tan 1992 Ford Escort. These are reasonably truthful, utterly meaningless facts.

As I read and file intake forms, I always wonder about the people. What do all the boxes of information represent? Is "home" an address or a place? Did anyone care for the person after the car accident? What if everything on the forms is a lie? When work is quiet, sometimes I fill out the forms for myself, creating new lives each time.

Each one is as true as my employment application. I don't like who I am, so I hide and pretend in order to get through the day. I've always wondered if my father took part of me with him when he died. Or if I would always have been like this.

When I was a child, I used to tell people my father was killed by a giant snake. Two lies and a truth. He did die because of a snake, but it wasn't very big, and it didn't kill him. A baby corn snake had crawled inside his car and decided to explore while he was driving. He freaked out and lost control of the car. A melaleuca tree killed my father.

The giant snake made his death sound heroic instead of meaningless. I would pretend that the snake had never crawled into his car or that I'd stepped on its egg, and it was never born. I would imagine a perfect life, with dad radiating at its center. At eight, I learned that little, harmless things could destroy everything without sense or reason.

The Florida Highway Patrol found my father in the waning moments of his life, clutching the tiny snake, screaming that it had killed him. They could have avoided putting that detail in the report, spared us knowing, but they didn't. It was one of those stories that ended up as yet one more Florida punchline. A story to be passed around so people can laugh at death instead of fear it.

My mother was unhappy with the obituary the *Sebring Herald* published based on the police report. It sounded like every other obit the paper ran, except for the snake. It read more like the snake's obituary.

"Walker Frances Miller died on Wednesday, September 22, 1976, in a freak car accident along State Road 70, east of Okeechobee. Mr. Miller had been distracted by a juvenile corn snake, a common nonvenomous reptile native to Central Florida, causing him to run off the road. He is survived by his wife of 10 years, Penelope (Penny) Dean Miller; his stepson, Michael John Dean (12); and daughter, Michelle Ann Miller (8). He was 41 years old."

Details like name, age, occupation, and surviving relatives were fill-in-the-blanks on death's *Mad Libs*. People sounded like they had always been corpses. Mom showed up at the small newspaper office and overwhelmed the editor. She demanded that they allow her to write a proper obituary for Dad. Her grief was still fierce and alive, and it showed in her work. Once he read what she'd written, he agreed to publish it. It may have been a slow news day.

Mom wrote about Dad as he had lived, about his favorite beer and his irrational hatred of avocados. She talked about him as a father and a husband. She described him as a man who rooted for the castaways to get off the island, knowing full well the show would be over if they did. Mom included a photo of him from when he had long, curly hair and a mustache. He was clean-shaven and balding when he died. Few people remembered he had ever had that much hair. It was my hair. He looked young and vibrant like he had just told a joke and was patiently waiting for you to get it.

People who didn't know my father suddenly missed him. People who had laughed at how he'd died felt guilty. And there was no mention of the snake. Mom made his death have meaning instead of being a punchline.

Dad provided my mother with an accidental vocation. After her version of the obit ran, people called the newspaper office asking for the person who wrote about the snake-accident guy—that kind of accident didn't happen in Florida as often as you might think—and people started asking my mother for help when they lost family members and friends. Especially when the dead guy was a bastard. My mother could make almost anyone sound respectable on a Sunday. Eventually, the newspaper asked if she wanted a job. There were a lot of old people in Florida, so obits were a good racket. Especially when you could get relatives to pay for photos and a few extra column inches to assuage their guilt for not coming to visit more often.

People told my mother their stories, and she created loving fictions for the dead. She made people sound like they lived as they'd always dreamed of living. She knew how to describe a rich and colorful life in three inches. She helped people who had almost faded out of existence come alive again. She understood grief. She often provided more closure than the funeral services. But, after her obit for Dad ran, we never talked about him or what had happened. We— she, my brother, and I—lacked what she could somehow give to other people.

Most of the obits were as truthful as my story about my father having been killed by a giant snake, but they were the truths people wanted to read and remember. Better yet, people paid to read them, to clip them and frame them next to photos that captured idealized moments at Sears Portrait Studios. Paid to remember things as they wanted them to be, not as they were. Memory can be bribed like that.

As I drive out to the highway, I think, "These are relatively safe memories. I can almost cope with these memories." The night voices are shrill and unreasonable, but the day voices aren't as bad. The irony that my father's death and obituaries are safe memories isn't lost on me. The bittersweet ache for my father has always been there. Memories of him, the few that I have, are always comforting.

I can feel other, more dangerous memories pounding to be let out. They are the ones that sneak through in the middle of the night and when certain songs come on the radio. I still can hear Sissy's laughter. I have fought to keep these memories contained for years.

The weight of the drive hits me as I pull onto I-75. I have at least seven, more like eight, hours of driving ahead of me. I crank the driver's side window all the way down, and sultry air fills the car. The sun starts rising hard and fast.

CHAPTER 2
PAST - SEPTEMBER 1984

"Chelle, do you think there's a nice way to say 'bigamy' that won't upset anyone?" my mother asked from the small Formica table that served as her desk.

I knew she was working on the obit for Purcell "Pucky" Matlock. This was a tough one. Two Mrs. Matlocks showed up at the hospital after Mr. Matlock's forklift accident. Apparently, his work called wife #1, and the hospital called wife #2. The hospital had him stabilized in intensive care, but seeing his wives together sent him straight to the cardiac care unit. He'd split his time between the two houses by telling his wives he was a long-haul truck driver. He was really a forklift driver for a construction company in Avon Park.

I thumbed through one of the multiple thesauruses we kept on hand and began searching for words. My childhood was filled with soothing synonyms.

"How about 'passionate about life'?" I suggested.

"Hmmm."

"Generously amorous?" I said.

"I guess I should find out which wife is paying for the obit first."

My mother, brother, and I lived in Paradise Acres in Lorida, Florida. Like most places with "Paradise" in the name, it was nothing of the sort. We also had a lot of "Estates" in our area. Orange Grove Estates and Coral Ridge Estates were trailer parks. Their names were the nicest things about them.

Paradise Acres was a small mobile home community, one of the few not specified as adults only. There was always a clear distinction that Paradise Acres was *not* a trailer park. We were also not a resort mobile home community, complete with golf carts and swimming pools. Those were for the rich poor people.

Nearby Coral Ridge Estates had as much coral as we had paradise. They were the kind of trailer park with exposed cinderblocks holding the trailers aloft. There was a pecking order to trailer parks, and covering the wheels somehow marked a better class of mobile home dwellers. Having a car, boat, or golf cart told the world you were enjoying an unfettered lifestyle on your own terms. There were obviously "good" and "bad" prefab homes, and ours was the relatively okay kind.

Our community had year-round residents, a few doublewides, cramped landscaping, fake potted flowers, and aggressively active, overly tanned Floridians. The "Acres" part of the name also overstated the situation. The forty mobile homes were located on about two acres, with an unpaved access road leading to two dead-end streets.

We lived just off Route 98, near Lake Istokpoga. Lorida proper existed along a one-mile stretch of Route 98 between Cowhouse Road and Arbuckle Creek Road. Lorida had a post office, bait stores, a few bars, a drive-through liquor store, several churches, lots of American flags, tin roofs, and not a single stoplight. The abundance of booze and churches told you all you needed to know: people in Lorida believed in other, better realities.

Lorida was one of those towns that exist so people have something to drive through on the way to somewhere else. Most of the time, people were headed to Sebring for the races, or they'd gotten lost on the way to Orlando. We were between I-75 and I-95, below Lake Kissimmee and above Lake Okeechobee. This area of Florida was something of a netherworld, a geographic purgatory between Mickey Mouse and *Miami Vice*. The older I got, the smaller the town got, as if we were growing in opposition.

Lorida was an old farming community, once home to Florida cowboys. According to my seventh grade history teacher, Lorida was originally known as Sunnyland. The town postmaster had spent time in Cuba, and she thought that the Spanish word *Florida*, which meant full of flowers, was a lovely name for a place. She dropped the F, and Sunnyland became Lorida in 1937. It didn't matter; people usually assumed the F fell off the sign. There were still cows and orchards, but they weren't enough to sustain a place like this.

Later, the area was packaged and sold as suburbs, but the families never really came. There were plenty of subdivisions and cul-de-sacs with tropical-sounding names, derelict for-sale signs, unpaved roads, and vacant lots. The ever-opportunistic developers decided old people loved Florida and created golf courses and fifty-five-plus communities, only the people who came died out, and their kids didn't want to be stuck in a backwater. Florida's history and future were perpetually shaped by people who knew how to package it for sale. The rest of us were stuck here.

Nearby Sebring fared better than Lorida. They had the highway and the Sebring Raceway. People had a reason to go to Sebring or at least stop there. Sebring had a Publix. Lorida had about nine hundred people to Sebring's ten thousand. I went to high school in Sebring.

CHAPTER 3
PAST - OCTOBER 1984

I was waiting for the after-school activities bus one afternoon when everything changed. I was sitting under the awning at the front of the school, leaning against a pole with a book in my lap. I was tired from swim practice. Bright white shoes and bare ankles approached and then stopped in front of me. I looked up and was eye level with a pair of sky-blue plaid shorts.

"I've got something better you can do while you are down there," said a ruddy-faced boy. As if the comment wasn't enough, he then pointed at his crotch and smiled. His vulgar attitude seemed at odds with the soft pastels he wore.

The comment was so disgusting it wasn't worth acknowledging. I gritted my teeth and ignored him, trying to focus on the reading assignment for Mr. Parrish's history class. The boy started to say something else when a reedy voice interrupted.

"Hey, Duane, so how *is* that gherkin hangin'?" I squinted up, and there was a short, stocky girl challenging him.

"Fuck you, Cecilia."

What she'd said worked because he left with a visible blush rising on his already reddened cheeks.

"Thanks," I said as I stood up.

"No problem," the girl said. "He's a total pervert." She spoke like she was wearing braces or a retainer, but I couldn't see anything on her teeth.

She came closer to me, and we began to size each other up in that way girls do. She had crimped dark hair with uneven highlights—was it Sun In?—and her bangs looked like a wave preparing to crest and break. She was deliberately tanned, not farm tanned. Her skirt was tight against fleshy thighs, and she was wearing a Benetton top. From her clothes and attitude, I assumed she was one of the rich kids. Her eyes were a dull brown color, but they were intense. They were outlined in blue with heavy black mascara. She smelled like fake strawberries.

There was something different about her. She was like one of those lenticular pictures of Jesus, looking pretty from one angle and homely from another. I wondered what she thought about me.

"What was that about?" I asked. "I mean, that was some verbal kryptonite."

"We went to middle school together. On a field trip to the Fort Pierce Inlet, he was fucking around on the jetty, showing off, and he fell into the water and completely freaked out. He'd gotten tangled in some seaweed and netting or something." The girl started laughing and lowered her voice conspiratorially. "He always kept his shorts tied loose so he could flash a few of his would-be pubes. He called the fluff his 'treasure trail.' *As if.* He started screaming that something had gotten ahold of him, and he jerked free of the shorts. He flailed his way to shore, and when he got there, he was completely naked. He cupped his hands over his doo-dad, but not before we all had a real good look. It was itty-bitty-teeny-tiny. Like a baby's. Seriously, there was nothing there to hide."

While she told her story, she mimicked his flailing and used her thumb to indicate his tiny penis. She was really funny.

I started laughing. "He's such an asshole. Thanks for doing that."

We smiled at each other for a minute, and before it got awkward, I said, "I'm Michelle." I wasn't sure what else I should say about myself, but my name seemed the best place to start.

"I'm Cecilia, but my friends call me Sissy," she said.

Already she had told me three lies.

The next day, I saw Sissy on my way to the bus lanes. I realized later she might have been waiting for me. When she saw me, she

waved and took off her headphones. She fiddled with the buttons
on her Walkman as we talked.

"Do you like Wham!?" she asked.

"A bit. I mean, when I hear them on the radio. I don't have any
tapes." It felt like a lame answer.

She started telling me about seeing INXS in concert in St. Peters-
burg over the summer. I really wanted to talk to her, but I didn't
want to have to call and tell my mother I missed the bus.

"I'm *really* sorry; I have to catch my bus." I tried to sound light and
friendly, like someone on a TV show talking to a classmate. It was
a casual conversation, only it wasn't. I had hoped that maybe this
year would be different, better than last year, but I hadn't made any
new friends yet. I wanted her to like me, and I didn't know why. I
was afraid she would think I didn't want to talk to her.

"Cool. See ya later," Sissy said, looking a little annoyed. Or maybe
she was just disappointed. It was hard to tell.

I replayed the conversation over and over on the bus ride home.
Did I sound friendly? Normal? Did I say the right things?

The next day she handed me a cassette tape when we ran into
each other between classes. Sissy had made me a tape of Wham!,
Kenny Loggins, Sade, Miami Sound Machine, Billy Ocean, and
more. I listened to it that night in my room on my brother's old
boombox. I was touched. No one had ever made me a mixtape before. She had included all the song names and written "Sissy's Mix
for Michelle" in a curly script on the spine.

I didn't have any real music of my own. Sometimes I taped songs
off the radio. I tended to listen to what my mom listened to, but
it wasn't cool to like the Bee Gees, Neil Diamond, or Elton John.
James Brown was awesome, but no one at school listened to him.
My brother wasn't as into music as he was cars. It seemed like
having a favorite band was a mandatory part of growing up, but I
wasn't sure who I should like.

Most of the kids at school identified with something – sports,
movies, clothes, or music. They built identities around teams, actors,
brands, and bands. I loved television, but that was somehow differ-

ent, maybe because it was free. You didn't have to make an effort to watch TV. There was no street cred in having never missed an episode of *Scarecrow and Mrs. King*. No one cared that you knew who voiced Charlie. My identity was built around a fuzzy UHF signal.

Now, though, I finally had some music of my own, thanks to Sissy. I listened to the tape three times that night.

I found Sissy near her locker the next day. I had written her a thank you note. It was folded into a complicated rectangle with an arrow directing her where to pull it open. I went to hand it to her, and I don't know why, but I got shy. I awkwardly pushed it at her and rushed off to class. I couldn't manage fake casual. Everything felt too important.

I was in eleventh grade at Ocean Breezes High School, but I hadn't met Sissy before. There were about two hundred kids in each grade, so it was easy to get lost in the crowd. I had been lost for a long time. I had friends and went to birthday parties when I was in grade school, but that started petering out in junior high, especially after my best friend Diana moved. I found making new friends difficult. Diana and I were inseparable for two years, and then suddenly she was gone. She didn't know where they would be living, so she couldn't give me her address. But she knew mine, and I never heard from her again. I missed not only Diana but that feeling of belonging her friendship gave me.

High school felt so isolating. I had a few friends and some acquaintances, but no one I was close with. It didn't help that only a handful of kids lived in Lorida. None of my friends lived nearby. Most were from Sebring and the surrounding areas. There were no kids my age at the mobile home park. At school, I spoke to people I knew, but I didn't go to sleepovers, and I certainly didn't go on dates. I swam, watched TV, and hung out at home with my mother and brother.

Then suddenly I had a best friend, and everything changed.

CHAPTER 4
PRESENT - JUNE 2001

I make it as far as Macon before I need to pee. I still have about seven hours to go. I pull off I-475 and find a Hardee's so I can use the restroom and order a biscuit and Mello Yello.

On a normal Thursday morning, I would be driving to work right now. Only it isn't a normal Thursday. I had been suspended at work for lying and forging documents. The patient, Gladys Anderson, F/58, was dead, and I was probably going to lose my job. I didn't mean to become a medical records clerk. I didn't even mean to come to Atlanta. I drifted there, like human jetsam.

My T-shirt is clinging to me as I get back in the car. It is already eighty-eight degrees, according to the truck stop sign. The air is oppressive. My brain is oppressive. The air conditioning in the Escort wheezes to life as I start the car.

The heat and exhaustion are breaking me down. I don't want to think about the life I left in Lorida. I consider turning around as I leave the Hardee's, but dread and guilt force me onto the southbound ramp. Maybe I deserve to feel like this. Maybe this is just a fraction of the punishment I deserve.

CHAPTER 5

PAST - OCTOBER 1984

There's the idea of high school, and then there's the reality. There are the kids everyone remembers—the star students, the hot guys, the beauties, the athletes, the bad boys, the troubled girls . . . and then there is everyone else. If you don't participate in any of it, it's easy to be anonymous. It's easy to be forgotten. Maybe there's an official school photo in the yearbook, or maybe you were absent that day, and no one noticed.

Ocean Breezes High School was a nice name, but it was as landlocked as you can get in Florida. You had rich kids, whose grandparents were often old Florida homesteaders who'd sold their land, or they were the people who sold the idea of Florida as a paradise to northern transplants. You had poor kids, usually old Florida poverty, having worked in the fields and orchards or at blue-collar jobs for generations. They got called crackers by everyone. There were also middle-class kids, but even middle class looks rich when you are poor.

The line between relatively rich and poor in Lorida was the electric bill. Rich kids had central air. They showed up looking refreshed and dry. Poor kids tossed and turned all night, seeking relief under box fans that shoved around torpid air and mosquitoes. If you were lucky, you had a screened-in Florida room, covered-in jalousie windows, and a huge ceiling fan. You could sleep in the room, on the magically cool tiled floor, when your sheets felt too hot to touch. We had one at our old house.

Rich kids had feathered and ironed hair that looked like delicate cotton candy. Poor kids had sticky, humid clumps that looked like collapsed scaffolding. We battled the heat, humidity, and bugs day and night. Rich kids never understood we were at war with the environment.

Ocean Breezes had kids who hailed from all over Mexico, the Caribbean, and Central America and a few from Vietnam. Some of their parents worked the local farms, and some were doctors and lawyers. Despite the statistical appearance of integration, the school had unwritten rules of class-based cliques and selective seg regation. Everyone knew that the white kids played baseball, and the Black kids played basketball. There was a perpetual state of unspoken tension based on race, income, and culture. People kept to themselves, suspicious of one another, and pretended everyone was okay with the situation. The school board patted themselves on the back for the appearance of a "melting pot."

Schools in Sebring had only integrated in the late 1960s, and that wasn't due to changing attitudes. It was because federal funding would have been cut if the schools didn't comply. There had been an all-Black high school until 1967, the year before I was born. Then students were thrown together, and new schools were built to accommodate the sudden overcrowding.

The usual cliques tended to break down further due to the size of the school. The rich kids self-sorted into the popular party kids and the ones who planned to take over their fathers' businesses or go to college. There were metalheads, but even they split into sub-groups. There were the ones who were angry at the world and others who just wanted to get stoned and listen to Iron Maiden. It seemed to me that loose-fitting cliques of girls came together and broke apart like flocks of birds. Murmurations of teenage girls. I could never figure out what they had in common or how to join. The nerds clung together for protection. Athletes hung out with their teammates and girlfriends.

I was an athlete—well, sort of—but I found myself in the flotsam and jetsam of the kids without a clique. I was a swimmer, but that was more about me and less about school. Swimming was something you largely did alone, aside from relay races.

If you didn't fit in somewhere, you were nameless and faceless. I was one of the kids who simply went to school, did what they were told, and went home at the end of the day. I was quiet. I was invisible. I was forgettable. At least that was how I thought of myself, but then Sissy noticed me. It was like she changed how I saw myself. I had shape and form under her gaze.

I could tell Sissy was rich, and that afforded her automatic social status. Even the most popular poor kids were still poor. They were still looked down on. Being rich meant you could dress the right way and knew the right way to do things.

Sissy and I had begun to leave each other notes in our respective lockers. She had a seemingly endless supply of Sanrio papers. I knew when I saw pink and blue paper peeking out of the slot in my locker that it would be a note from her. When she used the Little Twin Stars paper, she would write our initials on the characters. She called me all sorts of nicknames in the notes—Micha, Shelly, Mic, Mish, Elle, Shell, MM, Helga, and more. None ever stuck, but I thought it was sweet she wanted to give me a nickname. Her own special name for me. She was right, I figured: Michelle was a boring name. Mom and Michael called me Chelle, but they were the only ones.

We wrote notes during class, telling each other about the meaningless yet critically important minutia of our days. We told each other about the TV shows we watched, what music we liked, who we hated, and who she liked (I never confessed my crushes because I didn't have any), speculated about teachers, and complained endlessly about the daily hell of Ocean Breezes High School. We shared what we thought of as secrets. Oddly, we never mentioned our families, as if we only existed at school. We developed in-jokes that could get us laughing for no reason. I had never laughed so much before. We could just look at each other and start giggling.

What did we have in common? That's simple: we were lonely. I hadn't realized how lonely I was. How isolated I felt, especially at school. How one person could make that daily hurt go away. I had been pretending everything was okay, that I was okay when I wasn't. Sissy seemed more alone than lonely. I wasn't sure why she wanted to be my friend, but I was grateful she did. She told me about past friendships and how people had hurt her and let her down. Our friendship was so sudden and intense, like a summer storm, that sometimes I was afraid it would disappear just as quickly.

We didn't have any classes together, so we began meeting up at lunch at one of the disused bleachers by the portable classrooms. November in Florida offers the first waves of relief from endless summer. The afternoon thunderstorms become less frequent, and the volatility in the air subsides. The winds pick up, blowing mosquitoes away and allowing you to sit outside without every square inch of skin burning, sweating, and itching. We sat on the bleachers in our self-contained bubble amid the daily cacophony.

I had noticed that Sissy liked to change her look, and today, the big hair and heavy eye makeup were gone. Today, she had her hair softly feathered, and she was wearing a sleeveless shirt and a white skirt. Her eyes and lips looked sparkly and delicate. She looked pretty—not beautiful—but pretty.

"Is that bologna?" she asked.

I nodded and took a bite.

"What does it taste like? My mother said we shouldn't eat things like that."

Self-conscious, I busied myself opening the soda I had brought to go with the sandwich. I covered the store-brand label with my hand. I shrugged and tried to change the subject.

Sissy took the bait and started talking at length about a girl we both knew and what a loser she was for getting pregnant. I looked over at her lunch. She had perfectly cut carrots sticks in an orange Tupperware container and what looked to be salad dressing in a smaller green container. In another container were cubes of cheese. On the side was a plastic baggie with a peeled orange.

"Stupid bitch," she said.

"Who?"

"My mother. She knows I hate pepper jack."

"Your mother makes your lunch?"

"Of course. What else is she going to do with her day before it's time to start drinking?"

At the end of the day, there was a triangular note in my locker. In her curly script, Sissy asked if I wanted to hang out after school. It felt like a big deal. It was one thing to be school friends, friends by proximity and happenstance. It was another to be friends away from school. It wasn't a swim practice day, so I went to the pay phone at the front of the school and called my mother to ask if it was okay.

"Hi, Mom."

"Do you need a ride?"

"No, well, yes, but not right now. Would it be okay if I went over to Sissy's house?"

"Who?"

"The girl I told you about."

"Oh, yes, of course. Of course, you can. Go have a bit of fun. Let me know when to come get you."

Grinning, I hung up the phone and went in search of Sissy. The note said that she would be waiting at her car in the school parking lot until 3:45. I found her standing next to a tiny blue Mazda. I got in and threw my bag into the backseat. I tried to pretend like I did this sort of thing all the time. Not that I'd gone to anyone's house after school in years, but none of my other friends had cars. I tried not to let her see how excited I was. I felt so cool as we pulled out of the school parking lot.

Sissy lived between the school and my house in a development that bordered a golf course. Her house was at the end of a cul-de-sac. It's funny how cul-de-sac sounds all fancy; it makes it sound like you want to be trapped there, whereas my dead-end street implied you had made some kind of mistake and should turn back before it is too late. Sissy's house was a neutral stucco with a Spanish tile roof and real plants for landscaping. Squat palm trees rustled softly as we approached the front door. We stepped onto a terrazzo floor, and the central air caressed my skin. Her house smelled clean, like insecticide and lemons.

There was a small foyer that led down to a thickly-carpeted living room on the left or straight ahead to a large kitchen. Out back was a screened-in patio and a pristine pool that she said no one ever used. The kitchen was filled with appliances that she said went similarly untouched. There was more space for things that weren't used than there was in our whole trailer. I had been right about her being rich.

I didn't see anyone else, but the house didn't feel quite empty. She led me down a hall to her room. Against one wall was an unmade double bed covered in frilly pillows and stuffed animals. All the colors were soft and delicate—the walls, the bed, the windows. It didn't look like the room I had imagined. I was surprised to find it a bit childish. It was endearing in a way.

There was stuff *everywhere*. It was hard to take it all in. Clothes were heaped in piles around the room as if they exploded off her nightly. The mirrored closet doors were open, and I couldn't figure out how the closet still looked completely full, given all the clothes scattered around the room. There was a small, mirrored vanity with perfumes, lip balms, nail polish, and makeup and a white wicker shelf with knickknacks and weary stuffed animals. On the walls were posters and cut-outs from magazines. She had an entertainment center with a TV, cable box, VCR, and boombox surrounded by haphazard stacks of cassettes, VHS tapes, batteries, remotes, and magazines. There was an unplugged Atari system in the corner.

There was a door that led to a bathroom that connected to another bedroom. Sissy saw me looking and got up and closed the door.

"That's my sister's room."

Sissy had never mentioned her sister, but it didn't look like she lived there anymore. The bed was stripped, and the closet was filled with boxes and clothes. I wondered if she was at college.

Sissy made a big production of sweeping clothes, magazines, and schoolwork off a small, upholstered chair and set the chair next to her bed so we could watch TV. We found a movie on cable. The way the chair and mirrored closet doors were angled, I kept catching sight of myself. It was unsettling. I didn't like looking at myself. At home, the only mirror we had was a small one in the bathroom. I'd see myself brushing my teeth and catch glimpses getting in and out of the shower, and that was more than enough. If I wanted to see how an outfit looked, I had to stand on the edge of the tub and stretch up and down. How could Sissy stand to be in this room looking at herself all the time? I felt like I had a sense of myself in my head, but mirrors confused that. I was never sure if the me in my head was the right one or if everyone else saw someone completely different.

My eyes are hazel, my hair a frizzy, dark brown that droops to my shoulders, my limbs are long and muscular, my nose is angular. My lips aren't thin or full. I seldom smile wide because my teeth are crooked. I'm 5'7". There is a sprinkling of freckles across the bridge of my nose that fade out across high cheekbones. These are abstract descriptions because I have no clear idea what I look like. This is what I assume other people see when they look at me.

Sissy jumped up and left the room. While she was gone, I moved the chair, so I wasn't looking at my reflection. She reappeared with a bag of Doritos, a tub of cake frosting, two spoons, and a couple of cans of Diet Coke. She jumped back on her bed and kicked off her shoes. Her shoes were sparkling white Keds that smelled of fresh rubber. I tucked my yellowed, knock-off Keds that smelled of store-brand bleach under her bed.

We didn't have cable, or even a VCR, at home. Our crappy TV antenna barely brought in the stations from Tampa and St. Pete. I often had to go outside and spin it to get the best signal. One part of me was envious of Sissy, while the other part felt shitty for feeling that way. I wanted a life with central air, cable, and a pool, but I knew that wasn't a life my mother could afford. Did that make me disloyal? Was it wrong to want these things?

"Cecilia, I'm going out. Your father is with a client, but he should be home in about an hour."

I hadn't heard the woman approach the doorway and was startled by her voice. I expected Sissy to say something about me being there, but she didn't. I assumed the woman was her mother. She was taller than Sissy, almost as tall as me, with the kind of sleek blond hair that worked hard to look natural. She was thin in a deprived way, which was only accentuated by the draped, belted dress she wore.

"I left dinner in the fridge, or if you want, there is money on the counter for pizza,"

"Fine," Sissy said, with an eye-roll in my direction.

I looked for signs of drunkenness, but all I saw was tiredness. And something else I didn't understand. Like she was there and not there. She turned and looked at me, staring long enough to make me uncomfortable, and left as quietly as she had arrived.

When the movie was over, I called home and asked my mother to pick me up. She said she was in the middle of something but would send my brother. She put him on the phone, and I gave him directions with Sissy's help. Sissy insisted on coming out to the car to meet him.

When Michael got there, Sissy bounded ahead of me.

"Aren't you going to introduce us? You never told me you had a fine older brother!"

As I introduced them, I saw Michael was blushing. Sissy started asking him a bunch of questions. He answered quietly and politely. As he did, he looked at Sissy and back at her house.

I could also see Sissy looking at our car. The cracked dashboard and split plastic on the seats. The faded paint and the muffler rumble that sounded like a smoker's cough.

Your brother is a bit of a weirdo, isn't he?" she wrote in a note the next day.

I didn't know what she meant. I thought about it all of second and third period, trying to figure out what was weird about Michael. He never seemed weird to me. If anything, he was the poster child for normal. He was twenty, four years older than me. He was training to be a mechanic. Michael was usually quiet until he got to know you. He liked movies and wrestling and hated ketchup.

He was self-conscious about his teeth, which had some gaps, and would only smile for real if he trusted you. We'd often sit up with our mother and watch the late show, arguing over the proper way to eat French fries. He had always been a decent older brother to me. A lot of my friends hated their siblings, but Michael was alright. What was weird about him? How weird was I if I couldn't see how weird he was?

I asked her about it at lunch, and she laughed and said I had completely misunderstood her. She said she meant weirdo in a good way. She asked about our father, tiptoeing around the obvious fact that we looked nothing alike. Michael didn't even look like our mother. He was tall and wiry with wavy, sandy blond hair and gray eyes. Mom never said it, but I suspected he looked a lot like his father.

"We have different fathers. Michael's father isn't really around. He and my mother were together on and off for about a year when she got pregnant with Michael. He didn't handle it very well. They split up while she was pregnant. When Michael was a baby, my mom met my dad. My dad died when I was eight."

I rushed my explanation, hoping to get past the last sentence without her noticing. I had been avoiding telling her about my father. Having a dead parent marks you. You are the girl with the dead father when other children describe you at home. Kids whisper about it as if it is contagious. Teachers either forget and tell you they look forward to meeting your parents at back-to-school night, or they make a point of only mentioning your mother, making the absence just as pronounced.

My attempt to gloss it over didn't work. Sissy zeroed in on my father.

"Oh my god! How did he die? Do you mind talking about it?"

Once I started talking, I found I didn't mind. It was more awkward than painful. I liked thinking about my dad, but I didn't get much of a chance to talk about him. We didn't talk about him at home. It was too hard for my mother. He wasn't Michael's biological father, but he had been his dad for longer than he had been mine. We didn't talk about Dad, but he was always there. He was our spectral elephant in the room. Our own personal Spirit of '76. He died in 1976, and in my adolescent mind, the bicentennial celebrations and my dad's death had tangled together. The year after he died, I watched an episode of *In Search Of* about hauntings and kept hoping I would see his ghost. I would knock on things, hoping he would knock back, but he never did.

I told Sissy what I knew about him. I was only eight when he died, so there were stories I was sure I had experienced, but telling her, it dawned on me they had to have happened before I was born. The more she asked, the more I realized how many holes there were in what I knew. I was having trouble figuring out what I was told and what I remembered. I explained he died in a car accident. I didn't mention the snake.

In addition to the notes, we started calling each other every evening. She had a phone in her room, but it was harder at my house. My mother often needed the phone for work and the trailer afforded little privacy. I mentioned this to Sissy, and the next day, she thrust a Kmart bag into my hand

"Ta-da! I got you a present!"

Inside was a thirty-foot phone cord.

"Is it long enough? It is the longest one they had. Now you can have a bit of privacy and we can talk whenever we want."

I wasn't sure how thrilled my mother would be, but Sissy seemed quite pleased that she had solved the problem.

Through Sissy, I found out about all sorts of intrigue at school. Apparently, lots of people were having sex, including students and teachers. At least two of the teachers were drug addicts. There were also several drug dealers in our grade. Sissy said that people often confided in her and that was how she knew so much. I also found out about all the people who had treated her like shit in the past. She told me I was the best friend she had ever had. I almost burst when she said it.

There was something exhilarating about being around Sissy. She listened to me. She asked me questions no one had ever asked me.

She let me tell her things I had always kept inside. I found myself confiding in her in ways I had never done with other friends or even my family. I had started to tell her about how I felt about myself. How I felt like an outsider. How I missed my friend Diana. How I missed my father. She listened intently.

Sissy was always coming up with adventures for us. She made going to the school vending machines a quest. Who would we see? Who would we avoid? Who would we shun? Could we make people we encountered meow like a cat or snort like a pig? She spun through the halls in a brightly colored miniskirt laughing manically.

I felt a bit like Dorothy after she dropped into Oz. These people had all been there before, but around Sissy, they were transformed. There were witches and flying monkeys down one breezeway, and classmates were munchkins, dancing for our entertainment down another. I felt like I was living in Technicolor for the first time. Everything was fun, and I was having daily adventures with my best friend.

Normally I took the bus home, but one day Sissy offered to drive me. I was reluctant, and she seemed to sense that.

"Never mind. It's cool. See you tomorrow." It was most certainly not cool. Her voice had gone flat and cold.

She started to walk away, and I knew I had made a huge mistake. I knew she was angry with me. I was embarrassed by where we lived and was ashamed of feeling that way. I had seen the way she had looked at our car.

"Wait, Sissy, wait." I ran after her.

She stopped, arms crossed, and stared at me. That stare. How can it hurt to have someone look at you?

"I'm so sorry," I said, trying to apologize to her and my family simultaneously. I couldn't explain myself. I didn't know how. I didn't even know why. I just knew I didn't want her to be mad at me.

"I'm so stupid. That was totally rude of me. It's embarrassing. . . . I was hoping to see Mark Cutler on the bus today. That's all. I was being stupid. It isn't important. Would you please drive me home?" I had just lied and pretended I liked a kid in my Algebra II class.

"*Seriously? That kid?* He is probably fucking his sister."

"I know, it is really stupid. I'm so dumb. I'm sorry."

"Come on, let's go, dummy," she said with a laugh, but there was no humor in the way she said it.

And just like that, we were okay again, as long as I didn't think too hard about feeling scared inside.

She pulled in under the live oak tree by the rusty metal carport and parked her car. I assumed she was dropping me off, but she seemed to want to come inside. After my fuck-up earlier, I was willing to go along with whatever she wanted.

My mother was working at her table when I opened the front door. Sissy was back to her charming self, telling my mother what a lovely home we had and what a wonderful friend I was. Emboldened by her praise, I showed her my room. There were two bedrooms in the mobile home. My brother and I had shared a bedroom until I started junior high, and then he had moved to the pull-out couch in the living room. My mother had the bedroom at the front of the trailer.

I watched Sissy's eyes slink over the bunk bed, small bookshelf, dresser, and narrow closet with the broken accordion doors. She picked up the snow globe with a tiny Golden Gate Bridge inside and shook it. Most of my "treasures" were souvenirs from other people's vacations. I bought them at thrift stores and yard sales. I loved the idea that someone went to Arches National Park and wanted a spoon to remember the experience. Or a thimble from Las Vegas. I daydreamed about going places and the random things I would buy there to try and capture the memories.

It was the first time I had seen my bedroom through someone else's eyes. The dark synthetic paneling looked shabby. It smelled mildewy. The brown rug was threadbare. It felt dusty and dirty, even though I kept my room clean. Nothing matched. There was a hole in the paneling from when Michael and I had played with a bat years ago. Everything I had loved about my room was gone, replaced by glaring flaws I had never seen before.

My once cozy bunk bed looked rickety. Other people's souvenirs seemed pathetic through her eyes. Michael's boombox looked old and cheap. My mismatched desk and chair looked like we had gotten them at yard sales, which was true. My pretty sheets had holes in them. Even my swimming trophies looked dusty.

I should at least have had posters on the bare walls. I felt like there was nothing cool about me. The room showed all my nothingness. There was no TV in here, no VCR. No photos of my friends and adventures. My window looked onto Mrs. Swanson's trailer. One of the jalousies was cracked, so you had to crank it carefully when you opened and closed the window. I noticed a small gecko along the door frame. I prayed Sissy wouldn't see it.

I saw her taking it all in. Taking it all away from me. She walked over to the closet and looked inside.

"Michael also keeps his clothes in here," I said.

She wasn't sure where to sit down and eventually plopped down on the bunk bed, which shifted slightly. Pufnstuf jumped off the top bunk, causing Sissy to yelp. Pufnstuf was a kitten my brother had found a couple years ago. He was now a fat, gray tabby cat. He was a lethal lizard hunter when he wanted to be, but he mostly sat around demanding food and attention. Hence, the live gecko in my room. Sissy said she was allergic to cats and should probably go.

I wanted things to be normal the next day at school, but they weren't. Sissy was acting oddly and wouldn't look at me. I asked her what was wrong like I didn't know, and she said, "I didn't realize you had to live like that."

Here was everything I had feared about having Sissy drive me home. I hadn't realized there was anything wrong until I saw my life through her eyes. It was one thing to want a swimming pool and air conditioning. It was another to feel ashamed for being poor. I mean, I knew we didn't have a ton of money, but it had never mattered until she told me it mattered. Until Sissy made me feel like it mattered. Until I met Sissy, I thought I had what I needed. She made me feel like being poor was something I did wrong.

After that, we hung out at her house, and if she drove me home, she dropped me off and left. Down deep, I knew I was wrong for feeling ashamed. If I had been a better person, everything might have been different. Only I wasn't a good or strong person. And Sissy knew that, too.

CHAPTER 6
PAST - NOVEMBER 1984

When I was little, I loved to swim. I loved going to the beach. I'd angle to visit Mom's friend who lived in an apartment complex with a pool. It wasn't something I thought about being good or bad at, it was just something I enjoyed. When I started high school, I tried out for the swim team, not because I wanted to compete, but because I wanted regular access to a pool. None of my friends had pools. The ocean was too far to go to regularly. The tiny "beach" at the City Pier required Mom to drive me. I had tired of sneaking into apartment complexes to swim, and swimming in the local lakes was an invitation to brain-eating parasites or death by alligator or water moccasin.

I was put on the team, and, to my surprise, I was good at it. I was best at freestyle and relay because I had natural speed and stamina. I didn't do as well at the backstroke and breaststroke, but each year I got better at them. Coach Roberts pushed me hard. Some days I hated him for it.

Solomon Roberts was originally from the Bahamas. He taught health and drivers education and coached the swim team. He was lean and hard, with ropey muscles. His burnished arms looked like they had hidden gears and machinery under the skin. He was scary until he laughed, and then you wondered why you ever found him threatening. He yelled in a way that seemed friendly, but everyone listened to him. Even the stoners paid attention to him.

He regaled us with stories about his days as a diver in the Bahamas. By his telling, he was a legendary freediver, risking his life working unofficial salvage jobs. He made it sound secretive and dangerous. He was still fast and often challenged team members to race, usually beating us. We had no idea how old he was, but he was at least "parent old." He might even have been "grandparent old."

My mother didn't like to swim, and my brother seemed ambivalent, so swimming was all mine.

When you are young, you instinctively yearn for freedom. From that first time you break away and run down the supermarket aisle like it's an airplane runway to riding your bike out of sight of home. Swimming always gave me that sense of freedom. The water made me weightless and fast. I could go anywhere and in all directions. I could float, fly, or fall. I was by myself and yet surrounded. Sounds enveloped me. I could hear my own thoughts at the bottom of the pool. Salt water, fresh water, and chlorinated water all felt different, and each was special in its own way. I loved when the air and water temperatures were close to my body temperature so that only my breathing separated the two worlds.

In the water, I was free from the heat. I was free from being awkward. I was free of my frizzy, untamable hair. I was me in the water. Nothing mattered in the water but the water. Water could kill you or set you free.

I had made the varsity swim team, and we practiced on Tuesdays and Thursdays. We had occasional weekend practices if there wasn't a meet scheduled.

I was on the phone telling Sissy about our upcoming meet in Lake Wales.

"Would you like some of my sister's old bathing suits? I think they will fit you."

"She doesn't want them?"

"No, she doesn't need them anymore."

"Yeah, cool. My practice suits get trashed from the sun and chlorine after a while."

The next day I met her at her car, and she handed me two paper grocery bags filled with clothes. In addition to the swimsuits, which looked almost new, there were T-shirts, jeans, shorts, and two pairs of shoes.

"Thank you!" I squealed and hugged her. I was mirroring Sissy more and more. I had these flashes of seeing myself from the outside and was confused by this squealing new me.

Sissy seemed pleased. My mother less so when I came in the door holding the bags of clothing.

"Why did she give you all of this? Do you need clothes? Why didn't you tell me?"

"It's not like that."

"What is it like, Michelle? We don't need her charity." I wondered what Michael had said about her, about where she lived.

I hadn't seen it like that. Was that how Sissy saw it?

CHAPTER 7

By the time I reach Valdosta, GA, sweat is running along the under-wires of my bra. It is gathering in rivulets that soak the front of my shirt where the seat belt presses into my chest. It creeps through my hair and down my face and back. I'm having trouble focusing as the heat and sun dissolve the road surface into a mirage that shimmers like dark water. I no longer notice how hot the steering wheel feels under my hands. The overwhelmed air conditioner is swirling the heat around the car. I know that by stopping, I am delaying the inevitable. I know that by stopping, I stand every chance of getting back in the car, turning around, and heading straight back to Atlanta. I also know that I should have gotten gas last night but didn't because I planned on talking myself out of going. I look at the gas gauge and decide to stop, gas up, and clear the heat-induced fog out of my head. I am going stir-crazy after three hours on the road, simultaneously exhausted and wired.

I pull off the highway and find a gas station. They have Ca-jun-spiced boiled peanuts for sale. I buy a large cup and settle it in the otherwise useless console above the emergency brake. I'm not hungry, but cracking the shells gives me something to do while driving. It is something to focus on. A distraction. I haven't allowed myself to think about the past like this in years. Not since I left. I kept it all buried. My new life lets me pretend like my old one never existed.

It is now 9 a.m., and, as Anne, I should be starting my day at the hospital, grabbing a clipboard and going down to the nurses' station. I should be enjoying the hospital's southern-style air conditioning, cranked up far too high. I never thought I would miss trying to figure out if the name on the form was Ronald Jackson or Pomade Gorkam.

Three weeks ago, Gladys Anderson came into the ER and threw my life into disarray. For the last week, I've been sitting at home watching *Law and Order*, walking aimlessly, or sneaking into the swimming pool at the apartment complex a few blocks away from my apartment. When I am feeling especially bold, I sneak into the aquatic center at Emory University. I found an old swim team suit at the thrift store a few years ago, and it keeps people from questioning me.

The apartment complex pool is small, and I feel like I am pacing a cage. The Olympic-sized pool at Emory allows me to exhaust myself. I've always worked, sometimes two jobs. The sudden absence of work is terrifying.

I'm scared to admit it, but part of me wants to see my mother and brother. I've missed them, even if they haven't missed me. I know that seeing them will make me remember. I don't want to remember. I want the past to stay where I left it. I'm also scared that I will hurt them. Staying away meant they were safe from me.

I turn on the radio and sing along at random, trying to drown my buzzing thoughts with an off-key chorus. I eat the dripping peanuts, enjoying the almost potatoey taste. The juice drips onto my shirt, mixing with the sweat stains.

Further down the highway, the memories creep back in, past the formidable barriers of empty peanut shells, building traffic, Janet Jackson, and Destiny's Child. They go back to the five sentences that made me a monster. The five sentences that haunt me in the middle of the night.

SUSPECTED HOMICIDE NEAR LORIDA RULED A SUICIDE

Sebring, Fla. (AP) — *Police detectives have determined that the body found dead east of Lorida died by suicide.*

The body was found Wednesday morning near the railroad crossing at Cowhouse Road, east of Lorida. Investigators initially thought the death suspicious.

Sebring police Chief Bob Seafert said Friday that further investigation and an examination of the body determined the injuries were sustained when the victim was struck by a train. The person's identity hasn't been released pending notification of the next of kin.

CHAPTER 8

PAST - NOVEMBER 1985

Sissy teased me out of my shell. I didn't understand what a small-town kid I was until she showed me what freedom felt like. She had a car and seemingly few rules at home. She always had cash, even though she didn't have a job. Eventually, I learned where much of the money came from. She'd beg her mother for clothes, electronics, or some other portable item she *absolutely* needed or said she needed for school. She never took the tags off and returned items to whatever store they came from. She was polite and dressed nicely, and they always believed her. If they balked, she started to cry. She was an excellent liar. She would come up with stories that painted her as a hapless victim or helpful family member. She was, among other things, an unloved daughter, a heartbroken girlfriend, and a loving granddaughter. As far as I knew, she didn't even have grandparents anymore.

I often stood next to her, nodding or looking sad, providing silent support to her story. Occasionally, I played the role of sister or cousin when the lie got elaborate. The stores always took the return and gave her cash back or store credit. If they gave her store credit, she'd buy something and then wait a week or two, return it with the receipt, and get the cash back. Her mother never seemed to notice.

Sissy got bored easily. She'd spontaneously pick me up to go to Tastee Freez. Or, sometimes she said she was picking me up to go to Tastee Freez, and before I knew it, we were two counties over. She always had gas money, and everything was an adventure. We developed our own slang, filled with in-jokes. It was like she could read my mind half the time. Everything felt fun and exciting. All the TV shows and movies that made being a teenager seem like fun finally made sense. Junior high and high school had felt like an endurance test of shame and ridicule—until I met Sissy.

When we watched TV after school and on the weekends, Sissy would delight me by making fun of the characters. Sissy made jokes out of everything and was an artful mimic. I joined in, mocking Mallory Keaton for being a shallow bitch. It was so subtle that I didn't notice when the ridicule stopped being about fictional characters and Sissy started making comments about real people. I wanted her to like me, to think I was funny, so I laughed and, worse, joined in. After a while, I didn't even feel bad about what I said. I changed, becoming a person who said and thought hurtful things.

"You ever notice the mole on Charlene's face? It's like I can't even talk to her without zeroing in on the thing," Sissy said as she bit into a Pringle. "It's like a giant tick. I bet she's covered in fleas and ticks. We should get her a flea and tick collar and put it on her locker."

I knew how much the mole bothered Charlene, and yet I laughed.

Sometimes I felt like I wasn't myself anymore, but I wasn't sure who I was. Maybe this new me really was me. I didn't know. All I knew was that Sissy seemed to like the new me, so I tried to be that person.

We were walking to our respective classes when Cassie Littlejohn waved at me.

"You're friends with her? *Really?*" Sissy said under her breath.

"Yeah, we've known each other since elementary school."

"Oh? That's surprising."

"Why?"

"Never mind, I shouldn't say anything."

"What are you talking about?"

"Nothing, I probably misheard her."

"Would you tell me what you're talking about?"

Sissy lowered her voice and said, "I thought I heard her calling you trailer trash."

It was hardly the first time I had heard someone call me that, but it still stung. I thought Cassie and I were friends.

"Thanks for telling me," I said.

Sissy went to her class, and I walked further down the breezeway to mine. I was so glad Sissy was there for me. She was trying to protect me, and I appreciated it. I tried to focus on that instead of the hurt, but once again, I was left feeling like I was innately wrong.

CHAPTER 9
PAST - DECEMBER 1984

I was changing classes when I saw two kids get into a fight.

"*Hola, Falso. ¿Cómo estás?*"

"Fuck off, Ángel."

"How's your mother? You think maybe she would light my fire?"

The tall, skinny kid—the one who just threw down his books and got into Ángel's face—rode my bus. I thought his name was Morris or something like that. I remembered thinking of the 9Lives commercial the first time I heard it. No, wait, it was Morri*son*. Morrison Nuñez.

Morrison's frayed jean jacket was covered in band patches and buttons. His jeans hung low on his narrow hips. He wore beat-up Chuck Taylors with band names scrawled along the once-white soles. A blond devil's lock covered his right eye. He looked like a walking afterschool special warning about the dangers of punk rock.

Ángel started singing something I couldn't hear and thrusting his pelvis. Morrison grabbed Ángel and shoved him into the lockers without warning.

There was a sudden surge of kids surrounding them, waiting to see a fight. I was one of them. A couple of people cheered on Morrison, but most were rooting for Ángel. They circled each other, getting ready for this to turn serious.

From down the hall, someone yelled that the vice principal was coming. Ángel used the distraction to punch Morrison in the stomach. He then pivoted and headed down the breezeway as if nothing had happened. On cue, the rest of the crowd dispersed, leaving Morrison hunched over. I just stood there. The vice principal walked right past us.

"Are you okay?" I asked.

He didn't answer, just nodded and picked up his books, and walked away.

After school, I waited to get on the bus until the last minute. I was hoping that if Morrison was on the bus, I could "accidentally" sit near him. It sort of worked. He was stretched out on the seat, arms crossed, leaning against the window, making it obvious he didn't want anyone sitting next to him. I took the seat behind him. I was hoping there would be a natural moment to start a conversation, but he put headphones on and pulled a book out of his backpack.

All the way along Airport Road, I waited for an opportunity to catch his eye. I kept trying to see what he was reading. The bus bench was an impenetrable barrier. We turned onto Route 98, and I started feeling foolish. I stared out the window berating myself until we came to my stop. I wasn't sure why I wanted to talk to him. There was something about the hurt look on his face during the fight with Ángel. There was nothing tough or punk about his expression. There was a loneliness I recognized.

As I exited the bus, he looked up and said, "Thanks for checking on me," and then he dropped right back down and continued reading his book as if he had never uttered a word.

That was how my friendship with Morrison started. The next day he nodded at me when I got on the bus. That afternoon I mumbled, "Hi," as I passed him going to my seat, coincidentally, right behind him again. He completely ignored me. The next day I managed a more audible "Hey," and he responded with a nod. Finally, weeks later, after I had given up trying to talk to him, he asked what I was reading. It was *Their Eyes Were Watching God* for Ms. Leonard's English class.

He seemed unsure of what I had said until I lifted the book and showed him the cover. He nodded again and said he liked it, especially the description of the hurricane.

"Do you have Ms. Leonard for English?"

"Nah, not yet. I'm a grade behind you."

"How do you know what grade I'm in?"

He shrugged and said, "I know things," and let his devil's lock flop across his eye.

Before I could say another word, the bus came to a sudden stop, and I had to scramble to get off. I was forced to relive the interaction all weekend. What did he mean? How did he know what grade I was in? He read Zora Neale Hurston for fun? What teenage boy does that? I spent all weekend waiting for the Monday morning bus ride, but Morrison wasn't on the bus.

He was at school on Tuesday, and we went back to the cat-and-mouse game of talking/not talking on the bus. I asked what he was reading, and he produced a copy of *The World According to Garp*. I went to the school library at lunch, but the school didn't have a copy, and the librarian looked at me funny.

He did everything he could to make himself look hard and unapproachable, but it was an ill-fitting suit. He had the angry-looking band T-shirts, the sleeveless denim jacket with hostile sounding buttons, the tattered jeans, and that flop of hair hiding his blue eyes. I could see why he wore it like that because his eyes were the problem. There was something in his eyes that didn't fit the rest of him. His eyes were . . . soft and maybe a bit sad. It wasn't that they were especially pretty, just nice. In fact, I spent much of the winter trying to figure out if I had a crush on him or if I was inexplicably fascinated by him. I didn't imagine kissing him, so I assumed it was the latter.

I considered telling Sissy about him, but I was afraid she'd tell me something I didn't want to hear. Or that she would get mad. I had also lied to her twice about needing to get home so I could ride the bus. I decided to keep my curiosity to myself.

CHAPTER 10
PAST - DECEMBER 1984

Sissy and I talked every night and hung out most weekends. Morrison even managed three full sentences by the time I got off the bus on Friday. Everything felt good, which made me uneasy. Like I was waiting for something bad to happen.

December was always a hard month at home. My father's birthday was the sixteenth. My mother often retreated into herself around his birthday, but Septembers were worse. The dark cloud that usually settled over the house wasn't there this year.

On Christmas Day, Michael, my mother, and I made pancakes and lounged around the trailer. It was sixty-five degrees outside, nothing like the Christmases you see on TV, but it was cold enough by Florida standards. We had sweaters on. They smelled faintly moldy. We pretended to be colder than we were because TV and the movies taught us to be cold at Christmas. Pufnstuf stalked around, meowing with a new catnip toy in his mouth.

Mom was drinking coffee at the table. She seemed happy too.

"I hope you like it. I hear you listening to music all the time now and thought you might like one. The store told me which batteries to get. I wasn't sure if I should get you some tapes or what you would like."

My mother had gotten me a portable cassette player with headphones from Radio Shack. I couldn't wait to show Morrison on the bus next week. I wanted to go get one of the tapes Sissy had made for me and listen to it, but I didn't want to be rude. I was enjoying spending time with my family.

Mom had given Michael a set of metric sockets. We had gotten together and bought her two new shirts from Zayre's. By eleven a.m, it was too hot to wear the sweaters, and Mom changed into one of her new shirts.

Michael and I were playing Clue when the phone rang. It was still sitting in my room, the cord stretched from the kitchen, and I went back to answer it. As I got up, Pufnstuf launched himself on the Clue board and rolled onto his back, throwing Colonel Mustard under the couch with the candlestick.

"Hello?"

"Hey, when are we hanging out today?" asked Sissy.

"I'm, um, hanging out with my family right now." I was enjoying hanging out with my family, but I was afraid of disappointing her. "How about in a little while, before dinner?"

"Cool, I'll swing by and get you in about half an hour."

"Yeah, see you then."

I came back out and told my mother I would be going out with Sissy for a little while.

"On Christmas Day?" Mom asked.

"I'll only be gone for a little while," with what sounded like a whine in my voice.

"*Seriously*, Chelle? I'm pretty sure Sissy can live without you for a day. Or is it the other way around?" Michael said, now perched on the edge of the couch.

"Please, Mom. I won't be long." I started panicking. I didn't want to tell Sissy I couldn't come over.

"Michael, it's fine. Let her go." I saw her happiness had deflated a bit, and I felt horrible.

My brother began picking up the scattered pieces from Clue, tersely throwing them back in the box. I didn't want them to be mad at me. I didn't want Sissy to be mad at me. No matter what I did, someone was going to be upset.

Sissy picked me up and drove us back to her house. I was subdued, but she didn't seem to notice. She burst through her front door singing. I waved at her parents, who were sitting in the living room surrounded by scraps of wrapping paper. Sissy had finally introduced us, but I still felt awkward when they were around.

We went back to her room. Both doors to her sister's room were closed. I thought she might have come home for Christmas.

Pointing to the closed door, I started to ask, "Is she . . ." but Sissy cut me off.

She was so excited to show me all the stuff she got for Christmas, which included several new outfits, a small camera, a bunch of music, and cash. Then she handed me a neatly wrapped present.

My stomach dropped. I thought we were just hanging out. I hadn't bought her a gift. I had sent her a candy cane candygram at school before winter break, but that was it.

I started unwrapping it while she beamed at me. It was a silver Sony Walkman. A nice one, with fast forward and reverse.

"But wait, there's more!" she said.

Next, she handed me a package containing headphones. After that came a package with the soundtrack for *Footloose*, *Synchronicity* by the Police, Michael Jackson's *Thriller*, and a single of "Do They Know It's Christmas?."

I thought about the Radio Shack player I had been so happy with that morning. It was an unexpected punch to the gut. I felt like I had to choose between the Radio Shack player and the Walkman, between my mother and Sissy. She looked at me expectantly.

"Oh my god, this is amazing! Thank you so much!" I faked being happy. I gave her a hug that I hoped felt genuine. It was probably the most expensive gift I had ever received. I *should* have been ecstatic. Instead, it made me feel bad. I didn't even have anything to give her in return.

"I'm sorry, I forgot to bring your present."

"Don't worry about that, doofus. I know you can't afford much."

Sissy and I left her room to sit out by the pool to listen to music. On our way through, Sissy's mother stopped us.

"Michelle, dear, we're going over to the club for dinner later. Would you like to join us?"

What had Sissy had told her mother about me? About my family? "Thank you, Mrs. Davis. I appreciate the offer, but we have family coming over later." We never had family over. I didn't know much about my father's family, and my mother's family all lived out of state or had passed away. It wasn't like we expected Michael's dad to show up, twenty years late to dinner. It was just us. It felt like lying was the only way to survive.

When I got home, Michael was hunched over the TV, and my mother was grinning. The atmosphere was back to what it had been first thing this morning. I was confused and exhausted. Michael stepped aside to reveal a VCR.

"I got an extra bonus this year. Dead people are good business, I guess."

"Mom, that's great! I mean about the VCR, not the dead people."

"I thought we might like to watch movies sometimes. So, I opened up an account at the video shop yesterday so we could watch . . ." and with a flourish, she produced plastic cases with copies of *Raiders of the Lost Ark* and *Romancing the Stone* inside.

I rushed over and hugged her. I couldn't wait to watch movies whenever I wanted. Mom finished making dinner, and we heaped our plates and settled into our usual spots on the couch and comfy chair and pressed play. While we watched the movies, I debated what to do about the gifts from Sissy and my mother. Returning either one wasn't an option. I decided I would keep the Walkman Sissy gave me for school and bus use only, and the one my mother gave me would be for home use only. I would keep them separate.

After that, Sissy and I were together almost every day over Christmas break. One morning, she called and said we were going to the big mall in Fort Pierce. She said she wanted some new jeans for winter. Winter in Florida amounted to wearing pants. We went to Bloomingdale's, where she tried on a pair of painfully tight Jordache jeans. She said they fit perfectly and bought them. Next, she tried Burdines because she said she wanted a pair of Guess jeans. She grabbed a pair off the rack and went back to the dressing room.

She came out and threw them at the clerk and said they were defective. Was this how rich people shopped?

We wandered around the mall for over four hours. Sissy tried on ugly clothes she had no intention of buying, just to watch my reaction. Some of the outfits she put together were hysterical. She put on a lime green leotard over parachute pants, not caring that she was stretching the leotard to its limit. She topped the ensemble with a denim jacket with fringes and pranced up and down the dressing room hall like she was the hot girl in a music video. She gathered scarves, pants, and shirts in animal prints and day-glow colors and layered them until she looked like a kaleidoscope. I wished I had a camera. We were eventually thrown out of the dressing rooms at Bloomingdale's for being too loud.

We tried on over twenty pairs of sunglasses in one shop. At Sam Goody, we lingered at the listening station, blocking the junior high kids from taking a turn.

We continued to wander around until Sissy announced she was hungry and wanted Chick-fil-A. She ordered a sandwich, large fries, and a Coke and grabbed her tray. I checked my wallet. I had enough for small fries and not much else.

We sat at a sticky table with chairs bolted to the ground. I ate slowly, so I didn't finish ahead of her. We watched people walk past our table and pretended we were at the zoo. Parents struggled with feral toddlers. Predatory housewives stalked clearance sales. Teenage boys roved in musky packs. There were small schools of old people determinedly swimming laps around the mall. We were zookeepers in a cookie-scented cage.

Sissy finished her lunch and reached into her bag. She handed me a pair of sunglasses. They were sleek, mirrored Wayfarers. They were expensive and cool.

"I got these for you."

"Thanks! How do I look?" I said as I modeled them for her. "When did you get these?" I didn't remember her buying anything at the sunglass store. Did she steal them? *Of course* I wanted them, but if I accepted them, what did that mean? It was a corporate mall store, after all; it wasn't like she had stolen them from a person.

She gave me a mysterious grin, then—instead of commenting on the glasses—said, "So, like, what's up with your hair?"

It felt like a blow. I almost gagged on the French fry I had carefully placed in my mouth.

I wanted to tell her I had no idea. That I didn't know what to do with it. That all I wanted was a smooth, perfect Farrah feather or cascading ringlets. Or smooth, rollered, or ironed hair. Or anything that made it look like *something*. No matter what I did, it looked frizzy. The would-be curls kicked and screamed against the humidity, enraged by the constant exposure to chlorine.

My mother was no help. She had long ago settled on a simple bob with bangs for her mousey brown hair. It only required washing. She was perfectly content to look like an imitation Bonnie Franklin. I tried to hide my hair in a ponytail, but it broke easily, which only made it more disheveled. Occasionally, I used scrunchies and pretended the mess was intentionally teased. I wanted someone to come along and tell me what to do with it. I wanted to look beautiful, and my hair thwarted my every attempt. I hated my hair.

Instead, I said, "I like it like this." *Lies, lies, lies.*

These thoughts shoved aside my concerns about where the sunglasses had come from.

CHAPTER 11
PAST - JANUARY 1985

"Where you *is*, girl?" said an angry voice on the phone. The sleep cleared from my head, and I realized I was talking to my swim coach.

"What?" I said stupidly into the phone. I didn't remember answering it, but it was in my hand.

"The bus is leaving. Where you is? Never mind. I know the answer to that now. From the sound of it, you all snug in your bed. Michelle, this is one of our biggest meets." I heard the worry turn into disappointment.

"I'm sorry, Coach Roberts." I didn't even have an excuse. I had stayed out late with Sissy knowing full well that I had a meet today. It was the first big regional meet of the season, and we were in third place. I thought I could handle it. That I might be a little tired, but that it would be okay. I would sleep on the bus. Only, I forgot to set my alarm clock. I also forgot to tell my mother I needed a ride to the school early this morning.

I heard my mom in the kitchen. Swimming was my thing, and I didn't expect anyone else to be interested. After my freshman year, she usually only attended the big meets. . . . Like today's.

"Where's the meet? The address, I mean?"

He gave it to me, and I wrote it down. I told him I would do everything I could to be there. I went out to tell my mother what I had done. I explained the situation, took a breath, and asked if she would drive me to Fort Myers. I told her she didn't have to wait for me, that I would take the bus back.

She set the glass she was washing down beside the sink and turned to look at me. She was still wearing her nightgown even though I suspected she had been up for a few hours.

"Michelle . . . that's a whole tank of gas," she sighed.

"It's okay. Don't worry about it. It's my fault." I started to return to my room.

She dried her hands on a dishtowel and opened the cabinet above the stove. She pulled down the coffee can she kept house money in and fished out some fives and ones.

"Go on, get your stuff. What time do we need to be there?" she said, smiling at me.

As soon as I got home, I raced to my room and called Sissy. I started bouncing on my bed until it thumped precariously against the wall.

"Today was amazing! I thought I was going to have to miss the meet, but my mom drove me all the way to Fort Myers. I made it there just in time to compete. I didn't even know she could drive that fast."

"Really?"

I didn't catch the tone in her voice, so I kept going.

"Yes! She stayed to watch me race and I placed first in the 100-yard freestyle!" I was still wearing the medal around my neck. "We stopped for a celebratory dinner and ice cream, which is why I'm only calling now."

"Congratulations." Her voice was cold and distant.

I wasn't sure what I had said to upset her, but I apologized instinctively.

"I'm sorry."

"For what?"

"Would you like to come to the next meet?" I asked tentatively.

"We'll see. I gotta go," and she hung up.

My elation at having won evaporated. I wasn't sure what I had done, but I didn't want her mad at me. I was so tired.

Part of me wanted to call Sissy back, but I knew from experience that wouldn't end well when she was in a mood. Instead, I went out to the living room, slumped onto the couch, and started watching *T. J. Hooker*. I could hear Mom telling Michael about our day together.

"Michael, you should have seen her! She looked like a fish in the water. And then we had so much fun when we stopped for pizza in Lake Placid."

Michael looked pleased and said maybe he could come next time. I fell asleep to William Shatner saving someone's life.

Sissy didn't call me on Sunday. I pretended it didn't bother me, but it did. We usually saw or talked to each other every day. I couldn't figure out what I had done. I spent the day pretending I was tired from the meet so I could hide in my room. I willed the phone to ring. I was afraid to call her. I should have realized then that something wasn't right.

"What, no Sissy today?" Michael asked when he saw me slumped on the couch after dinner. Even he knew something was wrong.

When I saw her at school on Monday morning, she barely acknowledged me. I couldn't concentrate first and second period and slipped a note into her locker on the way to third, asking if we could talk at lunch.

She was already eating when I got to the bleachers.

"Hey."

She stared at me. Those eyes. Her stare made me feel dead inside.

"I'm sorry. What did I do?"

"Don't be stupid. You know what you did."

"I don't," I said, my voice getting close to a whine.

"Look, I get that you like to do your stupid swimming stuff, but do you have to rub it in my face that you have a mother who gives a shit about you?"

"*What?*" I was hurt and confused. I knew she was mad, but I certainly didn't think it had to do with my mother.

She got up to leave, and I grabbed her arm. "*Please*, can we talk about this?"

She rolled her eyes and reluctantly sat back down.

"I'm sorry. I really am. I didn't know that would bother you." I knew I was apologizing for something I shouldn't have been apologizing for, but I didn't know what else to do to get us back to being friends. All I wanted was for everything to be okay again. I hated her being mad at me.

"I guess I'm convenient when you want to go to the mall or someone to pay your way, but not when you need help. Not like an actual friend."

Is that what this was about? That I needed help and had asked my mother instead of her? It seemed ridiculous, but she was dead serious.

"There was no time," I said tentatively. "I should've called you. I would've, but there was no time. I overslept. I'm so sorry. I wish it had been you instead."

She started to look appeased, and I was flooded with relief.

"The swimming thing is stupid, anyway. Why even bother? I mean, it's not like you will ever go to the Olympics or could even become a Weeki Wachee mermaid. Ooh, look at me, I'm not drowning." She started flailing her arms around like this was a joke.

Is that what she thought of me? I had been so proud of myself on Saturday, and she took that away from me. Before I could stop myself, I blurted, "Fuck you."

I was as startled as Sissy. I usually didn't curse, and I'd never spoken to her in anger before. We were both frozen in that moment, unsure of what came next.

Her face crumpled into confusion. Hell, I was confused by what I said. I mean, I knew I liked to swim, but I didn't think I was that passionate about it. I was also ashamed that I was more protective of swimming than my own mother. I had been ready to sweep aside my mother's support to appease Sissy. That realization unsettled me. It felt like my insides were tumbling around, trying to find the surface.

"You don't understand," she said.

"No, I don't. And neither do you."

Then she started crying, and I was even more confused. How did we get here? I wasn't sure who was mad at who anymore. I wanted to talk, to fix things, and now everything was even worse.

"You don't understand what it's like with my family. What I've been through."

"What does that have to do with me swimming?" There was an edge in my voice I hadn't heard in months.

"You need to understand. You need to know if we're going to be friends. You need to understand why I get upset sometimes. Why some things bother me. Why you hurt me yesterday."

"Okay . . ."

"My sister is dead," she said.

"*What?* When? Why didn't you tell me?" I felt like a monster.

"I was ten when it happened. Jessica was fourteen. It was an accident. She was in a coma for a while before she died. Everything has been *so* fucked up since then."

"Why didn't you tell me?"

"It's hard to talk about. I think about it all the time."

She was still crying. I lived with grief every day in my house. I understood loss. I knew what it felt like to hold everything inside all the time, to not talk about the thing that you thought about almost every day. I didn't say this. I assumed she remembered I had lost my dad, and this would bring us closer together. Something else we had in common. Why hadn't she told me after I told her about my dad?

We were both calming down, but I still felt confused. Why were we even fighting in the first place?

"Please don't tell anyone, okay? Everyone judges you when you have a dead sister. Like there's something fucked up about you and your family. Do you know what it's like going to school with your sister lying in a coma for a month? Everyone was talking about me like I had done something wrong. Everyone judges you against her, and you can never live up to their memories of this perfect person. Sometimes I think I should kill myself so my parents will love me, too."

It hurt to hear her like this. I couldn't stay mad after she said that. I wanted to comfort her. I wanted to be her friend. I felt shaky inside as if I had just come off a roller coaster.

"You're like a sister to me. I care so much about you. I get all mixed up inside sometimes. I don't ever want to lose you. You're the best friend I've ever had," she said. I believed her.

"You're my best friend, too."

I felt horrible for making her tell me like this. For making her feel bad because her mother was so distant. For not understanding that she lost someone, too. For making her feel like swimming was more important to me than she was. For not being the friend she deserved.

We sat together through the next period, causing me to skip World History. I had never skipped a class before, but I couldn't leave her. She needed me.

When I got home from school, I saw that my mother had done my laundry. I had largely been wearing Sissy's sister's old clothes. There they were, folded neatly on top of my dresser. A dead girl's T-shirts and shorts.

I wasn't sure what to think about them. I decided they were a way of helping her remember her sister. You can decide to believe anything you want.

CHAPTER 12
PRESENT - JUNE 2001

Though my mother had suffered a cerebral hemorrhage Tuesday night, my brother waited until Wednesday evening to call me after they had to put her in a medically induced coma.

I think about that. He didn't call me right away. Why did he wait? Did he not want me to come? Or did he not expect me to come? They think she may have hit her head during the day on Tuesday. When Michael couldn't reach her Tuesday night or Wednesday morning, he went over to her house and found her unconscious. She could have been lying there for weeks and I wouldn't have noticed. Good thing he is there. I am useless as a daughter and sister.

The doctors aren't sure if she is going to make it. The next twenty-four hours are critical. I don't know what I can offer Michael. Or Mom. I think about the phone call and wonder if he asked me to come out of obligation, not expecting me to say yes. I can picture Michael telling me because it was the right thing to do, but not wanting me there. He has always been a decent person. Was I ever decent?

When you are a kid, you know right from wrong, but not necessarily good from evil. Even if you know something feels wrong, you don't know how to make sense of the feeling. Evil exists out in the open because it looks like everything else. You have nothing to compare it to. Evil can be banal. It can be part of everyday life. You can invite it in without realizing it. You can become evil without meaning to.

CHAPTER 13
PAST - JANUARY 1985

I expected to be closer to Sissy after our talk about her sister. Instead, she treated me like I had done something wrong. She didn't exactly shut me out, but things weren't the same. It was like there was an invisible barrier between us now. I could feel the old loneliness creeping in at the edges, only now it was worse because I knew what it felt like to have a best friend. An almost-sister. Part of me was missing, even though I could see it right in front of me.

The eleventh grade had an annual field trip to the South Florida Museum in Bradenton. It was a two-hour bus ride. It sounded like fun until the weather forecasters started freaking out in the days before the trip about an arctic blast spreading from Canada to Florida. We were already ill-equipped for the handful of days that dropped into the forties.

When I woke up the morning of the field trip, I could see my breath. The two portable heaters my mother had bought from Walmart were heating the bathroom and the kitchen. She was afraid the pipes would freeze. I didn't even know such a thing was possible.

I shivered under the covers, trying to get dressed without exposing any skin. I layered on pantyhose, jeans, a T-shirt, a long-sleeved shirt, the sweater I wore at Christmas, and a denim jacket of Michael's. I had never been so cold before. I couldn't feel my fingers. I attempted two pairs of socks, but they made my tennis shoes too tight.

When I went outside to catch the bus, everything was eerily quiet and still. There were no insects chirping or flying. The birds had gone quiet. I had never appreciated the constant soundtrack of birds, frogs, and insects until it was gone. There was a sudden absence of everything. Of life. It was creepy. I saw a few lizards, but they were just sitting there. None of them ran from me. I squatted to look at one and realized it was dead. It looked like it had fallen out of the tree. This wasn't normal. Shouldn't they have closed school? Maybe even closed Florida?

Sissy and I sat together on the bus to the museum. She had an actual ski jacket, hat, and gloves. She acted nonchalantly when she said they were from a trip to Tahoe. What was Tahoe? A store? A person? It didn't matter. She was comfortable and warm. Almost everyone else was shivering. The only kids who were semi-warm were the ones who sat near the front, near the heat vents. There were a few kids wearing what appeared to be oversized winter fashion from ten to twenty years ago, probably clothes their parents or grandparents had brought with them to Florida.

We passed orange groves and orchards that were sprayed with water during the night to protect the trees and crops. I wasn't sure how it worked, but the effect in the early morning sunlight was magical. The ice and icicles reflected sunlight in every direction, making it look like a frozen fairy tale. I wondered if this was what winter looked like up north. I never understood why people lived in cold places, but if they looked like this, it made sense.

Sissy seemed not to notice and wanted to talk about what had happened on *Dynasty* last week. I half-listened to her complain about Krystle Carrington while I shoved my hands under my thighs to keep them warm. The plastic seat felt hard and brittle. I was so glad I didn't have swim practice. I was pretty sure I would die.

Tammy Pruitt turned around in the seat ahead to talk to us. "Isn't the ice pretty? How do the plants not die from it? I'm sooooo cold." Like many of us, she had layered together an incoherent outfit. Tammy was abnormally cheerful. She had been that way since we met in sixth grade. She was a genuinely happy person.

I was fascinated by her and wondered what it would take to make her sad. Like, could she sit through *Love Story* with an unrelenting smile?

"Michelle, I totally forgot! I brought that tape you wanted to listen to." Sissy began rummaging in her bag and pulled out her Walkman. She fixed it so we could both listen using her headphones and pushed play on the Walkman.

Tammy hung over the back of the seat, waiting for a response. I was confused because it was a Duran Duran album we had listened to a ton of times at her house. It dawned on me that she thought she was saving me from having to talk to Tammy. Sissy referred to her as Totally Terrific Tammy, but I kind of liked her. I wished I was happy like that.

Tammy slid back down, turned around in her seat, and started talking to Donna Moore instead. I listened to the tape and went back to shivering and looking at Mother Nature's ice palace.

By the time we were done learning about the indigenous people of Florida, Marjory Stoneman Douglas, Henry Flagler, and meeting Snooty the manatee, the sun had warmed the air. All the ice was gone, and the fields had returned to their usual drabness. The unspoken frost between Sissy and me had melted too, and we spent the ride back to Sebring giggling and writing mean notes back and forth. It was everything I had wanted.

CHAPTER 14
PAST - MARCH 1985

Sissy and I settled into a routine that spring. I had finally figured out how to be the friend she wanted. Swim season was over, and my afternoons and weekends were free. I considered getting a job, but there wasn't much within walking distance of home. Instead, I usually went home with Sissy a few days a week, and we'd hang out all afternoon. We'd occasionally do homework, but we mostly watched TV, ate, and gossiped.

Sometimes I swam in her pool while she sunned on one of the loungers, or we'd rent a movie. I'd catch her mother staring at me while I swam.

"Does your mom mind me being here all the time?" Sissy looked up and saw her mother at the window.

"She likes you. She probably likes you more than she likes me."

"Okay, so why is she staring at me?"

"Maybe because Jessica liked to swim."

It dawned on me that I was wearing one of her sister's old swimsuits. Sissy wouldn't have given me the clothes without asking first, would she?

"Did Jessica drown?"

"No, and I don't want to talk about it."

She hadn't mentioned her sister again since our fight. I wondered about the accident and coma, but she never told me what had happened. Asking if she had drowned was the closest I had come to talking about it directly.

Often her mother would fix us dinner, and we'd eat and watch our *Must See TV.* The way we ate at home and the food at Sissy's house had little in common. I pretended to like the long grain wild rice but thought it tasted like chewy dirt. I liked Minute Rice. I liked Velveeta. I liked mac and cheese out of the box. I loved Beefaroni. Sissy's family ate none of that. I was shocked when I saw they threw out their S&H Green Stamps. At least we all agreed on Publix macaroni salad and potato salad.

I thought the way Sissy's family ate was how you were supposed to eat. I told my mother I didn't like instant mashed potatoes anymore. I did, but it seemed like a place to begin to make changes. To not be who I was. Instead, I asked for snacks like carrots and celery and ate them instead of Little Debbie cakes and Moon Pies. I hated carrots and celery, but I ate them because I thought they were right, and junk food was wrong. Well, wrong until it was time to watch TV, and then it was right again. Sissy's rules were arbitrary, but her snacks were always good.

I had a secret crush on Harry Anderson. *Night Court* was my favorite show. Sissy had a big TV in her room and cable instead of a crappy antenna. She'd tape it for me, and we'd watch that and whatever else Sissy had taped for us that week. On weekends, we went to the movies or the mall or just drove around. We talked alike and people commented on how we were inseparable. Everyone knew we were best friends. I realized I wasn't getting teased as much at school. I thought that was because of Sissy. I thought she made me better somehow. Or at least acceptable.

I was uncomfortable with Sissy usually paying when we went to the movies, but she said it was what friends did. The fight we had in January made me aware of the pain she hid. That no one really knew or understood her except me. She told me that. I knew I had to be more accepting if she said something that bothered me. I knew she didn't really mean it.

I was sliding into my desk in Health when Ruben Wilkerson turned around and asked me if Sissy was seeing anyone. I told him no and got out my notebook. I couldn't wait to tell Sissy that Ruben had asked about her. I knew he was on Sissy's list. Sissy had a list of boys she deemed acceptable. That was how she titled the list, "deemed acceptable." There were a few names crossed off in Sharpie, and I wondered who they were and what they had said or done.

Cassie, who I hadn't spoken to since Sissy told me what she had said about me, was sitting next to Ruben and rolled her eyes.

I turned and glared at her.

"She isn't very nice. Why are you even friends with her?" she said.

"How can you say that? You don't even know her. At least she isn't two-faced."

Cassie started laughing, and before I could argue further, the bell rang.

Cassie and I had become friends in second grade. It was after my dad died, and I had to switch schools. I didn't want to be there, and I didn't want to talk to anyone. I found a hiding place in the playground equipment and would hide there during recess. One day I fell asleep. The teacher was ready to panic, but Cassie said she thought she knew where I was. She led the teacher and the principal to me. Afterward, Cassie started sitting inside the metal structure with me at recess. She told me how she watched *Land of the Lost*, but the Sleestak scared her. She had the prettiest hair. Her braids were intricate and finished with beads. I loved the sound they made when she moved her head.

Eventually, I quit needing to hide, and by then, we had become friends. We'd go roller skating and see each other at birthday parties. We went to different junior highs, and the friendship fell apart. I had hoped we might be friends again when we met back up in high school, but she had new friends.

I seethed the whole class. I came up with rebuttal after rebuttal and couldn't wait for class to be over so I could let her have it. I was going to defend Sissy like she defended me. But I was so distracted by my internal tirade that I wasn't ready when the bell rang.

On the way out of class, Cassie dropped a note on my desk that read, "Michelle, I didn't mean to upset you. Really. You're a nice person and I don't want to see you get hurt. XO, Cass." What did that mean? Two-faced bitch. That's how I'd started thinking about people.

I saw Sissy at lunch and wanted to talk to her about what had happened, but she was busy reading the *CliffsNotes* for *Huckleberry Finn* for a test. Sissy had all sorts of ingenious ways to do and get what she needed. She was proud of the fact she had never read any of the assigned readings for English and still maintained a B average. The only book I had ever seen her read was *Go Ask Alice*, which she swore was a true story.

CHAPTER 15

I've spent so many years not remembering. Keeping my mind as blank and empty of the past as possible. I have pretended to be an orphaned only child from Atlanta. I act like my life started once I got to college. I dodge questions, pretending I don't understand, and answer with a derailing question of my own. When you don't want to talk about your past, even the most mundane small talk is filled with barbed triggers. I have avoided the past, and, in a way, I have avoided myself. Now I'm avoiding thinking about Mom dying and not being there, again.

For the last eleven years, I've collected forms, filed, processed patients in and out of the hospital, and pulled old records. For eleven years, I've found new ways to work and overwork to stay busy. I came in early and stayed late. I learned to touch-type. I deciphered doctor and patient handwriting. I was the only one who could make the ancient microfilm machine behave. There was a never-ending stream of patients and busywork.

I went straight from doing data entry as a work-study student to doing data entry at a hospital in Athens. The university career center had arranged the job via a temp agency, and I never left. When the hospital was sold, I had to face staying in Athens and being jobless or moving to Atlanta and taking a job at a new hospital. It felt like the decision was made for me. I just had to do as I was told.

I had always wanted to live in a city. I thought it would be exciting. Instead, I found that being surrounded by millions of people instead of thousands was even lonelier. I was lost in a concrete ocean. The tides of patient intake and discharge paperwork were the same. I would occasionally go out with co-workers after work, floundering for connection. I was so lonely but felt incapable of offering or accepting friendship.

As Anne, I'm the person patients have to talk to in order to get care or leave the hospital. I am the human embodiment of paperwork. All they want to do is see a doctor or go home, and I am in the way. They never remember me.

My bosses see Anne as "a hard worker" and "team player." My co-workers love that I will always cover their shifts. I'm that co-worker without kids, parents, or family they can always count on to help them out. Anne is a work of fiction. What they don't know is that I don't want to go back to my empty apartment.

I had forgotten how intense everything felt those years. The memories are just as intense. Everything I have kept at bay is flooding back, filling years of calculated emptiness with waves of emotion I can't handle. I worked so hard to repress everything. I am confused and startled to find some good memories mixed in with the bad. I thought everything would be tainted, but it isn't.

But those are the ones that hurt the most.

CHAPTER 16

I was standing outside, waiting for the bus, which was conspicu-ously absent. A few minutes later, the vice-principal stormed over, spluttering something about the bus breaking down and needing to double us up with another route. He said this as if we had some-thing to do with the breakdown. He stood there, wild-eyed, fervent-ly pointing at an idling bus with his walkie-talkie.

Most of the seats were taken when I got on. I found an empty one and slid in. Seconds later, I felt the bounce of someone sitting beside me. I looked over, and Morrison shrugged at me. We had progressed to occasional small talk on the bus, but nothing more. He started reading his book, and I stared out the window.

"You ever see *Invasion of the Body Snatchers?*" he said, still looking at his book.

"Which one? The one with Kevin McCarthy or Donald Suther-land?"

"I was thinking of the one with Donald Sutherland. That's what Vice Principal Polk looked like, pointing at the bus. Like Donald Sutherland at the end of the movie," and he started laughing.

I didn't even know he could laugh. I started laughing.

After that, we started sitting together on the bus. We usually saw each other in the morning, if he came to school, and in the after-noon, if I didn't go home with Sissy. Neither of us said anything about the change. Once he asked if we could switch seats, and I thought he liked the window.

"Can we switch seats?" he asked the next day.

"I thought you liked the window?"

"It's not that." He started to point to his ear and said, "My left ear is a little fucked up."

I switched with him.

"Thanks. If it is quiet, I am fine, but the background bus noise is the worst. I can't make sense of what anyone is saying."

After that, I automatically sat or walked on his right.

He usually wore a sleeveless denim jacket with patches and T-shirts with bands I had never heard of. His jeans were ripped, the strings fluttering in the wind created by the open windows. He wore thick bracelets around his thin wrists. He would prop his knees against the back of the seat and let his feet dangle. He wore Converse sneakers, the soles smooth from wear. Sometimes we read, sometimes he shared his music with me, sometimes we talked about TV and movies, but mostly we provided each other unspoken shelter from the aggressive din of high school students, unfettered from the rules of school or home. The bus was a no man's land.

Most of the people at Ocean Breezes High School looked and acted like variations of one another. Morrison and I did not. In some ways, our friendship seemed inevitable.

One day, we started talking about a movie we had both watched the night before.

"I like movies because even when things are wrong, they are right. People say the right thing. There are endings. There are answers. Mistakes get fixed. Even evil people make sense. Everything has a place or is part of the story. It all works out somehow. Real life isn't like that."

It was the most personal thing Morrison had ever said to me. We had avoided personal topics, sticking to safe subjects like school, books, music, movies, and TV.

Morrison knew I lived at Paradise Acres, he saw me get on and off the bus, but I didn't know where he lived. Now that we were finally sitting next to each other, I was emboldened to ask him that simple question. It shouldn't have been so hard to talk to him, but it was. He had a wall around him that was only just starting to come down.

"So where do you live?"

"Down off Cowhouse Road."

I knew where he meant. It wasn't far from my house. He probably lived at Coral Ridge Trailer Park.

"Do you live with your parents?"

"Just my mom. She's a waitress. Don't go imagining *Alice* or some shit like that. She works at a roadhouse on the other side of the lake. She works nights, so I can pretty much do what I want." He wanted to sound cool, but instead, he sounded defensive.

"It's just me and my mom and half-brother." I wasn't sure why I referred to Michael as my half-brother. I always called him my brother.

We didn't mention our fathers. We each made assumptions, none of them right.

I learned that his grandmother lived in Whispering Pines when he was little, and he sometimes lived with her, but mostly he lived with his mother. They moved to Miami for about a year when he was in ninth grade, but they came back to Lorida when that didn't work out. He got into punk the year he was in Miami. His mom's boyfriend was in a band, and he let Morrison hang out with him.

He said he liked punk because he could feel it better than he could hear it. He said that punk didn't care if he couldn't hear one hundred percent because it wasn't meant to be perfect. That nothing was perfect.

CHAPTER 17
PAST - MAY 1985

Michael offered to drop me off at Sissy's on his way to work one Saturday morning. I wondered what Morrison did on the weekends. I imagined him going to concerts or parties. I enjoyed sitting with him in the mornings and afternoons. He had been on the morning bus every day for two weeks now, which was a record.

As Michael and I got into the car, he said, "Chelle, I wanted to talk to you about something. I get that you . . . that you and Sissy are friends. Mom was really happy about you having a new friend, at first, I mean." He was hesitating as if he was trying to remember what he wanted to say instead of simply talking with me.

"We're worried about how much time you spend at Sissy's. We wonder why you never spend time with her at our house. Why is that? Mom is uncomfortable with all the stuff she gives you." The more he spoke, the more rehearsed it sounded. I could hear my mother's words in his mouth.

"She's my best friend. So, why does that even matter to you and Mom?"

"Because . . . because you aren't the same when you are around her."

"*What? So?*"

"Chelle, I don't want to fight with you about this. We're just worried, is all."

"*About what? Me finally having a real friend?*" I shouted. I was afraid Mom might try and stop me from hanging out with Sissy.

I could see Michael was getting frustrated. I was glad we were pulling up in front of Sissy's house. I got out, and he looped the cul-de-sac.

I could hear Sissy yelling as I walked up to the front door. I considered waving and asking Michael to wait, but he was already at the corner. I didn't want to give him any more ammunition after our "talk."

"You fucking bitch! You can't do this!"

"Cecilia, you are going, and that is final! Enough is enough. Quit acting like a spoiled brat." I heard Mrs. Davis yell.

"I won't fucking go!" she screamed.

I was frozen on the front porch. The door swung open and slammed against something on the inside. Sissy barreled out the door with her keys in her fist. Mrs. Davis stood in the open doorway, looking every bit as dangerous as Sissy.

Sissy saw me and said, "Get in the fucking car."

Before I could buckle up, she was peeling out, speeding past the stop sign. I prayed that my brother was long gone.

"That fucking goddamned Nazi bitch!" she screamed as she turned hard onto the highway, skidding on the gravel shoulder. I knew she was speeding worse than usual, but I was afraid to say anything.

"What happened?"

"My mother is a fucking cunt. That's what happened. They are punishing me for something I didn't do."

"What?"

"Never mind. Let's go shopping."

With the mood she was in, whatever Sissy wanted to do was fine with me. My response was upbeat, and I hoped it pacified her. She floored it all the way to Fort Pierce. I felt a little car sick by the time we got there, but I didn't say anything.

She stalked into Bloomingdale's like she was on a mission. She wasn't even looking at price tags or trying things. She just thrust her credit card at clerks over and over again. Three hours later, her purchase of a new stereo system at Peaches was denied. She smiled at the clerk as if that was what she had been waiting for.

With cash, she bought us lunch at Sbarro. I wanted to ask what happened, but her mood felt too dangerous still. I could feel the anger radiating off her. Instead, we ate our pizza in silence. I knew the fight she'd had was with her mother, but I still felt like her anger was somehow my fault. Like I failed at making her feel better about whatever had happened.

On the walk back through Bloomingdale's, she stopped at the perfume counter and started spraying me with perfume, saying she needed to cover up my stink. She laughed as she did it, but there was something about the way she said it. She wasn't kidding. Did I smell bad? What else was wrong with me? I knew that my breath stank. Sissy often offered me mints, but I noticed she didn't eat them.

She'd tell me what I was doing wrong in small ways in general. I had loved my waterproof Timex watch until she jokingly compared it to her Swatch and said it looked like something a creepy old man would wear. I knew she was trying to help, but I ended up feeling bad about things I didn't know I was doing wrong.

There were so many ways to be wrong.

If you were smart, you were wrong. If you were dumb, you were wrong. Tall? Wrong. Short? Wrong. If you were pretty, obviously, you were stuck up. If you were ugly, you were also stupid. If you were poor, you were dirty and lazy. Outie instead of an innie? Wrong. As if the act of being born was a mistake. No boobs, and you were a frigid freak. Big boobs, and you were a slut. You had to be feminine, but not too much or too little, or you faced being labeled as high maintenance or a dyke. Guys needed to be men, no exceptions. Women had to eradicate body hair, but men had to be able to grow a full mustache. No matter how hard you tried, you were still wrong, and no one ever told you how to be right.

I started brushing my teeth three times a day, shaving my legs and underarms daily until my skin was so irritated, I had to stop and kept my watch for swim season only. I tried so hard to be right. To be okay. To be acceptable. Sissy seemed to feel better as we drove home, but I felt worse and worse.

CHAPTER 18
PRESENT - JUNE 2001

Lovebugs are splattering against the windshield, causing me to use the wipers and window washer fluid to ineffectively clear them. I'm passing Gainesville as I notice my dashboard's temperature needle is in the red zone. I'm so hot that it takes me a minute to comprehend the car is overheating, too.

I exit at Micanopy and look for a service station. Thankfully, there is one right off the highway. Is this a sign I should turn back? To what? To my empty apartment and *Law and Order*?

Three weeks ago, a middle-aged woman, Gladys A. Anderson, came into the ER with a friend. Gladys was having trouble speaking. I asked if her friend, Lillian, could help me with the intake form. The trouble started when I asked about her marital status. The friend hesitated, and Gladys began thrashing, shaking her head no.

I indicated no on the form. When I asked about next of kin, Lillian didn't know how to answer, and Gladys couldn't speak.

Within two days, Gladys was on life support. Lillian had stayed by her side the whole time. On the third day, Gladys's husband showed up, demanding that Lillian be barred from sitting with his dying wife.

I hadn't thought anything of the blank spaces on the form the day I admitted Gladys. I was just doing my job. I knew all too well it is the little, harmless things that can destroy everything.

I saw Lillian sobbing on one of the concrete benches outside the hospital.

She looked up as I walked by.

"*Wait, wait.* You were in the ER when we came in," she said, tears running down her cheeks.

I stopped and nodded.

"What does 'next of kin' mean? Who can be next of kin? Is it only blood or legal relatives?"

I explained that the patient could name anyone next of kin. It doesn't have to be a spouse or a child. That it isn't the same as a will or anything.

"So, if I was next of kin, I could be with her?"

That was when she told me that Gladys's soon-to-be ex-husband had assumed the role of next of kin and wouldn't let Lillian be with her.

The next morning, I got to work early, found the intake form, and listed Lillian as the next of kin. I called and let her know she should be okay to visit. What I didn't know was that the forms had already been scanned. What I didn't know was that the husband would be challenged to provide proof of marriage because the form said Gladys was unmarried. What I didn't know was that the forms would be pulled and compared. I would find all of this out after I was called into a meeting with the hospital administration and lied myself into a corner.

What I did know was that Gladys would die alone because the hospital, Lillian, and Gladys's not-quite-ex-husband were busy fighting. No one got a second chance.

Gladys A. Anderson shook me out of my inertia.

After what feels like forever standing under a merciless sun, the mechanic takes a look at my car. I explain that I am on my way to Sebring from Atlanta. He pops the hood and makes a few grunting noises. He says it needs to cool down before he can say for sure what is wrong. He thinks it might just need a rest and some coolant. A rest? It's a car, not a horse.

He shoves a greasy rag into his back pocket and shuffles back inside the garage.

"How long will it take to cool down?" I shout to his retreating back.

"'Bout an hour before I can check it right. We got drinks in the store." He motions to the attached minimart.

I can't sit still. It's too hot to sit in the car. I look around to see if there is anything else to walk to. A fireworks stand is open. Across the street is a restaurant. All I can make out is "Café" from where I stand. I walk over, thinking I will get lunch to kill time, but I get there and realize that the full name is Café Risqué, and I am about to walk into a strip club/diner. I'm not prepared to deal with all that. I throw my hands up, abandon any hope of a sandwich and walk back to the gas station. Impatient and aggravated, I buy an iced tea and bag of chips and find a tree near the air pump. I all but throw myself on the ground in a huff. About thirty seconds later, I notice I am sitting next to a fire ant nest and scramble up. I am waiting for all this to be funny.

I find a spot in relative shade and sit down on a parking block, doing what I can to avoid the venomous grass and treacherous sun. I eat the chips like I have a grudge against them, having fixated on making things better with a sandwich. The ritual of greeting, menu, drink, order, eat, and pay would easily have killed thirty minutes.

I finish the iced tea and chips and look at my watch, willing time to move. It is barely fifteen minutes later. *Shit.* I should call Michael. There is no way I am going to be there when I said I would. I rummage in my purse for change.

I go back into the minimart connected to the gas station and ask them for change for three dollars. While I wait, I notice a dead fly in the pickled eggs jar. It's as pink as the brine surrounding the eggs. How long has it been there? How many have they sold with the pickled fly floating around with the pickled eggs? Are there also pickled fly eggs for sale? I have momentarily distracted myself from thinking about my own life by focusing on the dead fly.

They also have artificially dyed nuts under a heat lamp near the register. I wonder if they too come with a side of insect eggs. There is a pay phone around the side of the gas station. I dial Michael's phone number, and the automated voice instructs me to insert $1.25 for the next three minutes. He picks up on the first ring.

"Hello?"

"Michael?"

"Michelle? Are you close?"

"Not exactly."

"Are you even coming?" he says flatly.

"I am. I really am. I broke down in Micanopy. I am waiting for the guy to look at my car."

"So you're on your way?"

"Yes, I will be there. Please, just give me a few hours. If there is something wrong with the car, I will try and get a bus to Sebring, okay? I'll figure something out." I realize as I say it that I mean it. I was looking for an excuse to run back to Atlanta, but his voice has shamed me to my core. I've missed him so much.

"Hospital visiting hours end at eight. Will you be here by then?"

"Yes." No. I don't know.

"Are you sure?"

"I'll be there, I promise. I just don't know exactly when."

"I'm glad you're coming. Bye, Chelle."

"Bye."

Chelle. No one has called me Chelle in a long, long time.

We hang up just as the automated voice starts to ask for more money. I will get there, somehow.

I walk to the fireworks stand and look around. Everything on display exclaims its potency and seems like a medical history intake form waiting to happen. I watch men come and go from Café Risqué. I wonder if there are daily specials. Eventually, I wander back to my parking block, but a car is parked there now. The others are in the sun, so I stand under a tree to wait.

The mechanic comes back out and slowly removes the radiator cap. He nods to himself, goes back inside, and returns with a bottle of coolant and a funnel. He tinkers under the hood for about ten minutes.

"Ma'am, far as I can tell, yer coolant was low, and ya overheated.

Yer belts and hoses seem okay, and the water pump is working. If there's a more serious problem, you'll know soon enough, and ya can come right back here. If not, just take 'er easy in this heat and stop and let 'er rest and cool down a bit if she gets all het up. That's a bitty engine in there for all that driving. You also need an oil change, but that's best left for another day, I imagine. That'll be $25."

I pay him and get back on the highway, obsessively watching the needle for movement. It bobs up and down a bit but stays clear of the red. I keep heading south, compulsively watching the gauges and listening to the engine.

CHAPTER 19
PAST - JUNE 1985

I was hesitant to go over to Sissy's house for a week or so after the blowup, so we mostly hung out at the strip mall in Sebring or over by the Tastee Freez. It was raining hard Thursday afternoon when we drove to her house. Her parents weren't home when we got there, which was a relief. We went to her room, and she left to get us towels and Cokes.

Sissy's room was always messy, but it looked like she had recently trashed it. There was a crack in one of the mirrored closet doors. I didn't mean to snoop, but a brochure for Serenity Ranch was sitting on her desk. Everything else that had been on the desk was now on the floor. The brochure looked like it had been crumpled and smoothed out again.

Serenity Ranch will help repair your family and enable your troubled teen to heal. Their journey begins with our wilderness therapy ranch.

Reconnecting with the environment will help them reconnect with life. Teenagers will form bonds with their peers, who are also struggling. They will learn to rely on one another and forge newfound strength and determination.

Campers will learn orienteering, survival skills, basic cooking, and daily exercise to prepare them for three week-long hikes in the beautiful Wasatch Mountains.

Our highly trained staff will keep your teen safe and help guide them to a new beginning.

I now understood what the fight with her mother had been about.

I was sitting in my usual spot, flicking through the channels to see what was on, when she walked back in. She hadn't said anything more about the fight and never mentioned the camp. I certainly wasn't going to bring it up. I wondered if she had left the brochure out for me to see. Was it her way of telling me? I wondered what her parents considered "behavior issues"? Was this about her spending?

That weekend she told me she was going to be away for much of the summer. She told me she had been accepted to attend a camp for the talented and gifted. I didn't let on that I had seen the brochure. I figured she was embarrassed. I acted impressed and told her that was awesome. We were both lying, but it was okay. She said they only accepted eighty kids from all over the country. The camp was in Utah, and she'd be leaving right after the end of school. She told me again and again how much she was going to miss me.

Of course, she saw this as an excuse to go shopping. She said she'd need clothes like they wear in Utah. I had no idea what that meant, but she interpreted it as several pairs of short shorts and a few tube tops.

I wanted to tell Sissy about Morrison. I was worried she would see us talking at school. I worried she wouldn't like him. She seemed enthusiastic about the camp, and I didn't want to set her off, so I decided not to bring it up.

Coach Roberts sent a flyer to the homerooms of swim team members. Sweetwater Shores, a country club on the outskirts of Sebring, needed lifeguards, caddies, and servers for the summer. It wasn't that far from home.

I took the flyer home and talked to my mom and Michael. I had rehearsed a speech in my head. I told them I wanted to get a job. I wanted my own money, and I wanted to contribute to the house money. Only after they had agreed to the wonderfulness of my idea did I explain that I'd need rides to and from work. It was too far to walk, and I didn't have a bike.

"I'm surprised Sissy hasn't already arranged that for you," Michael said.

"Hush, Michael," my mother said, "This will be good for her."

They agreed they would drive me back and forth. I told them I would pay for gas. My mother asked Michael to drive me there Saturday morning, so I could apply for a lifeguard position.

I didn't tell Michael that Sissy was going away. I didn't allow myself to give voice to the thought that I wouldn't be getting a job if Sissy was going to be around for the summer. I imagined she would tell me I didn't need a job, that she could pay for everything. That she might get mad if I said I was getting a job. As if I was rejecting her for wanting my own money. I didn't like how I felt thinking like that. She was my best friend.

Monday morning on the bus, I excitedly told Morrison I got a summer job. I rummaged in my backpack for the flyer and showed it to him.

"They still hiring for caddies?"

"I don't know."

I didn't see him on the bus that afternoon.

"I got a job, too," he said casually the next morning.

"Where?"

"That country club you told me about. I traded a kid a couple of tapes for a ride yesterday and did the application and all. I think they were desperate because they made it clear I would be wearing a uniform and said I would have to keep my hair under a baseball hat."

The end of school melted into the shimmering heat of Florida in summer. *Grease* taught me that the end of school should be ecstatic and involve a flying car. Instead, there were false promises to "K.I.T." and "Have a GREEEAT Summer!!! XOXO" Girls hugged each other like they were being sent to a gulag.

In Sissy's case, that was sort of the case, but no one knew that but me, and I wasn't supposed to know. She made us say goodbye about ten times: once on the last day of school, again at her house, and then she called me right before leaving for the airport. And then she was gone. The air felt both heavy and light. I felt lonely, but I also felt a little bit free. The now silent phone sat next to my bed until I eventually moved it back into the kitchen.

A few days into summer break, Michael was driving me to lifeguard training when we spotted a skinny kid on a rickety ten-speed on Route 98. I asked Michael to slow down. We pulled alongside the kid.

Morrison didn't look over, just shouted, "Fuck off, you fucking pervert-dipshit-dildo-punks!"

"Morrison!"

He glanced over and saw it was me, and the scowl turned into a lopsided grin, "Oh, hey!"

"Meet us up the road."

We drove ahead until we could pull off the road and waited for him. He huffed into the lot a few minutes later, his face red and sweaty.

"You going to the country club?"

"Yeah, it's my first day. I didn't know six miles was so fucking far."

"Throw your bike in the trunk," Michael said.

He did and hopped in the car.

"Thank you so much, man."

That afternoon, my mother picked us both up, and Morrison picked his bike up from our house. We compared schedules, and our days and hours mostly overlapped. Mom and Michael were happy to drive him as well, so he biked or walked to our place in the morning, and we drove from there. He also contributed for gas and often bought Michael and me drinks and snacks at the Circle K in the afternoon. Outside of school, Morrison seemed more at ease. The hard edges softened. He looked nothing like himself in the work-issued khaki pants, polo shirt, and baseball cap.

Before she left, Sissy made me promise to write her every day, which I tried to do. I told her that I was so bored and lonely without her that I got a job as a lifeguard. I made it sound miserable. I told her about the monstrous kids. I told her about the questionable Speedos. I told her about the bad boob jobs and about the mothers who disappeared for "tennis lessons." I made the last one up because I thought she could use some salacious gossip. I tried to make my days sound like an episode of *Dynasty*. I usually mailed my letters every three to four days, a nice thick envelope filled with melodramatic life at Sweetwater Shores Country Club.

About two weeks after she left, I received my first letter from Sissy, postmarked Ogden, UT. I knew she had traveled, but my most exotic trips were to Busch Gardens and Weeki Wachee. This was my first real letter from another state.

She told me about life at the camp. How she was pretty sure she was going to die from heat exhaustion. How dry it was there. She said she met some kids who were nice. She said she was happier than she had been in a while. That she was learning a lot about herself at the camp. She told me about Jason, a boy from New York, who liked her, but they hadn't kissed yet. She also told me how much she missed me. Most of her letters were similar, but I supposed mine were as well.

With our first paychecks, Morrison and I splurged and got lunch at Denny's and went to see *The Goonies*. After it was over, we pretended to go to the bathroom and snuck into *Return to Oz*. We exited the theater spooked and satisfied at twilight. I found a payphone and called my mom and asked if she could pick us up. We waited for her on the curb outside the movie theater.

"I'm so freaked out right now. That was fucking scarier than *Cannibal Holocaust*. Who does that to children? I'm, like, afraid of rocks and roller derby now," Morrison said, mock shivering.

I tucked my head inside my shirt, pretending to be headless.

"Knock it off. That's some fucked up shit."

"You were the one who wanted to sneak in to see it."

"The punishment didn't fit the crime."

I laughed, and I had an unfair, flickering thought that I didn't miss Sissy like I thought I would. I shut the thought down and told myself I was a bad friend. In my head, I promised I would write her an extra-long letter tomorrow.

CHAPTER 20

PAST - JUNE 1985

Morrison called me on one of our days off.

"Do you know where Stoner Couch is?"

"I've heard of it, but I have never been there." Everyone had heard of Stoner Couch. It was the source of middle school legend. Everyone knew someone who had either stumbled across a stoner orgy there (unlikely) or found woodland fairy porn there (more likely).

"Go to the end of Prescott Lane, and when you come to the end of the road, keep walking. There is a trailer with a mean dog back there, so keep to the trees on the left. Go across the clearing and look for the old washing machine."

"Washing machine?"

"Hey, I don't make the landmarks, okay? The couch is under the trees to the right of the washing machine. Meet me there at five-thirty. I want to show you something."

"Okay."

I underestimated the walk to Stoner Couch. I assumed if stoners went there, it would be an easy walk. It wasn't. I had to navigate fallen trees, oppressive humidity, sticker burrs, and swarms of gnats and mosquitoes. The drone of bug and bird noises got louder and louder the closer I got to the lake. I couldn't see it, but I knew it was there. Some of the most beautiful, elegant birds have the ugliest cries, and they were all coming from the same direction. I listened to the chalkboard screech of herons and guttural croak of egrets as

I fought my way through the grass.

I found the washing machine tilted on its side and covered with layers of rust and graffiti. I also saw the rusted husk of what might have been a tractor. I finally made it to the couch and found Morrison waiting for me.

I was aggravated from the mosquitoes and had sticker burrs covering my socks, creeping up to poke my calves. Sweat was dripping down the sides of my face and gathering under my breasts. Hair had flung itself loose from my ponytail and was either plastered to my forehead or standing on high alert for danger. Morrison sat on the couch with a smile that was hard to read.

He jumped up and said, "Come on, I want to show you something."

He plunged into the trees and ferns bordering the lake, and I had to scramble to keep up with his long legs. A few minutes later, we were standing under a massive live oak tree draped in Spanish moss. It looked like an octopus, with arms curving out from a thick trunk. I stood there waiting for the big reveal.

"What? What is it?" I said, slapping at my face and legs.

At that prompting, he disappeared around the tree and reappeared above my head.

"Come on up!"

I crept around the back, stepping over gnarled roots protruding along the ground. I guessed at where he disappeared and looked up. Along the tree, I saw pieces of two-by-fours nailed along the trunk, creating a ladder of sorts. I put my hand on one and my foot on another. I was up in seconds. I found him at the crux of the tree, which was covered by a square of plywood. Tree limbs split around the crux soaring above and around us. The limbs extended out and bowed towards the ground. On his lap was a scuffed, plastic dry bag. He was rummaging inside of it. He tossed me a bottle of Avon Skin So Soft.

"Rub it on. It helps with the mosquitoes. I hate the smell of Off! and if I spray it here, it kills other bugs. They belong here. I'm just a squatter. That should keep the mosquitoes off you. And you'll smell springtime fresh."

I did as he suggested, and it helped with the mosquitos, but I didn't feel springtime fresh. I felt oily on top of feeling sweaty. It was gross. He did the same and then moved onto one of the large limbs. I moved onto another limb, and he lifted the plywood, replacing the bag in a natural crevasse beneath the board. "What is this place?"

"It's my tree. I mean, it isn't mine, but I come here. My mother seems to think I should be out being a teenager, but I usually just want to read and think, so I tell her I go to parties and come here. If my eyes are bloodshot from reading in the dark, she thinks I've been smoking weed. She'd prefer the latter."

He lifted the board and rummaged in the bag again. He pulled out two warm Cokes and handed one over.

"Sorry, they are hot."

I didn't care. I was thirsty and drank it half-down without stopping. The soda fizzed in my nose. I moved to the branch opposite Morrison and sat down. I could see Lake Istokpoga from up here. It was closer than I realized. You don't go swimming in a place like Lake Istokpoga. Only drunks, rednecks on a dare (probably drunk), and out-of-towners swam in water the color of a gator. Lake Istokpoga is also really shallow, about four feet on average, despite its size. It is five miles long and ten miles wide, one of the biggest freshwater lakes in Florida.

I seldom went to the lake, despite living near it, but I knew all about the history from school. According to my fifth-grade social studies teacher, it was named by Seminole Indians, and the rough translation was "lake where people were killed or died." Legend held that a group of Seminoles tried to cross the lake and got caught in the muck and died. The more dramatic versions of the legend included whirlpools.

Legends usually have some basis in fact. Most likely, a wind came up. The lake got choppy fast when it was windy. Alligators could also have been involved. This was all meant to keep us away from the real and imagined dangers of the lake. It had worked on me. I never went there. Not until I met Morrison.

People fished the lake for bass. Most of the fishing camps were along the southern edges of the lake, but a few people entered the lake from the north side, by where we were. I saw a few boats out on the lake and heard an airboat in the distance. The water was completely flat today. Pond lilies covered the surface of the water near shore. Billowing clouds glided along the horizon. There were bald cypress trees along the water's edge, their knobby knees protruding around the bases of the trees.

I looked around at the herons and egrets nesting along the periphery of the lake, which explained some of the noises I had heard earlier. Now that the mosquitoes were leaving me alone, I was enjoying this peek into Morrison's world.

He fussed with the bag again, and as he did, I saw a thin blanket, rope, and a few books. There was a blue tarp sticking out from under the board. I wondered if he camped out here.

"What do you think?"

"This is pretty cool," I almost shouted. The cicadas, frogs, and maybe crickets sang so loudly that I needed to raise my voice to be heard.

We talked about work for a while. We discovered that his worst regular caddying job was for the father of one of the kids I loathed. That kid had caused us to close the pool twice so far. The kid was known among the pool staff as The Tootsie Roll Devil. He threw Tootsie Rolls into the pool and then yelled, "Poop!" Every time the pool had to be cleared while we investigated the "poop" and made a production of retesting the water. I also had to watch him because he liked to hold his little sister underwater until she freaked out. He would then pretend to save her, making a big show of my "negligence" to their mother. This usually earned him a Twin Pop and me dirty looks.

Morrison told me that he occasionally dropped spare balls on the green to make things more interesting. He confessed that he snuck and picked oranges and limes from the groves that bordered the golf course. He pretended to go looking for a ball and pocketed the fruit.

He also told me that he opened new Columbia House accounts for every one of his mother's boyfriends. He had long ago exhausted the catalog for the tapes he wanted, so now he mostly ordered stuff like Lynyrd Skynyrd, AC/DC, and Rush. He used the tapes as currency, trading them for cash or favors. When he was particularly broke, he would forge the signature of the least popular band member—to make it more plausible—and play it up as a collectible. His punk attire, which made him a routine subject of ridicule, gave him sudden respectability when it came to selling musical memorabilia.

"Lynyrd Skynyrd fans are so gullible that it is actually kind of sweet. The only time I almost got caught was a Pink Floyd fan. Those are some obsessive motherfuckers," he said, bemused.

Morrison looked at home here. Relaxed. He stretched out along the tree limb as much as gravity would allow. He usually seemed so guarded. I asked him something I had wondered about for months.

"Hey, what was that fight that happened at school?"

He knew what I meant because his face shut down. At first, he pretended he didn't know what I was talking about. I wanted to know because in the few months we'd been friends, I had never seen that side of Morrison again. He had lost it that day. I had wondered why ever since.

He brushed me off and said that Ángel was an asshole and tried to change the subject. I could see he was uncomfortable and dropped it. We went back to talking about Morrison's Columbia House scam, but my question hung between us.

The sun was starting the get low, but the heat didn't abate and wouldn't for months. I started to wonder about getting out of the woods in the dark.

Morrison seemed to read my mind. "I have a flashlight," he said. He went back into the dry bag and fished one out. It was like Mary Poppins's magical bag.

I started to get up.

"Ángel was making fun of my mother," he said quietly in the

growing darkness. I strained to hear him over the trilling, chirps, and squawks.

I settled back into my branch, and he continued, his voice low and serious. I leaned in to listen.

"My mother . . . my mother is cool and all. She was really young when she had me." He faltered here.

"It's cool. You don't have to tell me." I knew what it was like not wanting to explain your family. I still hadn't told him about my dad.

"My mom went down to Miami with a group of high school friends. To that Jim Morrison concert at Dinner Key. You know, the one where he got arrested for showing his dick? Well, the sight of that must have been an aphrodisiac because she met my father that night. Unfortunately, she never got the guy's name. A few months later, she figured out she was pregnant. She was sixteen and living at home. She left school and got a job at a canning factory.

"She met this guy Juan at work. They were the solution to one another's problems. My mom wanted to get out of the house, despite the fact she needed my grandmother to watch me, and Juan wanted a green card so he could eventually bring his family up from the Dominican Republic. I was born two months early, but they managed to get married right before I was born. I got his last name and a fake father on my birth certificate. Morrison F. Nuñez, the paper son of Juan J. Nuñez."

I listened and thought about Michael's invisible father and how my dad had become his dad. Sissy had a father, but he was barely home. I had never seen him hug her. I remembered my father hugging Michael and me all the time. Morrison's father didn't even know he existed.

Morrison continued, "As you may have noticed, I'm blond-haired and blue-eyed. Apparently, the stud at the Doors concert was, too. Juan was most definitely not, and everyone knew the marriage was a sham. Juan was nice enough. We all lived together until he could bring his real family to the States, and my mother could afford a place on her own. He tried to stay in touch, but we moved around a lot. I haven't seen him in years.

"I'm stuck with Morrison as a first name, and I fucking hate the Doors. And then Nuñez as a last name, which I kind of like, but the actual Hispanic kids love to poke fun because they know I'm not really Hispanic. I was friends with Ángel in elementary school. He was the last person I told, and afterward he wouldn't stop making fun of my mother and me. I got in trouble for asking the teacher what a *puta* was."

"Wait, wait, your mother told you all of this when you were just a kid?" I was incredulous. I mean, I could barely get my mother to talk about my dad or anything family-related, and Morrison's mother had told him he was the product of a one-night stand when he was in elementary school.

Now, Morrison sounded angry and defensive. "It isn't like that. I mean, it is, but it isn't. My mother isn't a slut. She has this thing about celebrating Jim Morrison's birthday. That's always been a thing with us. She's never lied to me, and she could have if she wanted to." His voice softened, and he continued, "My mother never really got a chance to be a teenager, and because of that, she's never quite gotten around to being a grown-up. She wants me to have all of the fun she missed out on, but it doesn't work like that."

I wanted to say something, but I was careful not to sound like I pitied him because I didn't. At least now I understood what had happened that day and why he was so guarded. Instead, I said, "I hate the Doors, too." I guess it was the right thing to say because he smiled at me, looking relieved.

"My dad is dead," I added.

"I know. Someone at school told me. Was it really a snake?"

"No, it was a car accident. Everyone remembers the snake, but no one remembers my dad."

"Hey, I'm sorry."

"It's okay. Really. I just miss him sometimes."

"I miss having one to miss. The only paternal story I have involves another man's dick."

"What does the F. stand for?"

"I'll take that secret to my grave." He looked at the sky and said,

"Let's get you home. There is a shortcut to your house."
    "Why didn't you send me that way earlier?"
    "Because it amused me to make you bushwhack to Stoner Couch."
    "Asshole."

CHAPTER 21
PAST - JULY 1985

I wondered what my mother thought I got up to when I disappeared with Morrison. I'm pretty sure she would rather we were having sex instead of sitting in a tree surrounded by alligators, water moccasins, wild pigs, and bears. My mother held a particularly strong grudge against snakes, understandably so.

We were deep into summer, and we hung out at the tree after work and on our days off. One evening, we descended the tree at dusk, heat lightning flickering where we could see the sky through the trees. The day insects and night insects were singing together. The mosquitoes were overwhelming, despite the Skin So Soft. I dropped down and found myself standing so close to Morrison that I could feel his breath tickling the hair by my cheek. I felt close to him and wanted to show it but didn't know how. Asking for a hug seemed stupid and childish. I felt dull-witted and impulsive from the heat. I leaned up to kiss him.

He flinched. I cringed. My cheeks burned and shame roared blood in my ears. I wasn't even sure if I liked him that way. I wasn't sure how I was supposed to feel about him.

I mumbled, "I'm sorry," and began walking towards home as quickly as possible.

"Please, wait. I'm sorry."

I kept walking.

"Chelle, please."

He jogged to catch up and asked me to come back to his house.

"You don't understand . . ." he trailed off.

I kept walking and he grabbed me.

"*Please*, stop!"

I finally brought myself to look at him and he was as upset as I was. Neither one of us knew what to say.

"Michelle, *please*. Let me try to explain. Please don't leave. *Please*."

I began to follow him home. We walked in silence for fifteen minutes. He didn't live in Coral Ridge like I thought, but he did live in a trailer. It was on a scraggly plot of land down the road from the trailer park. The trailer looked like it was semi-feral and trying to return to the wild. It was varying shades of green from the moss, mildew, and algae covering the sides. It was up on exposed cinderblocks and even those were shades of green.

Morrison banged the front door open and invited me inside. It was dark and musty. It felt chaotic. The couch was red and orange, but I couldn't tell if it was a pattern or flowers. There was stuffing coming out of one arm and the back corner was patched with duct tape. The floor was dirty linoleum. There were shell and macramé hangings dangling from the low ceiling.

He motioned to the couch and sat beside me. There was a cluttered low table in front of the couch. It was covered in dirty dishes, beer cans, and an ashtray with several scrawny cigarette butts.

He covered his face with his hair and looked at the floor. He plucked at the loose strings on his jeans. From underneath his hair he said, "I'm sorry. I want to like you like that, but I . . ."

I felt my face getting hot again. This was humiliating. It was a stupid mistake. I wanted to cry, but there was an itch of anger forming. What *was* he saying?

"Fine. I'm going home," I said and got up to leave.

"I think I like guys," he said.

I sat back down. I felt twice as stupid. Neither of us knew how to handle this.

He sat there, his face in his hands and hair, hiding from me.

"Okay, that makes sense," I said.

"What? Why? *What the fuck does that mean?*"

"It just makes sense is all."

"I'm so sorry. I am. I want to like you. I mean, you're fucking gorgeous and cool and funny. I've tried being with girls, but it doesn't feel right. I dated this girl in ninth grade, Samantha. I liked her as a friend. She was my best friend. You know that pressure everyone puts on you, like being friends isn't enough, there has to be more. So, we started dating. But it didn't feel like everyone told me it should. Sex didn't feel like everyone told me it should. I just wanted my friend, but in order to keep my friend I had to be this different person. We were making out one night and . . . never mind." It was obvious he was saying more than he meant to.

"No, no, please go on."

"It's embarrassing."

"I think you owe me one, because I'm feeling incredibly stupid right now."

He stopped and ran his hands through his hair, "We were making out. *Buck Rogers* was on in the background. The only times I was interested . . . the only times I was interested was when Gil Gerard was on TV. I mean, even Princess Ardala did nothing for me. That was when I knew for sure."

We sat in silence for a moment, but I couldn't help myself.

"What about the little penis-shaped robot?" I said as I snorted a little laugh.

"It's not funny! Okay, maybe it's a little funny. Look, I really like you. You're my best friend and I don't want to fuck that up. I fucked things up last time, and Sam stopped talking to me. I'm afraid that no matter what I do or say I am going to fuck things up again. Please, tell me we are okay?"

The pleading in his voice hurt to hear. This was my fault. All I wanted to do was tell him how much he meant to me. I still had no idea how to do it. At least I now knew that kissing was totally the wrong way to go about it.

"We're okay."

I still felt stupid and wanted to go home, but I didn't want to leave him in this dirty, lonely trailer. Morrison was looking at me, waiting for the rejection he was sure was coming. He thought I hated him. Nothing could have been further from the truth.

"Wanna watch something?" I asked.

He nodded. I got up and started turning the channels until we found a staticky rerun of *M*A*S*H*. We let the TV fill the silence. I wondered when I could leave without it being awkward. Thank god it wasn't the episode where Hawkeye and Hot Lips kiss.

And "fucking gorgeous"? Bullshit. I wondered how much truth there was in anything he said. I fixated on that comment more than him telling me he was gay. That he knew he liked guys made sense. I still didn't understand why I didn't like anyone.

"I meant what I said," he said.

"What, that you have the hots for Gil Gerard?"

"No, that you're beautiful. You are. If I liked girls like I like boys I'd be so happy right now. I'm just happy you don't hate me."

I had no idea how to process this. I couldn't accept the compliment because that would have felt like I was agreeing with him, and that seemed vain and disingenuous. I didn't want to argue and say I wasn't because it would seem like I was fishing for him to say more, and I wasn't. I was uncomfortable enough as it was. I was left with only one response, deflection.

"Yeah, well, I like boys too, but not nearly as much as I like fictional characters."

"Well, duh. They make the best, and least disappointing, boyfriends."

We started laughing.

"Are we really okay?" he asked.

"Yes, we are *really* okay."

I punched his arm. I should have just punched him at the tree. Why didn't I think of that sooner? Morrison seemed so relieved our friendship didn't implode. I didn't know how to tell him it wasn't so much that I like-liked him as I didn't know how to tell him I loved him as a friend. We ended up at the same place.

"Okay, so what guys do you like?" he asked me.

I knew he wanted to tell me about the ones he liked, so it seemed time to finally admit my long-standing crush on Harry Anderson. He admitted that he liked Patrick McGoohan. This prompted me to reveal my nerdiest crush of all—Peter Davison, but only as The Doctor. People seemed to hate him when he became The Doctor after Tom Baker, but that floppy hair and those sad eyes did it for me. Were floppy hair and sad eyes my thing?

CHAPTER 22

I spent part of my day off with my mother. The dryer had stopped working a few months earlier, so we went to the laundromat in the morning and went food shopping in between loads. I met up with Morrison at the tree in the afternoon. We were talking, but the air was heavy and still. It was a narcoleptic heat. My eyelids felt forced down by the weight of the heat. I must have nodded off.

When I woke up, I was at an odd angle, pressed against Morrison's bony shoulder, his arm around me. I was surprised by how comforting it felt. I pretended to be asleep for a while longer until something bit my ankle, and I couldn't resist swatting at it.

"Sorry, you fell asleep and you started sliding. I was afraid you were going to fall out of the tree," he said.

"Thanks."

I wanted to make a joke, but I couldn't. I was touched. I mean, literally I was touching Morrison, but it was more than that. I was worried after he told me he was gay that everything would be weird. If anything, it made things better. It took down the rest of our barriers. It made us closer. We stayed that way for a while, even though I was no longer in danger of falling out of the tree.

I heard what sounded like a horn or that noise eighteen wheelers make when they slow down, but we were fairly far from the highway. It didn't sound like the airboats that were always out on the lake, either. Morrison swung over to a branch and walked out onto the limb so he could look across Lake Istokpoga. The noise started spreading, coming from other areas of the lake.

"There!" he yelled, pointing to an area of shoreline where the water appeared to be vibrating.

"What's going on?"

"It's alligator sexy talk!"

He was so excited that I didn't want to tell him I thought it was time to go home, like immediately.

"This is so awesome!" he said excitedly.

"This isn't going to turn into some *Bridge to Terabithia* shit, right Morrison?"

"No, you aren't going to die. The alligators aren't interested in you, and they certainly don't want to have sex with you."

So, we sat together in the tree, listening to horny alligators sounding like truck horns and tubas as if it was the most amazing thing in the world. And maybe it was.

CHAPTER 23
PAST - JULY 1985

Morrison and I looked for ourselves in ourselves and couldn't find what we needed. We looked in each other and came up empty-handed. We looked to TV, movies, and music, but we weren't there, either. Not in total. There were parts, but the best we could do was create a patchwork. A hodgepodge that provided no clear sense of self. We had no role models and no one guiding us. We were told we should know these things instinctively, but we didn't. We were floundering, but at least we were floundering together.

For better or worse, TV was my view of the world outside of Lorida, but according to TV, interesting people lived in cities and suburbs and idiots lived in rural areas. I didn't see families like mine on TV. I wanted to see a regular girl from a regular town. TV shows set in rural areas were either filled with hillbillies or were set in a different century.

As much as I loved Sabrina, Jill, and Kelly, and even Diana Prince, they weren't the role models I needed. Then one night after Sissy had fallen asleep during *Dynasty* I started watching *Hotel*. I was transfixed by Shari Belafonte. As Julie Gillette, she was young. She didn't have fabulous hair. She had a regular job.

I tried to find out as much as I could about Shari Belafonte. She was in *Vogue*, *Teen Beat*, and *Jet*. I pestered my mother to buy me copies when we went to the grocery store. She was so beautiful. I remembered my father had some Harry Belafonte records and asked my mother if we could play them, because he was her father.

As much as I was enamored by Shari Belafonte, it was really Julie Gillette who spoke to me. I had no idea how much I needed her until she appeared. Sometimes I would imagine what Julie Gillette would do in my shoes and it gave me confidence.

Morrison had similar conflicts. He could be gay, but everything said he had to fit a certain mold, and that mold didn't work for a nowhere town in central Florida. Or he could be a punk, and in some ways that mold was even more rigid. A gay punk who loved nature? Were he and I the only ones of our kind? Would Marlon Perkins whisper outside our windows describing our strange behaviors, the eating of TV dinners, and how we were the only known specimens in captivity?

Sissy seemed comfortable trying on different personas. I thought I needed to pick one. I felt this push to figure it all out. To figure myself out. Morrison and I were safe not knowing who we were with each other. We were safe trying to figure that out. Maybe we would have figured everything out if we had had the chance.

CHAPTER 24

Every day was hot. The days blurred together. The only thing that distinguished them was whether we worked or not. We usually worked weekends and three days during the week, with two weekdays off. We convinced our respective supervisors to give us the same schedule, which guaranteed us both showing up. Morrison hauled bags around for the same fat guys day-after-day and I listened to the shrieking of their obnoxious kids. As far as I could tell, adults knew better than to get in the water. The job changed how I felt about swimming pools. I'd rather swim in Lake Istokpoga than in a pool with small children.

My mother and brother took turns dropping us off and picking us up. Morrison had finally admitted that he hated going home to the empty trailer. My mother seemed to sense this and started inviting him for dinner. My brother also seemed to like him.

After dinner at my house, we'd often walk to the tree. We were exchanging the day's work stories when we heard a loud crash of thunder. We peered around the leaves and, sure enough, there was a huge, dark cloud bearing down on us from the west. It was a fast-moving storm and we both knew there wasn't enough time to get to either of our homes before the rain started.

He began rummaging under the board where he kept his dry bag and pulled out a small blue tarp. It was barely big enough for one person, let alone two. Fat, heavy drops thudded through the leafy canopy. We huddled together and made ourselves as small as possible and each took an end of the tarp. A gust of wind almost ripped it from my hand.

For five minutes the air around us boomed, but most of the lightning strikes were to the south, over the lake. The tarp was useless, and we were completely soaked. We should have just enjoyed the rain. If you accept you are going to get wet, a warm thunderstorm can be a joy. It was only when you resisted the rain that it seemed bad.

As soon as it was over, frogs began trilling all around us. I was still wearing my bathing suit from work under shorts and a T-shirt. I was prepared to get wet all day every day. Morrison, on the other hand, was wearing his regulation polo shirt and khakis.

"Shit, this was my clean set. I need these for work. I need to go home so I can get these off and hang them to dry."

I decided to go with him since it was still light out and I didn't have anything better to do.

We climbed down the tree and started towards Morrison's house, our shoes making squelching noises as we walked. The sun was back out and you'd never have known there had been a downpour. It felt like a sauna. The mosquitoes were vicious as sunset approached. We beat a rhythm of squishing and slapping as we walked. I suspected that there was no way Morrison was going to get his clothes dry short of going to the laundromat. The air was just too humid, and the sun was going down.

We got to the trailer and went inside. I was startled someone else was home. I had never met Morrison's mother.

"Hello, Rebecca!" Morrison said when he saw her on the couch. He seemed surprised to see her, too.

I was stunned by him calling her by her name and even more stunned by her lighthearted response.

"Sunny, quit being a jerk."

"Okay, *Mom*," he said with mom drawn out as long as possible.

"*Morrison . . .*"

"Sorry. Rebecca Joy Sawyer, please meet Michelle, the friend I was telling you about. Michelle, please meet Joy. Absolutely not Rebecca. Definitely not Becky, just Joy."

She bounced off the couch and came over to me. As she jumped up, her loosely tied top shifted, briefly exposing a breast, and then she grabbed me in a hug. She was wearing short shorts, no bra, and dirty flip-flops. The hug was overly enthusiastic, and I felt the ash from her cigarette fall onto my arm. She was somehow a blonde with blond roots showing. She was at least ten years younger than my mother. She looked more like Morrison's sister. She was everything I expected, but I was still surprised.

"Please call me Joy. I'm *so* happy to meet you! Sunshine has told me all about you. You're *lovely!*"

She either neglected to notice we were soaking wet, or she simply didn't care. She started talking to me, rapidly asking questions, not waiting for an answer before moving on to the next question. She overwhelmed me. I now understood why Morrison spent so much time up in a tree.

Morrison reappeared in dry clothes, holding his wet clothes. He motioned for me to follow him outside. He wrung them out and pinned the shirt and pants to the sagging clothesline behind the trailer.

"What *exactly* did you tell your mother about me, Sunshine?"

"That you're a girl, and your name is Michelle. That was pretty much enough for her to decide we were having earthshattering, but completely protected, sex at least three times a day."

"How does she know it's protected?"

"Because she gave me a fistful of condoms. In fact, she keeps giving them to me. I bet when we go back inside, she'll give you some, too. I keep leaving them in bathrooms with the hopes that the inbred motherfuckers around here won't make more little inbred motherfuckers. Also, if you ever tell anyone my nickname is Sunshine, I will tell the world about your crush on Harry Anderson."

Morrison was still damp the next morning. He said he got the shirt mostly dry using a blow dryer. It was not mostly dry.

Working as a lifeguard was tedious. I thought I would be swimming every day. Saving lives. I thought I would be rescuing children from drowning. Instead, I avoided the water, knowing how few kids got out to use the restroom. Thus far, my rescues had been limited to fishing out the toads and lizards the horrible kids threw into the water. The reality was that the pool was an afterthought so that bored wives could gossip and let their spawn run wild. You had to watch the kids and tell them not to run. You had to tell them the pool was only five feet deep and that diving might break their little necks. You had to tell them not to pour Coke into the pool. You had to listen to, "Mom, watch this! *Mommmy!* Watch me!" seven thousand times a day. It was babysitting with a whistle.

We were waiting for my mother to pick us up, and Morrison had this look on his face like he could barely contain himself.

"What?"

"We need to get away from here first."

My mother pulled up, and we got in the car, rolling the rest of the windows down and opening the vents as fast as we could, but the hot air outside merely traded places with the hot air inside the car. Mom started talking about an obit she was working on for a local guy who she thought must have been in the mob. Generally speaking, most of the obits she wrote were for regular old retirees and unremarkable locals, so this guy made her day more interesting.

"I've never had so many phone calls from New Jersey in my entire life. They talk weird. It took me three tries to realize they were saying orange, as in Orange, NJ. The family just kept calling, wanting to add more and more to the obituary. They want two photos, one of him and one of him and the whole family. There were like thirty-five people in the photo," she said. "And how were your days?"

"Hot. Tedious. I'm never having kids," I said.

"Fine," Morrison said, making a weird coughing noise, trying to stifle what sounded like laughter.

"Morrison, I am going to make mac and cheese later. How's that sound?"

"Great, thank you, Mrs. Miller."

We pulled up in front of the trailer, and Morrison and I hung back, waiting for my mom to go inside. I looked at him, and he lost it. He started laughing, tears forming in his eyes.

"*What?!*"

"Okay, okay. You know I was caddying for Jeb Covington, the big sugar guy, right?"

"Yeah, I saw him yelling at his kid by the pool today."

"The guy is a first-class asshole. He talks about all the women he is fucking, and he uses the N-word even when he's talking about inanimate objects. I hate the motherfucker. So today, we were at the tenth hole, and I had to pee bad. I asked if I could step away for a minute to run back to the clubhouse. He says, 'Son, play with your dick on your own time.'" Morrison stopped to let a giggle escape.

"Around the twelfth hole, I couldn't hold it any longer. I had no choice."

"*What* did you do?"

"He was looking for his ball in the sand trap. So, I used the distraction to do what I had to do. I was going to pee myself."

"*What* did you do?"

"I stealthily peed in his golf bag. I figured it would drain out of the holes in the bottom, and the bag would be well dry by the eighteenth hole."

"You didn't!" I said, laughing.

"He left me no choice!"

He was openly giggling now. "Wait, there's more. It was hot today, and he's doing that fat, bald guy flop sweat thing. He starts to blame the sweat in his eyes on his bad game. He comes over to the bag, and I think he's getting another club. He isn't. He reaches down inside and pulls out a small towel. I had no idea it was in there, I swear! He wipes the sweat off his face but realizes as he does that it's wet. It's too late. He has rubbed the piss on his face."

"Oh, my god! Morrison, you're going to get fired!"

"I was sure I was going to get worse than fired. I was getting ready to run. I mean, really, there's no way to apologize for something like that. Before I can say anything, he throws the whole bag into the lake and storms off. I can hear him yelling all the way to the clubhouse. Apparently, his kid spite pees around the house, and he assumed it was the kid."

A small part of me thought I should feel bad for the kid getting the blame, but it felt too much like karma. His kid, Jeb Jr., was The Tootsie Roll Devil.

We laughed until our sides ached. We were still laughing when my mother popped her head out the door and asked if we wanted some iced tea she had just mixed up.

CHAPTER 25
PAST - AUGUST 1985

I went over to Morrison's trailer to see if he wanted to go to the movies with Michael and me. I had called, but I kept getting a busy signal. I knocked, and he answered a few seconds later. He was home alone.

"Is your mom working?" I asked.

"Nah, she's out with Jack," said Morrison.

"I thought she broke up with Jack."

"She did. I call all her boyfriends Jack—short for Jackoff. I mean, they never last long, so why get to know them? Plus, I find it funny to say, 'Hi, Jack,' and make them paranoid that she is seeing other people. Once, she accidentally called one of them Jack. That didn't end well."

I saw the phone on the floor. It looked like it had been ripped out of the wall. I didn't ask.

"Want to go to the movies?"

"But what if Gil Gerard calls while we are out?" He looked down at the broken phone, shrugged, and said, "Let's go."

"Chelle, Sissy called three times while you were out," my mother said as Michael and I walked through the door.

I knew Sissy was flying home today, she had said so in her last letter, but I wasn't sure when. Morrison and I had gone to see *Pee-wee's Big Adventure*. He made that stupid laugh the whole drive home.

I raced to my room and dialed her phone number. I hadn't heard her voice in months. It rang six times before she picked up.

"Yes."

"Hey!" I squealed. I hadn't squealed all summer.

"Hi. I called. You were out. What were you up to?" Her words were casual, but her voice wasn't. I began to panic. I knew I needed to tell her about Morrison. What had my mother said to her? She had been alone at that camp all summer, and I was here making another best friend. What if she hated him? Was it okay to have two best friends? I realized I was sweating. The knot in my stomach that had loosened over the summer was back. I scrambled to think of a response.

"I was out . . . with a work friend." I wanted to get off this subject as quickly as possible and launched into questions before she could respond. "How was the camp? What is Utah like? Did you meet any cool people? I've missed you so much! It was awful here without you. When can we get together?"

That was all it took. She sounded like Sissy again when she asked what I was doing tomorrow.

"I work until five. Could I come by after work?"

"Yep."

We talked a little while longer, and she told me she had hated the camp but that she had made some new friends. She started telling me about Vicki, who lived in West Palm Beach. She had never mentioned Vicki in her letters. She had also never mentioned hating the camp until now. Then again, she had never mentioned it was a camp for kids with behavioral issues either.

The next day when my mom picked Morrison and me up from work, she dropped me off at Sissy's on the way home. Morrison was sitting in the front seat, still wearing his caddy uniform. Mom had already made it clear Morrison was coming home with her for dinner. I felt bad that I hadn't thought about that when I made plans to hang out with Sissy.

Sissy saw us pull up and ran out and hugged me. She looked over my shoulder as they drove away. She missed nothing and immediately asked me about the guy in the car.

"Is that the one you went out with last night?"

"No. Yes," I stammered.

"What?"

"Yes, that is the one I was out with last night, but it wasn't, like, a date."

She arched her eyebrows at me.

We stopped hugging and headed towards her front door. She looked different. She looked older. She was thinner. The baby fat was gone. Her clothes were different, too, and she sounded like someone else when she talked. The blue mascara and heavy eye makeup were gone, with a more sophisticated look taking its place. Maybe the camp was good for her after all. I wondered if I looked any different to her. Probably not.

We went into her kitchen to look for snacks. I was starving after work. Her mother was there. Mrs. Davis gave me a half-smile and said, "I'll leave you girls to it," and left the room.

Sissy's room looked completely different. It was clean for a start. Everything was put away. I could see the rug again. The cracked mirror on the closet door had been replaced. The stuffed animals that had littered her bed were now on the wicker shelf.

We resumed our usual spots as if the last three months hadn't passed. She found a movie on cable that we had seen a million times and put it on for background noise, then immediately launched into her time at the camp.

"Oh my god, it was so awful. They watched everything we did. They had these group meetings twice a day. You had to write how you felt all the time and then talk about it. It was so fucking tedious. The food was so gross, and at least once a week, we had to take overnight hikes and then week-long hikes in the mountains. One girl almost died."

I was confused. "But in your letters, it sounded like you were having an okay time?"

"Oh, those. They read our mail before they sent it. If they thought you were following the program, you'd get extra privileges. We figured out they were reading letters after one girl got raided and her stash confiscated. We started writing fake letters of happiness and joy, and *ta-da*, we had all sorts of privileges being bestowed. They were so fucking proud of us. We were model prisoners."

Stash of what, I wondered. Who was we? "Did you make some friends at least?"

Sissy had dropped the pretense that this was a camp for the gifted and talented, and I didn't question her because I had always known the truth.

"I told you about Vicki. And there was this girl, Dana, who was pretty cool. I had sex with Gary, one of the counselors." She seemed to have forgotten that we'd watched *Little Darlings* like a hundred times on cable.

"Mostly, I hung out with Vicki, the one from West Palm. She introduced me to a few things."

She left the last sentence hanging there like she wanted me to ask. When I didn't, she got up off the bed and walked in front of me.

"Notice anything different?" She spun in a graceless circle.

"You look *really* good." Actually, she looked a bit too thin. I could see hollows near her collarbones.

"Don't I? I lost like twenty pounds, thanks to Vicki's little secret."

My mind raced to every afterschool special I'd seen; I worried that Sissy was going to vomit up the Pringles she'd been eating.

Instead, she went to her dresser and showed me a vial of white powder.

"It's coke. Want a bump?"

CHAPTER 26

We had about two weeks before work ended and school started. Sissy's father had a membership at Sweetwater Shores, so she'd come over to the pool while I worked. She enjoyed showing off her new body. I had never seen her flirting with this type of determination, and it often ended with her leaving with some guy before I finished my shift. On one of my days off, she said she wanted to go back-to-school shopping, which seemed ridiculous because she shopped year-round. I agreed to go along, and she said I should ask my "work friend" if he wanted to go, too. I asked Morrison, and he shrugged and said he had nothing better to do. I knew he was as curious about her as she was of him.

Sissy pulled up in front of the trailer and honked. She was smoking a freshly lit cigarette when we got in the car. That was another habit she had picked up at summer camp. She was still new to smoking, and her inhalations were more theatrical than practical.

Morrison was dressed like real Morrison and not caddy Morrison, and Sissy seemed taken aback. Did she recognize him from school? I was worried she realized I had lied to her. I told Morrison about Sissy, but I never told him I hid him from her. He could see I was nervous. I maneuvered it so that he was sitting in the backseat, and I was going to try and steer the conversation from the front seat.

Instead, Sissy launched into a story from "bummer camp," as she referred to her months away, about a nymphomaniac kid from Arkansas. For much of the day, she kept making lewd jokes at our expense. She was certain that Morrison and I were a couple and treated us as such.

"Sissy, it's not like that," I tried to explain.

"You are such a fucking prude."

"But . . ."

"Don't be such a fucking weirdo. Sex is normal and healthy. It's nothing to be ashamed of, right Morrison?"

I looked over at Morrison apologetically, and he began batting his eyelashes at me. I started laughing. Sissy thought I was laughing at what she said, somehow admitting that we were having sex, and she started laughing, too. We were all laughing at nothing. I thought it would all be okay.

CHAPTER 27
PAST - SEPTEMBER 1985

School started, and we went back to our old routines, with a few changes. Sissy decided Morrison should be included when we hung out. She had also started dating, if you could call it that, so our hang-out times tended to be after school and during the day on weekends.

The first time Morrison came home with us after school was a bit awkward. I recognized my own first reactions to her house in his expressions. I was still envious of the pool, and he stared at her father's stereo system with open desire. He wasn't sure where to sit in Sissy's room. Sissy took her place on the bed, and I dropped into my usual chair. Sissy eventually threw him a pillow, and he leaned against her bedframe. We put on MTV and did our usual nothing. After several hours of nothing, a bag of Wise BBQ chips, Doritos, three Cokes, two Sprites, a Tab, and a bag of Reese's Pieces, Sissy drove us home.

That became our ritual. Morrison would insist on getting out at my house, and Sissy would wink at us as I shut the car door. I knew Morrison didn't want her to drive him home, and I knew why. My mother seemed disappointed when we started staying at Sissy's in the evenings. Michael was irritated with me too. I didn't think it was fair that they were making me choose between them and Sissy.

One day I made the situation worse when I forgot to call home after school to let them know we were going home with Sissy. When we weren't home by seven, she made my brother drive to

Sissy's to find us. I had forgotten she was making a special dinner. She had wanted to celebrate Michael's promotion at work. I had also forgotten it was the anniversary of my father's death.

Michael waited until Morrison left with a plate wrapped in tin fold to lay into me.

"Chelle, we talked about this! You can't act like we don't exist. Like Dad didn't exist."

"I can't pretend like Dad didn't exist?! Do you even hear yourself?" The irony of what he said was overwhelming. I knew we were having the argument outside so our mother wouldn't hear us talking about our father.

I went inside the trailer so that I didn't have to deal with Michael. My mother was in the kitchen tersely putting the remains of dinner into the refrigerator.

"Michelle, I am tired of this. Tonight was the last straw. It was simply inconsiderate."

She was right, but why hadn't she just said something? Why did I have to carry the burden of her grief, as well as my own? I felt like I had to constantly be present for the pain we all felt, but I could never talk about it. It was smothering. I realized far too late that she was trying to fight against the annual fog of grief.

I went to my room and shut the door.

I lay there, everything feeling exposed and raw inside. I hadn't meant to hurt them. I was ashamed I had forgotten what the date meant. It was my last year of high school, and I wanted to be with my friends, which made me feel petulant. I had started to think about what it would be like to leave and what that would mean.

Over the summer, Morrison's mom had started dating a new guy, Travis. Morrison didn't like him, so I didn't like him, either. We avoided his house after Travis showed up. Travis was always there, usually smoking pot, even when Morrison's mother was at work. He said that his mother usually dated for a few months, and either the guy left, or she kicked him out. He was waiting for them to break up.

He told me he liked a few of her boyfriends, especially the one who was in the band. That one would bring him albums and T-shirts when he went on tour. He said he was around for almost a year, probably because he was on the road much of the time. He also liked Mike, who had taught him about the woods and animals. He said Mike was a hunter and insisted on taking Morrison out to "teach him how to be a man." That was how he found the tree. It had been an old hunting blind. Morrison didn't want to kill anything, and the gunshots bothered his ear. He figured out if he talked loudly, pretending to be deafer than he really was, he would scare the animals away. It irritated Mike until Morrison started asking about everything they saw. Mike enjoyed being an expert, so he would explain the animals, plants, birds, lizards, and trees to him. Mike was long gone, but Morrison kept learning from books.

He told me that his mother made sure none of them abused him outright, but she seemed oblivious to the fact that most of them didn't want him around. Travis was worse than most.

At school, people saw us together and assumed we were dating, as Sissy still did. It was easier to let everyone think that than try and explain that Morrison and I both thought Greg Louganis was hot. The reality was that Morrison provided as much cover for me as I did for him. I still didn't like-like anyone at school. I didn't get crushes. I didn't want to go on dates. I had seen my friends go "boy crazy" in grade school and middle school. I had waited for it to happen to me, but it never did. I would get what I assumed were crushes on fictional characters, but not on real people. It made me feel like a freak sometimes. Letting people think Morrison was my boyfriend made me look and feel normal without having to actually date someone. As for Sissy . . . I assumed that there would be a natural point to tell her that Morrison and I had broken up and were just friends.

For the time being, "we" still amused her. Sissy decided we were going on a double date with her and one of the guys she was seeing. Tim? Tom? My mom dropped us off at Sissy's house, and we all went to pick up Todd(?). He seemed put out that she was driving and kept talking about his truck.

"Yes, Thad, but you can't fit four people in your truck."

Thad, that was it. He was the one in FFA who was going to take over his father's cattle business.

"Yeah, but you sure can fit two people in the truck bed." He made a noise that I suspect he thought sounded sexy but that I thought mimicked constipation.

We drove up to the drive-in in Avon Park. The kids' movie was playing when we got there. We went and got popcorn and walked around a bit. We were there to see *Return of the Living Dead*.

We spread a blanket in front of the car and relaxed while *Teen Wolf* played on the screen. Sissy started talking to Morrison, which I could see was pissing off Thad. He tried to talk to me, but we ran out of small talk fairly quickly when I told him I wasn't all that interested in the Avon Park-Sebring football rivalry.

Whether he'd admit it or not, Morrison liked the attention Sissy gave him. It took me a month to ask Morrison a personal question, but Sissy had no such inhibitions. She asked him all sorts of questions. She asked about his name, and he said his mother liked the Doors. There was no mention of the concert or the one-night stand.

"Some people think I'm named after Van Morrison, which might be worse. Nah, nothing is as bad as an ardent Doors fan. They *feeeel* things, soooo many things, *man*."

Sissy used that as a tangent to tell us all how hot Sting was and how she loved the Police. This further pissed off Thad, who muttered something about Sting being a homo.

Morrison ignored Thad, rolling his eyes at Sissy instead. "He is the Pat Boone of British rock."

I waited for the explosion, but it didn't come. Sissy would get upset if I contradicted her, but she challenged Morrison back and demanded to know what kind of music he liked.

"Billy Idol, The Clash, Bad Brains," he said smugly.

Sissy jumped up and started putting on a bad Billy Idol impression, re-enacting the music video for "White Wedding." At that, he launched into the worst rendition of "Every Breath You Take" imaginable, pretending to choke himself as he sang. They sparred back and forth about music for a while, genuinely laughing.

I was so happy. She seemed to like him. I was afraid they would hate each other. The three of us together made me feel like I truly belonged somewhere. Thad, on the other hand, seemed to sense he was irrelevant, wasn't going to have sex tonight, and said he was going for a smoke. He never came back, and none of us minded.

CHAPTER 28
PAST - OCTOBER 1985

I was headed to meet Sissy for lunch when Coach Roberts waved me into his classroom. He walked over to his desk and invited me to sit down at a nearby desk. I was aware he taught driver's education and health, but I had never had one of his classes. I only knew him from the swim team. He usually wore shorts and a school T-shirt to swim practice, but now he was in his teacher clothes, a button-up short-sleeve shirt, and dark polyester pants with a stitched crease. I could see a gold chain with a shark's tooth hanging just below his collar. Around the room were posters decrying the perils of drinking and driving and not using your turn signal with equal gravitas.

"Michelle, are you making any plans?"

"What? When?"

"For after school."

"Today?"

He sighed. "Michelle, are you applying to college?"

"Oh! Um, well, I . . ." I wasn't sure what to say to him. I wasn't sure what I was doing or what he wanted to hear. "I thought maybe I would go to community college or maybe get a job."

"That's what I was afraid of," he said, settling back into his chair.

"My friends are here." It sounded like an excuse as soon as I said it. An excuse for what, though?

"There is more than what is right in front of you."

I nodded because that seemed to be what he wanted me to do. Nobody I knew thought about what they were "going to be" when they grew up, at least not after elementary school. The what-if dreams just petered out, and they did what they needed to do to survive. I wasn't sure what my mother once wanted to be, but she wrote about dead people for a living now. Michael wanted to be an astronaut for a while, and now he fixed cars. Daydreams about the future felt like a luxury.

Coach Roberts continued. "Michelle, you know I was a diver back home, right? It was what I was good at. I reached a point where my mama and I knew I had a choice. I could swim myself off the island, or I could stay, find a nice girl, make some beautiful babies, and never look past the life I knew. That was right for many of my friends. It wasn't for me. I wanted more."

I noticed the happy-go-lucky island accent had all but disappeared. It made me wonder more about him.

"I know you think I'm just some stupid old man who teaches kids how not to drive like maniacs, but my life is more than what you see here. If I hadn't left home, I would never have become the man I am. I don't want to see you cut yourself short."

He stopped, and we stared at each other for a long moment. He knew. He could plainly see the internal conflict I was only beginning to acknowledge.

"Doreen . . . Ms. Washington, and I think you can swim yourself off this island . . . if you want."

Ms. Washington was my English teacher. They had been talking about me? He continued, "The University of Georgia has a good swimming program. It is a good school. I talked to the coach there. They are interested in seeing what you got, but you need to apply. I will help, but you need to want to do this. You need to want more in order to get it."

I wasn't sure what to say. I wasn't sure how I felt about any of this.

"Go, think about it, and come see me tomorrow, okay?"

"Yes, sir. Thank you."

"Michelle, I could have spent my life pulling up conches and lobsters for tourists. I chose to be here. Choose your life before it gets chosen for you."

I did think about it. All night. As far as I knew, no one in my family had gone to college. I wasn't sure what my mother had hoped for, but I suspected our life in Lorida wasn't it. When I thought about the future, it was vague. I felt vague. I knew I wanted more, but not what more meant. I knew I didn't want to spend my life in a trailer in Lorida. That thought always made me feel disloyal and like I was looking down on my mother. I wasn't. I was sure she could sense this, and I thought it was one of the reasons we were growing apart.

I knew they didn't like me being friends with Sissy, but I needed my own life. We didn't talk about Sissy being rich, but I assumed that was the problem. We also didn't talk about the future. Did they think I was going to stay in Lorida forever?

I knocked on Coach Roberts's classroom door after school the next day.

"Come in."

He was at his desk grading practice exams for the driver's test.

"Coach Roberts, could you tell me more about what we talked about yesterday?"

A smile broke across his face. "Good, good." He reached into his desk, pulled out a manila envelope, and handed it to me. Inside was information about the University of Georgia, an application, a stamped envelope, and two letters of recommendation. One from him and one from Ms. Washington. There was also a sealed letter to someone named Buck Williams in the athletic department. My face fell when I saw there was a fee to apply.

Coach Roberts saw that and reached down into his desk again and handed me a money order.

"I can pay you back," I said, accepting it.

"You can pay me back if you want, but I'm not worried about it. I'm more worried about you not having a plan. Even if you don't do this, will you promise to start thinking about what you want to do? Also, there may be someone from Georgia at the next meet. Put everything you've got into it."

It wasn't until years later that I appreciated how much I owed to Mr. Roberts and how clever he was. If he had just given me the application, I would have procrastinated, scared of my own future, and probably never applied. The money order meant I had to apply. I wasn't going to take his money and not apply. I wish I had understood sooner. I wished I had thanked him.

I spent the next week reading and re-reading the application, wondering what my life would sound like to a stranger. I was expected to distill myself and my future into 1,000 words. Essays for English class came easy to me, but this was different. How could I talk about my life, my family, with strangers? Heroes? Could I wax on about Shari Belafonte and expect to get into college? Life-altering experiences? Hobbies? I liked to watch TV and sit in a tree.

I hid in the school library, using the electric typewriter to write and re-write my essay. I wrote and threw out multiple drafts. I kept the manila envelope under my mattress at home. I was hiding an imaginary future life that didn't exist. I wanted to talk to my mother, but I didn't know how. Would she and Michael think this was Sissy's influence? We didn't mention it again, but Mom and Michael had been acting aloof with me ever since I had missed dinner that night.

I was afraid of hurting my mother and brother by even thinking of leaving—and I was also afraid Sissy would hate me. I didn't tell Morrison about the application, but somehow, I thought he might understand.

After far more angst than I thought possible, I drafted an essay about swimming. About what the water felt like against my skin. How it felt to soar and glide through the water. Speeding and floating. How water made me feel free and protected. How I loved the smells of salt and chlorine. Loving to swim was the most truthful thing I could think of to say about myself.

CHAPTER 29

I didn't write that I had always been afraid of the ocean. It wasn't sharks or the sheer power of the water; I was afraid I would start swimming and not know when to turn back. I wanted to see how far I could swim, but I was afraid I wouldn't stop.

The great paradox of the ocean is that you can go from being confined by land to utterly free and completely alone a matter of yards from shore. You can see people on shore and enter a void where you can be lost in seconds.

How far is too far to swim? You don't know that until it has happened, and by then, it is too late. You can't get back.

I wanted to see how far I could swim from Lorida, but I always meant to come back. Was it so wrong to want more than I knew? Instead, I got stuck in the void, surrounded by nothingness, caught in a rip current that wouldn't let go. It was what I deserved.

CHAPTER 30
PAST - NOVEMBER 1985

Squatting at the base of a bald cypress, Morrison began digging around the debris at the bottom of the tree with a small stick. The way the tree grew, it looked like it was on tiptoes. There were little tunnels created by the arched roots. He said he was looking for salamanders.

"Fuck! Fuck! Fuck!" he shouted.

"What happened?" I asked.

"Fucking scorpion stung me. Fuck, ouch."

"Oh god, are you going to die? Should I run for help?" I asked, panicked.

"What? No. Don't be stupid. It just fucking hurts. I've been stung before. It's not like with Jessica." He said, shaking his hand.

"What?"

"Sissy's sister. You know, how she died."

I stared at him, momentarily stunned. "Sissy only told me she was in a coma from an accident and died."

"The coma was from getting stung by like a million bees or something. Jessica had kicked a nest. Sissy tried to save her. Jessica was allergic or something. There was nothing Sissy could do."

Why had Sissy never told me this? Why had she told Morrison, who she barely knew, when she had never told me? I was hurt that she had told him and not me.

"I didn't know she saw it happen."

"Yeah, it fucked her up pretty bad. Anyhow, it was just a little

striped asshole scorpion. The deadly ones don't live around here."
He was still cradling his hand, wincing.

"How do you know all of this shit?" I asked.

"Why aren't you more curious?" he retorted.

I was curious. I was also afraid of getting stung. I didn't like making mistakes. I also didn't like that Sissy had told Morrison about her sister, and feeling like that made me feel like a shitty person. I didn't want to feel jealous over something like her sister's death, but I did.

CHAPTER 31

The three of us were flopped around Sissy's room talking, while MTV droned on in the background. Sissy had been pestering us to let her give us each a makeover. I was now wearing too much eye makeup, and it made my face itch. She was trying to do something to Morrison's hair, but there wasn't much to do with it.

"Let me cut it," she demanded.

"No problem, but only if I get to cut yours first."

"Yeah, no."

"You sure?" he said, grabbing the scissors and reaching for her hair.

"How about we dye yours instead?" she said, moving out of his reach.

Morrison shrugged and agreed to that. Sissy didn't have any dye or even Kool-Aid, so she was applying black mascara to his hair instead. Robert Smith had nothing to fear.

I was quietly sucking all the flavor off a Dorito and feeling the chip dissolve in my mouth. Sissy had caught me doing this before and made fun of me, but I didn't think that Doritos tasted as good when you simply ate them.

A commercial came on for Swanson's Hungry-Man dinners.

"Ewww, who eats that shit," she said.

I ate that shit. Morrison probably ate that shit. But you'd never know it from our silence.

I liked spooning out the crevasses. I liked the little burnt edges of mashed potatoes. The apple cranberry in the turkey dinner was my favorite.

His hair now sticky and mottled, Morrison put his arms behind his head and asked us, "What comes after school?"

I knew he was asking the big question. I had been trying to figure out how to bring this up for weeks. It was all I had been thinking about.

"I'm not even sure what I want to do this weekend, let alone with my life. Maybe college could help me figure that out. I don't know," I said. There, I said it. College.

"Neither do I. I was hoping someone else had answers." Morrison said. He hadn't said much about Travis lately, but I knew things were difficult at home.

"I'm going to be rich and famous," Sissy said. "Like Alexis Carrington."

"How do you plan on doing that?" Morrison asked.

"I don't know. I'll win the lottery. Or my dad will die or something, and I'll inherit his money."

Morrison and I exchanged a look.

Oblivious, Sissy continued, "I don't think I'm going to bother with college. I can get a job with what I already know. I learn fast. I'm a people person. Why waste four years when I can hit the ground running, right? I'm in FBLA, and I'm taking accounting and typing this year. I feel like I could easily move into an executive track. I know some people aren't ready for the real world right away, but I am."

I had mentioned college like it was a real possibility. Mostly, I wanted to know what they thought of the idea. I wanted to talk more about this, but it seemed like a dead subject already. I was hoping they would have some opinion, but I didn't want to push it. I didn't want to tell them I was thinking of going to a college in another state. I knew I probably wasn't going, but I still found myself daydreaming about the idea.

"If you guys want to use my sister's room, it's cool," Sissy said.

"To do what?" I asked.

"To do *it*, stupid," Sissy said. *"Jesus, you two are such prudes."*

"We, um, I . . ." I stammered. I still hadn't told her we were just friends. I was afraid she would get jealous of Morrison. I should have said something before now. Was this the opportunity I had been waiting for to tell her we had "broken up"? Sissy stared at me, waiting for me to finish my sentence. *Do I keep up the lie or tell her the truth?*

The moment ended when Morrison grabbed the remote and changed the channel to ABC. Sissy glared at him. She controlled the remote, but it was almost time for *Dynasty*. He had initially mocked us for watching it, singing about having a TV party, and rolling his eyes. Now he was as sucked in as we were.

During one of the commercial breaks, Sissy abruptly said, "Oh! I forgot to tell you! I had sex with Karl the other night. You know, the one going with Sherylynn, little Ms. Perfect Orange Blossom Princess?"

"Aren't you afraid of getting pregnant?" Morrison asked.

Sissy laughed.

"Hardly. You can't get pregnant from a hand job. I tell them I'm on my period and jerk them off. If I'm horny, I let them go down on me. If I call it sex, they think they had sex. They are just happy for someone to touch it. It's over in like thirty seconds and much less gross. What's great is that they aren't sure if they really cheated or not. It's fun to see them in school and wave with my talented little hand. Derek Colding almost died when I did that to him when he was sitting with Kandy."

Sissy saw the expressions on our faces and laughed. "What? I'm practically performing a community service."

"How exactly do you figure that?" Morrison asked.

"Do you know how many boys I've saved from going blind by helping them avoid the sins of masturbation?"

We erupted into a pile of giggles that evolved into a pillow fight that pretty much trashed her room.

I was happy that fall. Sissy didn't seem to mind me being at swim practice as much. Either she was with one of her guys, or she and

Morrison were hanging out. I was swimming better than ever. I swam my personal best at one of the regionals. We had a good shot at the state finals for the first time in twenty-two years. Things were still tense at home, but I had Sissy and Morrison, and they felt like family.

CHAPTER 32
PAST - NOVEMBER 1985

"You lying fucking bitch!" Sissy screamed at me over the phone.

"What's wrong?"

"You never fucking told me that Morrison was a homo."

What could I say to that? I hadn't. She kept insisting Morrison and I were a couple. We could have told her the truth, but we didn't. The assumption made our lives easier at school and with Sissy. She had accepted him, thinking he was my boyfriend. According to school rules, if you are dating someone, there must be something okay about you; you weren't a total loser. So, yes, we let everyone think what they wanted to think.

I kept apologizing, but she wasn't mollified and slammed the phone down. I asked Morrison what happened on the bus the next morning. He said they were hanging out while I was at swim practice. They were watching a movie, and she went to the bathroom. He said when she came back, she seemed kind of hyper and started messing around tickling him. He said it was weird. At first, he thought she was joking. Then she started kissing his neck, and he backed away. He said he started to bluff and keep up our pretense of being a couple, but that only seemed to make her madder.

He said she started losing it, screaming at him. He finally blurted he was gay. That seemed to stop the fury, and she threw him out. He said he hitchhiked home.

Sissy thought Morrison and I were dating. She had tried to kiss him, thinking he was my boyfriend. Was she going to have sex with him? She was furious with me for not telling her he was gay, but shouldn't I have been mad at her too? What if he had been my boyfriend? Sissy didn't speak to either of us at school the next day or the rest of the week.

I had been home all day Saturday, moving listlessly between the small rooms.

"Chelle, baby, you okay?" Mom asked as she made notes about the recently deceased at the kitchen table.

I wanted to tell her no, I wasn't okay. I wanted to curl up on the couch with my head in her lap and have her stroke my back. I wanted to talk to someone about my friendship with Sissy and how it made me feel bad a lot of the time, but that I felt like I needed her. I was ashamed of how Sissy made me feel.

Maybe if I'd talked to my mom about it then, she would've helped me see who Sissy was. Would that have changed what happened? Instead, I said I was fine and went back to my room and shut the door.

Sunday afternoon, I decided to take a walk and see if Morrison was at the tree. It was late, and the sun was getting low, but there was still plenty of light filtering through the woods. There was a breeze keeping the bugs at bay. He was sitting in his usual spot with a pair of jeans and a razor blade. I hoisted myself up onto my branch and looked at him quizzically. He began cutting the knees with small cuts and then rubbing and fraying the edges against the bark. He did this repeatedly.

"What are you doing?"

"What? They look cool like this."

"You make fake punk clothes instead of letting it happen naturally?"

"This is natural. We're sitting in nature, right?"

I laughed.

"Sissy talk to you?" he asked.

"No. You?"

"No."

We let it drop. We were both nervous about her silence. Morrison was also nervous about what she was going to do with what she knew. She was right to be mad at us. We both had lied to her by not telling her the truth when we had the chance.

"Did you have to read *The Great Gatsby* for Mr. Thomason?" he asked.

"I didn't have Mr. Thomason. I had Mrs. Leonard, but I read it for her."

"What did you think?"

"I liked *Great Expectations* more." I wasn't sure what he was getting at, and I didn't want to sound stupid.

"That doesn't answer my question."

"I wasn't crazy about it. I didn't hate it or anything, but why are they teaching it to us? How am I supposed to relate other than understanding that the poor stay poor? I already know that."

"Okay, good, it wasn't just me."

"If you're reading the same books this year, *Brave New World* was pretty good. I found *The French Lieutenant's Woman* kind of tedious."

"I already read *Brave New World*. I saw it at the library, and it looked interesting. I liked it. I come out here to read. It's not so much that I like to read as much as I need to escape. I can't afford cable or drugs or booze, but I can always get books from the library."

I knew he read a lot, but I hadn't known why. I sometimes read for fun, but it was usually trashy stuff. I didn't want to admit that I was currently reading V.C. Andrews.

He continued, "I like to read about fucked-up people and families. It makes me feel a bit better about my own life to know other people are just as fucked up. Or weird stuff, like *Chariots of the Gods*. I like knowing there are people out there thinking crazy shit that they feel compelled to share."

We sat there for a bit, and then he said, "I lied. About the pants. They do look cool like this, but the reason I'm not letting nature take its punk rock course is that I've been growing lately. Some asshole at school mocked me for wearing highwaters. I can only let them ride so low before my dick is hanging out. If I shred out the knees and add a few other well-placed cuts, the legs hang a bit longer."

I nodded. "I get it. I've done similar things." I thought of how I went through a phase asking for clothes a size or two too big, so I wouldn't get made fun of again for wearing clothes that were too tight or short when I started growing. I told my mom it was the style. Instead, I got made fun of for wearing too-big hand-me-downs.

On Tuesday, Sissy left a note in my locker asking me to meet at the bleachers at lunch. Morrison was there when I got there. He was skipping a class to be there. We looked at each other. We had each received a note from Sissy. She bounded up a few minutes later.

"I was really mad that you both lied to me, but I've thought about it and decided to forgive you."

"We didn't mean to lie to you," I said.

"Hey, I'm sorry, I should have said something," Morrison chimed in.

"Why did you lie?" she asked me.

"I, um . . ." I said, faltering, not wanting to say that I was afraid she would be jealous of Morrison.

"Because I asked her to," Morrison cut in. "I had some bad experiences with other people, and I wasn't sure if you would be cool with me."

I couldn't believe it. Morrison was lying to her to protect me. He knew I had been scared about them meeting but never asked why.

Sissy looked at Morrison. "There's one thing I'd like to know," she said.

"Yeah, what's that?" he replied warily.

She leaned in and whispered, "Do you have AIDS? It's okay if you do. I thought maybe that was why you lied. I mean, you're so thin. Is that it?"

"No, I don't have AIDS," he said flatly.

If I didn't know better, I would have thought Sissy was disappointed in his answer.

When I got home that night, my mother was watching the news.

There was a story about a boy in Indiana suing to get to go to school. He had AIDS. The Indiana Department of Education had ruled he could go to school after being barred all year. Parents were in an uproar. I thought about the conversation with Sissy earlier.

Life returned to normal, with one exception. After we reconciled, Sissy presented Morrison with his own bean bag chair. He no longer had to lean against her bedframe when we watched TV or listened to music. She asked if we wanted to sleep over the Saturday after Thanksgiving. We did, and when she picked us up, we went and rented a stack of movies and bought two bags of snacks.

We walked into her house, and Sissy loudly announced that we would both be sleeping over. Mrs. Davis looked up at us from the couch. I don't know if she was going to say anything or not. It didn't matter. Sissy acted as if she objected and said, "It's okay, mom. He's a fag." She turned and led us to her bedroom.

She had never mentioned the sleepover to her mother. I wanted to apologize. I mean, she knew how Sissy was, but still.

Morrison looked agitated once we were all gathered in Sissy's room. It seemed too small for the first time.

"What?" Sissy asked peevishly.

"Not fucking cool. That's my personal business, not yours to use against your mother."

"I'm not the bad guy here. You should be glad that I'm cool with you being gay and all."

"I didn't realize I should be grateful that you accept me as a human being. To be fair, I'm cool with you being known as the hand job queen of Ocean Breezes High."

"Whoa, calm down," I said. "Let's just put the movie in, okay?" I grabbed the plastic container and put the tape into the machine. It immediately began playing. Sissy threw herself onto her bed, and Morrison threw himself onto his bean bag.

We began watching *Purple Rain*. After about twenty minutes, Sissy broke the tense silence.

"Am I really known as the hand job queen of Ocean Breezes

High?"

Morrison made a jerk off motion with one hand and slowly began raising his middle finger on the other. I started laughing. Sissy started laughing, too. Morrison wasn't laughing.

CHAPTER 33
PRESENT - JUNE 2001

Florida is a series of strip malls glued together by car dealerships, gas stations, fast food, and other invasive species. The land is leveling out, the bumpy horizon stretching into nothingness. The three-lane highway reduces down to two lanes. Cars and concrete are replaced with trucks and cattle. Telephone poles beat out a steady rhythm alongside the highway. Egrets stand in roadside drainage canals. Swarms of trucks ping rocks off my windshield. I opened all of the windows to make the drive bearable, and now there are dead and dying lovebugs littering the backseat.

Traffic starts backing up. The afternoon sun is unrelenting. The road ahead looks wet from the heat mirage. I look at the other cars, with their rolled-up windows, enjoying functioning air conditioning. The needle is twitching towards red on the temperature gauge. I am finally able to exit off the Turnpike and onto US-27. I have to drive a few miles before I find a gas station/produce stand. I gas up, taking the opportunity to scrape off some of the lovebugs splattered on the windshield. I get something to drink and pace under the gas station awning. I am tired of driving, I am tired of snack foods, and I am tired of myself. I hope fifteen minutes is enough time to let the engine cool off.

I'm mad at myself, remembering now how Sissy had reacted and not holding her responsible for what she had done, or rather, what she'd tried to do by coming on to Morrison. I was so sure it had all been my fault. Why had I even sought her forgiveness? That had been yet one more chance for us to break free of one another before it was too late.

I get back in the car, and the lighter traffic and slower local roads keep the needle steady. I continue slogging my way south. I can see thunderheads building to the west.

CHAPTER 34
PAST - DECEMBER 1985

My mother dropped us off at Sissy's one foggy Saturday morning. We were going to go to the movies later, and I offered to call and get the times. I was listening to the recording as Sissy and Morrison sparred.

"What would you do if I told your mother your secret?" Sissy asked Morrison. Sissy had never met Morrison's mother, and he aimed to keep it that way.

"What secret?"

"That you're a homo."

"That isn't a secret. I don't think she would care. If anything, it would mean I would have twice the condoms to get rid of at school."

"What if I told the kids at school?"

"What if you did? You and I both know the assholes there already hate me for not looking or acting like the rest of the sheep. Tell them I'm gay, and you put me in actual physical danger. I'll drop out before I deal with that shit from these redneck assholes." Morrison didn't find her game funny in the slightest.

Sissy acted like it was all a joke, and Morrison was crazy for getting mad. I wasn't sure what Sissy was up to, but she stopped for a change. All kidding aside, we knew it was dangerous for him. We all knew the rumors about what happened to the kids people assumed were gay. We had heard what happened to Charlie Klepner and the "accident" in gym class. He had dropped out instead of coming back to school.

I had put as much of my lifeguarding money into the bank as possible. By the end of the summer, I had about $600 in my account. I wasn't sure what all I would need it for, but I knew I would need some at Christmas. I still felt bad about not getting Sissy a gift last year. I went to the bank with my mother and took out $100 to get gifts for everyone.

I got Sissy and my mother perfume and Michael cologne. I felt grown up buying the bottles at the Macy's counter. Morrison didn't seem like a cologne kind of guy. I wandered around Peaches Records and Tapes for forty-five minutes, but I was afraid he either had the tapes or would think the ones I picked were dumb. I ended up getting him a multi-use pocketknife and a Clash patch for his jacket. I wanted his gift to be perfect. I knew it wasn't.

Morrison and I exchanged gifts before we went over to Sissy's. He seemed especially pleased with the new patch and said he would sew it onto his jacket tomorrow. He handed me a small box wrapped in the Sunday comics section. Inside was a leather keychain.

"I made it in shop," he said.

On the smooth side, "HA!" had been punched into the leather. "Do you get it?"

I stared at it again. What was I missing?

"H.A. Harry Anderson. He has the key to your heart, right?"

I punched his shoulder and hugged him. I loved it. His gift was perfect.

Sissy picked us up a few minutes later, and we went back to her house. She had gotten Morrison a new denim jacket. He put it on right away, and I immediately missed the ratty jacket he always wore. She had gotten me a hair set with a curling iron, brush, and rollers. I wasn't sure what to say. I had no idea what it would do to my hair. I pretended like I couldn't wait to use it. It scared the shit out of me.

Morrison had gotten Sissy a tape by Echo and the Bunnymen. She said thanks and tossed it onto the precarious stack of tapes by her boombox. When she opened my gift, she barely said anything. It was like I had done something wrong, but I didn't know what. Morrison could see I was hurt. He made a big deal about wanting the Clash patch to be the first one he added to the new jacket. I had spent $25 on her perfume, which was more than I had spent on anyone else. I'm not sure what I was expecting or what I wanted, but I felt bad, and I didn't know why.

CHAPTER 35

In the summer, the woods around the tree were thick. Everything was thick—the air, the bugs, the trees, the ferns, the vines, the Spanish moss. In the fall, the light softened, and the cypress trees turned a golden color. Now, in winter, there were bare patches, allowing a clearer view of the lake and woods. Live oaks kept their leaves in winter and shed them as new growth appeared in the spring, so our tree still offered cover and shade.

It was still just our tree. We never brought Sissy here. We knew it wouldn't mean anything to her.

Winter meant the return of elderly human snowbirds pretending to be locals. Wearing shorts when it was sixty degrees always gave them away. A pair of sandhill cranes must have decided they had a good point and had been hanging around the woods all year. I'd watch them preening and pecking at the ground and wondered why they decided to stay. They were programmed to migrate. What made them stay when they knew they should leave? What made the other birds leave when it was nice and warm here all year-round? Maybe being nice and warm wasn't enough.

Morrison taught me a lot about the woods. I told him about the owl that lived near me. One morning I heard it as we were leaving for work. That was when I found out that my owl was a mourning dove.

The truth had always been there, but I couldn't see it. I had imagined it was an owl because that was what I thought an owl should sound like. Morrison taught me how to listen and to see with my ears as much as with my eyes. I could never tell if he heard things differently because of his hearing loss or if the loss made him that much more aware of what he could hear.

I began to appreciate the woods differently. I had noticed the changing light and how the dense canopy of the summer yielded, and light filtered down to the understory. I knew there had to be a word for the way the light looked, but I couldn't find the right one. Dappled was good, but it described how the light fell, not how it felt. The light had a texture all its own. Spangled and marbled weren't right either. It was like saying the sky was blue and red when what you were trying to describe was that explosion of color that occurs just after sunset. Blue and red aren't wrong, but they are crude descriptions for something so beautiful that it makes your heart ache. Maybe there wasn't a word that described the texture of light penetrating live oaks and bald cypress on a perfect autumn day in Florida. Maybe some experiences shouldn't be made into words. They needed to be seen. Felt.

CHAPTER 36

"Let's go to West Palm this weekend. Winter break is almost over," Sissy said.

"Why West Palm?" I asked.

"There is a bar there—*a gay bar*. My friend Vicki, from camp, told me about it. It is only about an hour away. It will be super cool! We can dance or whatever and not have to worry about assholes bothering us. Right, Morrison?"

"How would I know?"

Morrison and I remained unconvinced, but she was insistent, telling us how much fun it would be. When we still didn't show the expected enthusiasm, she berated us and said she would pick us up at 7:00 p.m. at my house.

She pulled up wearing too much makeup, a mini skirt, boots, a crop top, and a denim jacket. She looked at us, dressed in our usual jeans and T-shirts, and sighed. She drove down Highway 710, speeding past Lake Okeechobee. It was mostly two-lane roads in the middle of cattle pastures and swamps. It was closer to two hours than the hour she promised. Eventually, we could see the light pollution illuminating the sky along the coast, and traffic began to increase.

Sissy had a map and some crude directions written out. I had only been to this part of the state for swimming tournaments. This was postcard Florida. Even in the darkness, everything was bright and clean. The palm trees were perfect silhouettes. Here, the Spanish moss looked more like artfully placed decoration. We got to West Palm Beach and started driving along US 1, looking for Sentinel Street. We found it and started looking for Roman's Place. We'd driven up and down the street three times, growing increasingly frustrated, before she finally spotted the street number we were looking for and parked. There was no sign indicating it was a bar or even a business. It didn't look open, whatever it was. The businesses on either side were closed for the night. We were arguing about what to do when we saw a tall woman walk up to the door and go inside.

Sissy grabbed her purse and got out of the car before we could argue further. We walked inside, and it was . . . boring. I'm not sure what I was expecting a gay bar to be, but this wasn't it. I got the feeling that Morrison was thinking the same thing. He seemed a bit nervous. I wondered what he had been expecting. There was a guy behind a small bar and a customer talking to him. There were a few round tables, a row of five stools wrapping around the bar, and a pool table further back in the room. The walls had a few posters for beers and alcohol, age warnings, and a poster for Campari. Music was playing in the background. I didn't see the woman who had entered the bar before us.

Sissy walked up to the bar and sat on a stool as if it was the most natural thing in the world. We followed her and took seats beside her. The bartender came over and looked at us with a bemused smirk. He was in his twenties with shaggy blond hair and a small mustache. I felt self-conscious and out of place.

Sissy asked for a gin and tonic. The bartender asked for ID. She smiled and said she had forgotten it in her car, but she was nineteen and grandfathered in under the old drinking age.

Florida had raised the drinking age to twenty-one that July, but if you were nineteen before the change, you could still drink. Sissy's lie was so smooth. I was impressed. Sissy did look at least nineteen. She could easily pass for twenty-five, so the little lie of nineteen seemed reasonable. Morrison and I both looked young, and she didn't bother lying for us. She opened her wallet, flashed a bit of cash, and asked if she could buy the bartender a drink. He laughed and gave her the drink.

"Would you two like a Roy Roger? Maybe a Shirley Temple?" the bartender asked.

I actually liked Shirley Temples but felt humiliated and asked for a Sprite.

We sat there awkwardly for a few minutes. I started gulping my Sprite with the hope we'd be leaving soon. This was basically a room with a small bar and a handful of tables and chairs. I figured Sissy's friend had gotten it wrong, and this wasn't a gay bar. It was barely a bar at all.

Morrison was looking around like he was trying to figure things out. Sissy kept looking at him like he would explain everything.

We were ready to leave when three guys burst through the front door. They were loud and shouted hello to the bartender. And then they were gone, disappearing down a hallway that I had assumed led to a storeroom or bathrooms. Another guy came in and slipped down the hallway. All at once, we understood what we had been missing.

Sissy waved to the bartender. "What's back there?"

The bemused smirk returned, which I was beginning to hate. "That's nothing for you, dearie. It's just a Friends of Dorothy meeting, nothing that would interest you."

Sissy smirked back, finished her drink, and walked straight down the hallway. She returned a few minutes later, excitedly waving at us to follow her.

We walked down the hallway to a door at the end of the corridor. There was a sign on the door that said "When in Rome" in bold script. The building must have been longer than it looked from the outside. As we got closer, the music got louder. The minute the door opened, the sound hit us.

There was a stage and dance floor with alcoves tucked into the walls. On stage was a woman who looked like a tall version of Dolly Parton singing "9 to 5." Sissy found a second, larger bar in the corner and ordered three gin and tonics. She thrust them into our hands. She was loving this. I wanted to go home. I felt awkward, like a kid playing dress-up. I had never been to a bar before.

Tall Dolly shook her tits and ass at the audience. As she finished singing, *"It's a rich man's game no matter what they call it. And you spend your life puttin' money in his wallet,"* she walked up to an audience member, demanded money, and shoved it into her bra.

She strutted off stage, and a beautiful Latina woman came out and said, "Please give it up for Ima Tucker! How you fuckers doing tonight?! Drink up. We get prettier as you do. Next up, we have Coco Butter. Give her a big round of applause, you fucking perverts!"

The music went up again, and a heavyset woman came out to the opening chords of "Private Dancer." I split my time between watching Coco Butter and watching Sissy and Morrison. Their eyes were hungrily roving the crowd. Sissy said her friend might be there. I wasn't sure what Morrison was looking for.

I took a sip of the drink Sissy had ordered for me and didn't like it. I was scared of getting drunk. I pretended to drink it but only ate the ice cubes. Morrison, on the other hand, finished his and ordered another round, letting Sissy pay for the drinks.

"She's pretty good," I said to Morrison.

He nodded.

"I mean, her voice sounds just like Tina Turner's."

Sissy started laughing. Morrison leaned over and said, "He's lip-syncing."

"He?"

"You know this is a drag show, right?"

I didn't know. I felt like some kind of small-town idiot.

Morrison leaned over and whispered into my ear, "Hey, it's cool. I've only read about them. It didn't dawn on me until I saw the Adam's apple on Dolly. You're fine." He grabbed my hand and squeezed it.

Coco exited the small stage and the MC, who introduced herself as Infidel Castro, started talking to the audience.

She sashayed over and pointed the microphone at me and asked,

"So are you a pussy-eater or what?" A spotlight landed on me.

I blushed and felt my ears go hot. Morrison, who I didn't realize was already drunk, shouted, "Nah, she has a thing for Harry Anderson."

"Really? Because I have a *thing* for Harry Johnson!" The audience whistled and clapped.

Infidel Castro moved on to another victim, singling out a guy not paying attention to her act. She got off the stage, took his drink, and got back on stage.

Sissy laughed so hard she sloshed her drink. "Really, Harry Anderson?" She was gasping for breath. "Is *that* why we have to watch *Night Court* all the time?"

I decided that death could come and take me in that instant.

Infidel Castro came back to where we were standing. She looked down at Sissy and said, "I hope you cut the bitch who did that to your hair. Also, baby, here's a dollar to buy a lightbulb so you can see when you put your eye make-up on."

Morrison seemed to sober up immediately. By now, he had experience with Sissy's mood swings when challenged.

Sissy went still and then started laughing. She was enjoying the attention. Infidel Castro winked at her and started introducing the next performer.

Morrison and Sissy were having the time of their lives. They were dancing and singing along. They were both drunk. After a while, Sissy disappeared. I assumed she had gone to the bathroom, but she came back with some new friends. I could tell she had had some cocaine while she was gone. I had begun to see that look more frequently since she had come back from camp. Sissy eventually drifted away with her new friends, who turned out to be hairdressers from Jupiter. They were whooping it up as each new performer came out on stage. She was throwing herself around on the dance floor. The hairdressers were treating her like a cute little drug-sharing pet.

Morrison went to the bathroom and thankfully came back without an entourage. He leaned over and told me I should go see the men's room. I was expecting something scandalous. Instead, he laughed and said, "They have Anita Bryant's face taped to the inside of the urinal. For target practice."

Morrison, who had had at least four gin and tonics, started talking to a couple of guys. One was wearing a crop top and cut-off shorts, and the other a polo shirt with the collar popped. A punk, a preppy, and a jock walk into a gay bar. . . .

I decided to go back to the bar at the front of the building. It was all a bit too much for me. I wanted to wait for them where I could hear myself think. At the bar was one of the performers I had seen earlier drinking a beer. He waved me over and moved his wig off the barstool beside him. He introduced himself as Willy Wonky but said I could call him Bill. On stage, he was dominating as Cher, but at the bar, he seemed warm and friendly.

"Where you from? I've never seen you or your friends here before."

"Lorida, near Sebring."

"Lorida? Is that a real place?"

"I'm not sure some days."

At this, Bill barked out a laugh that sounded incredibly masculine, which jarred me for a second. "You okay, kid?"

"Yeah, yeah. My friends are having a great time."

"Are you?"

"I'm cool. The noise and crowd got to me. I'm not used to it. I don't even go to school dances."

He reached for his cigarettes and slid a pack of matches out of the cellophane. He struck a match and lit one.

Exhaling, he said, "You can hang out here with me. I'll let you in on a secret . . . I'm from Gibsonton. Small towns, small minds, even smaller dicks. I was raised on brimstone, circus freaks, and repressed hillbillies. My attire makes more sense now, doesn't it?" He smiled at me, and I started to relax.

The bartender came over and gave Bill a fresh beer and slid a Shirley Temple toward me with a friendly wink this time. Bill clinked his bottle against my glass.

Bill was easy to talk to. He started asking me questions and listened to the answers. Before I knew what happened, I was telling a
stranger about my life. I told him I was scared to go to college, but
I didn't feel like I belonged in Lorida, either. I told him things I had
trouble admitting to myself.

"Try and remember something—fitting in and belonging are two
different things. Fitting in means changing yourself to fit the situation. It's either a lie or becomes your new truth. Belonging means
you are accepted just the way you are. I couldn't have fit into my
family or Gibsonton if I had wanted to. I had to find where I belonged."

Bill started telling me a story, something about a bear, when Morrison and Sissy burst through the corridor with the hairdressers
from Jupiter. They were a kinetic bundle of noise. I could see Morrison was quite drunk, but Sissy was overly alert. They said goodbye,
with Sissy hugging all of her new best friends goodbye. Morrison
waved goodbye to the wall.

The neighborhood outside the bar was absolutely silent. We got
into Sissy's car, and I used the dash light to read her directions in
reverse to get us home.

"You should be more like those guys, Morrison. They were fun!"
she said, but thankfully he had already fallen asleep in the backseat.

The roads were empty at that time of night. Bright eyes caught in
our headlights and darted alongside the road. Sissy was wired, and I
found myself gripping the dashboard. I glanced over, and she was
doing seventy-five in the pitch-black night. She was singing along
to the radio, thumping the steering wheel to the beat. I had told my
mother I was sleeping over at Sissy's. I imagined the cops coming
to tell her I had had an accident so far from home.

CHAPTER 37
PAST - JANUARY 1986

Things changed after that night at the bar. Morrison and Sissy started hanging out alone. I couldn't tell if they were treating me like
a little kid or if I was just acting like one. He usually went home
with her when I had swim practice and occasionally when I didn't.
Sometimes they disappeared after school, and I rode the bus home
alone. One day, I noticed that Sissy was standing on Morrison's
right side, and it was intentional. It was ridiculous to be territorial
of someone's good ear, but I was. I should have been happy they
were friends. I should have been relieved that she didn't feel like I
was choosing swimming over her like she used to. Instead, I was
resentful and jealous, and I didn't like myself for it. I was used
to having in-jokes with Sissy that Morrison didn't understand and
with Morrison that Sissy didn't understand. Now they had in-jokes
I didn't understand. They had a favorite night shift waitress at the
Denny's in Sebring. He seemed to be better at making her happy
than I ever was. I worried about what they said about me.

"Mom, can you drop me off at school Saturday morning?" I said.
    "Swim practice? What time?"
    "Um, no, it is some test the school makes us take."
    "On a Saturday?"
    "Yeah, it won't take long. I just need to be there at 9 a.m. and will
be done by noon."
    The lies came easily. I wasn't sure whose feelings I was protect-

ing—hers or mine. In reality, I would be taking the SAT. It was the last piece I needed to complete my application for the University of Georgia.

I had decided on an all-or-nothing approach. Either I would go to the University of Georgia on a scholarship, or I would get a job when I graduated. I treated the idea of going to college like a fantasy. Taking the test felt like a childish hope, but I went nevertheless. Logically, I knew I could go to South Florida Community College, but I wasn't sure what I would do there. Pay to go to school to work at a hotel, or just go work at a hotel? Plus, that seemed like I was taking my Shari Belafonte fixation a little too far.

Going anywhere else meant trying to figure out how to live between school and home. There weren't many options close to Lorida and I didn't have a car. It wasn't like I could ask Sissy to drive me. I couldn't afford to live on my own and go to school. I couldn't ask my mother for money or take out a loan to figure out my life. They probably wouldn't give me a school loan if I didn't have a plan, and I certainly didn't have a plan. If Georgia gave me a scholarship, they would tell me what to do and where to live. If not, I'd get a job and get on with life. I convinced myself that my lack of options was a plan.

Michael picked me up at noon.

As I got in the car, he asked, "So what test did the school make you take on a Saturday?"

"It was just standard testing."

He looked at me and shook his head. He knew I was lying. We were quiet as he drove me back to the house and went on to work. He was working as a mechanic at a garage near Okeechobee. He was using mom's car but almost had enough saved up for one. He worked second shift and usually got home around midnight.

As I walked in the door, Mom said she had gone to the grocery store, and there was some Hi-C and macaroni salad for lunch. I didn't know why, but the Hi-C made me angry. I had just gone and taken a test that could decide my future, and she was offering me a child's drink. I said I wasn't hungry, even though I was, and went to my room. I called Sissy and asked if she wanted to hang out.

She and Morrison picked me up an hour later. Morrison showed me the new boots Sissy had bought him. Sissy had been making Morrison over slowly. All of his old, worn-out clothes were being replaced. He was also filling out. The skinny, scruffy kid was disappearing.

As we sped along Route 98, Sissy said, "Michelle, that reminds me, can you give me back my belt? The black one with the studs on it."

"I don't have it," I said. I couldn't even remember seeing it since her mother cleaned her room over the summer.

"Look, I'll give you stuff if you need it, but I don't appreciate you stealing from me."

"I didn't, I swear." Had I ever even mentioned liking the belt? I couldn't remember.

"Whatever."

Sissy, Morrison, and I went to the movies on Friday night. I had agreed to go on the condition that we went to the 7:00 p.m. show, and I went straight home afterward. Sissy agreed but made comments about how her schedule had to revolve around me all night. About how we were stuck with *Iron Eagle* or *The Best of Times* because we didn't have time to drive to "a decent theater." She knew the reason I wanted to be home early. Saturday was the last big swim meet before the state finals.

"A movie about high school football rivals—wow, Michelle, that was a great choice. We should have brought Thad along so you would have someone to talk football with." Sissy said sarcastically as we pulled out of the parking lot.

Morrison laughed at her joke. I hadn't even picked the movie. *Iron Eagle* had started at 6:45 p.m., and *The Best of Times* started at 7:15 p.m. We were too late for *Iron Eagle*. It felt like she was picking a fight with me.

Out of nowhere, she said, "Remember what you said about college?"

"What do you mean?" I felt heat start rising in my face. "Duh, how you said you thought you might go. Are you going to apply anywhere?"

"I don't know, maybe."

"What does *that* mean? Where? Have you applied?"

"No. Yes."

"Which is it?"

"Coach Roberts made me apply to one, so I did."

"Where?"

I didn't want it coming out like this. I wasn't even going to say anything. I was going to forget about the whole thing when I didn't get the scholarship.

"It doesn't matter. It isn't going to happen."

"*Where?*" she shouted. "Tell me the fucking truth!"

Truth? Was there a truth? I didn't know anymore. I wasn't sure what was true or a lie, a fantasy or the future.

"The University of Georgia," slipped out in a whisper. Like I was admitting to a crime.

Morrison, who had been quiet in the backseat the whole time, got quieter.

Sissy started laughing, which was scarier than when she was yelling at me. "Georgia? You're going to fucking Georgia? So, when were you going to tell us?"

"I—I'm not going. It was just something Coach Roberts made me do. I'm going to stay here. I'm not going to get in, and even if I do, I don't have to go."

"You're right. You probably won't get in. And how would you ever afford it? You can't even afford your own movie tickets. Still, you thought about leaving us. Why? You never told us you applied. Why would you do that?"

"I don't know."

"It really fucking hurts to be treated like this. Do you hate us that much? This isn't the first time you've lied, either."

"I'm sorry."

"That's probably a lie, too."

"It isn't. I swear, I'm telling the truth." There was that word again.

Sissy stopped in front of my house. I got out and pushed the seat up for Morrison to get out, but Sissy told him to get back in the car. He looked at me and back at Sissy and got back in the car. He looked hurt.

I went inside, barely acknowledging my mother, and went to bed. I flopped back and forth for hours. By 3:00 a.m., my self-hatred had swallowed me whole.

I hadn't asked my mother to come to the swim meet, and Morrison and Sissy never showed up, so the only people who saw me win two races and place second in a third were my teammates and coach. It put us in place for the state championships. I swam as hard as I could, trying to escape through the water.

On Monday, I had people congratulating me in the halls at school. Morrison said he was sorry he hadn't been there but that Sissy hadn't wanted to go and he hadn't had any other way to get there. Sissy had been ignoring me. I wanted to be excited. Instead, I felt alone. Adrift.

Mom came home that afternoon and placed that day's newspaper down beside me. I was flopped down on the couch in front of the TV. Someone from the *Sebring Herald*, the newspaper where my mother worked, must have been at the meet. On the front page, below the fold, was an article and photo about the swim team going to the state finals for the first time in twenty-two years.

"Chelle, I didn't realize that was such a big meet."

She stopped and waited for me to say something. I burrowed deeper into the coarse fabric on the couch.

"I know you have your friends now, and I appreciate that, but I wish you would have told me about the meet. I would like to have gone. These are your last few meets. I would have stayed out of your way."

"Mom, I'm sorry," I said into the cushion.

"Baby, are you okay?"

"I'm fine, just tired."

She sat there a few more minutes, neither of us saying anything until she got up to start dinner. I knew I should try and explain, but I didn't know how.

Sissy never said anything to me about the fight. She just started talking to me again, acting as if nothing had happened. The first time that had happened, it was devastating. It still stung, but not as much. At least I knew she would eventually forgive me. With Morrison, I felt like we pretended things were normal. We avoided talking about how I had lied to him about applying to college. I could tell he was hurt. I often felt unwanted when we were all together. I wanted things to go back to the way they had been.

CHAPTER 38
PAST - FEBRUARY 1986

Senior portraits were on Monday. I had an idea, but I was nervous.

"I want to cut my hair," I said to Morrison.

"Like how?"

Morrison and I were talking, sitting on our usual branches in the tree. It was the kind of day that made me understand why people came to Florida in winter. It wasn't hot or cold. It was the very definition of pleasant. The weather seemed to match Morrison's mood. He was different since our night at the bar. He was more upbeat than he used to be. I was glad, but I was also a bit envious. I was lonely and more unsure than ever. I had trouble finding time to talk with him alone. He and Sissy were together all the time now. We still hadn't talked about my college application, and I felt it sitting between us.

"I was thinking of going short. Like Shari Belafonte's. Or Mia Farrow's."

"Seriously?"

"Yeah. What do you think? Would it look dumb?"

"I think that could look pretty awesome on you."

"I might see if I can go to the beauty school in Sebring. They do cheap cuts on training days."

"I can cut your hair."

I stopped and stared at him.

"Seriously, if you just want it cut short like that all the way around, I can do that. And before you go stereotyping me, I learned to cut hair because we had this dog with thick hair, and he was miserable from the heat and fleas. It made finding ticks easier. I started clipping him short once a month. I got bored, so sometimes, I would cut his hair into actual styles. I still have all the supplies. I cut my own hair if you haven't noticed."

"Sure, why not. It can't be worse than this mess I have now."

"Thanks for the vote of confidence."

"When?"

"Now?"

Why not? I had felt bad for a long time. My hair was one of the things I hated about myself. I decided it was the easiest place to start making changes. I watched as brittle chunks of hair floated to the cracked linoleum floor in Morrison's trailer. The hair itself weighed next to nothing, but the weight it carried had been immense. I kept going to run my fingers through it, expecting them to catch in tangles, only to find them hovering above my head.

Morrison loved it. My mother loved it. Even Michael, who was still mostly avoiding me, said he thought I looked pretty. I walked into school on Monday morning with my shoulders thrown back, feeling better than I had in a long time. It was the first time I had ever felt good about my hair.

It took about five minutes for that to evaporate when some kid I didn't know shouted, "Hey, Pat Benatar!" His laughter echoed down the hallway.

I had wanted to surprise Sissy with my new look and hadn't told her when we had talked last night. She was always changing her style. It was finally my turn.

When she saw me, she gasped and said, "Oh my god, what happened?"

"Morrison cut it."

"You *let* him do this to you?"

I felt my eyes welling with tears. It was stupid to cry over hair, but I wasn't crying about my hair. I felt good about myself, and that had been ripped away, yet again.

Sissy came over to me and put her arm around me. She comforted me and said, "Oh, Michelle, why did you do this? You look like a boy. I would've told you not to do this if you had said something. Maybe we can get you a wig."

She stood there with me at the lockers until I pulled myself together and went to class. I slumped into my chair in first period. Theresa Polk told me I looked great, and another girl, one who had teased me in the past, said it looked rad. Some guy nodded at me and smiled. I was so sure they were making fun of me.

My photo slot was after lunch. I took off my shirt and slid into the black V-necked drape that all the girls had to wear for their photos. I didn't feel like smiling and stared ahead as the photographer tried her best to get a forced, toothy smile.

Sissy came in for her appointment as I went to change back into my shirt. I stood at the back of the gym, waiting for her. She threw one smile after another. She arched her back. She knew how to pose and tilt her head just right. The photographer had her change positions a few times.

Sissy had ordered a deluxe package. I had ordered the cheapest package, one 8x10 and eight wallets, so there was only one pose. Only one chance to get it right.

CHAPTER 39

The state championships were the first week of February. They were held at the regional sports complex in Stuart. The school had arranged an extra bus for students and parents. Morrison, my mom, and my brother all said they would be there. Sissy seemed to be over being mad at me and was acting like my biggest cheerleader. Sissy, who had actively hated me swimming until we were contenders for the state championship.

They all thought I was nervous about the meet. I was nervous about what the meet meant. I was as scared of winning, knowing that might lock my spot at the University of Georgia, as I was of losing, which would lock my spot in Lorida.

When I came in first place for the 200 meters freestyle, I could hear Sissy screaming from the stands. I looked up and saw my mom, Michael, Sissy, and Morrison all waving and clapping.

We also placed first in the 500 meters relay. Mr. Roberts's accent was all over the place that day.

Once the medals were awarded, I raced over to the stands to find them. I hugged them all. I was so happy they were all there, and I didn't have to choose at that moment.

"Coach Roberts wants to take us out to celebrate. Is that okay, Mom?"

Before she could answer, Sissy said, "Awesome! Where are we going?"

"I mean the team. He's taking the team."

"Yes, of course, baby. You go and have fun and celebrate. You all earned it. I'm so proud of you," Mom said.

"So, I'm not invited?" Sissy said.

"No, no," I stammered, "It's not that."

I saw my mother and brother exchange a look. Michael started to say something, but my mother grabbed his arm and said, "Sissy, dear, how about we plan a celebration for Michelle at home? Where we can all celebrate her win together."

Sissy turned away from them and rolled her eyes at me.

"Michelle, go celebrate with your team. It's okay," Michael added. I could see he wanted to say more but was holding back.

"Whatever, go do your stuff." Sissy with her fake smile. Morrison and I could tell she was really irritated. I worried about what she would do or say on the bus ride back.

My mom had brought a small camera and took pictures of us. I was wearing the medals around my neck.

I think Sissy expected me to buckle and come back on the bus with them, but I didn't. More than celebrating with the team, I wanted time away from all of them to think about what the win meant. I wasn't sure I could do that on the bus surrounded by everyone. I should have realized the mistakes I was making. What my choices would mean. I had no idea what they would cost me later.

CHAPTER 40
PRESENT - JUNE 2001

I've been driving for over an hour, watching the storm move in from the west. From the signs, I'm somewhere near Lake Wales. I'm close.

When the sky finally exhales, it's a sweet-smelling gust of charged air, and then rain is pelting the car in fat, swollen drops. Within seconds I can barely see out the window. It is a low grumbling storm, the thunder a murmur that ripples gently around me.

I want the rain to be a relief, but it isn't. It begins to spatter the interior of the car. I roll up the driver-side window and turn on the defogger. That causes the needle to start twitching. I turn it off, and the windshield starts fogging up.

If I open the driver-side window, I get smacked in the face with rain, yet I can't reach any of the other windows to close them. It is a losing battle. I give up and pull over on US-27 into the driveway of an overgrown, vacant house. I crawl around the car, rolling the windows up, leaving just a crack at the top for air. I'm sweating and start to feel like a PSA about leaving an animal in a hot car. It looks like the kind of storm that will be over in a few minutes. There are clear skies at the edge of the dark cloud.

I stare at the house through sheets of rain. There is anonymity in Florida. People often come here to escape or disappear. It is like the heat and overgrowth swallow them. Nothing stays the same in Florida, but somehow it always *feels* the same. I've experienced this storm thousands of times before.

By all rights, people shouldn't live here. There is a perennial battle against nature. It is home to wild things—storms, trees, plants,
animals, bugs—and all can and will take over again given a chance.
Have you ever seen an abandoned house in Florida? Within a few
years, it is obscured by plants and trees. In a decade, insects destroy
the wood. Storms and sun beat it down. The structure blurs. It dis-
appears into the landscape. That can happen to people, too.

CHAPTER 41
PAST - MARCH 1986

Sissy and I had moved our lunch spot from the forlorn bleachers to one of the tiled tables in the courtyard. I was eating my lunch, reviewing my civics notes for an upcoming test, while Sissy read the *CliffsNotes* for *Heart of Darkness*, and a junior named Mark rubbed her shoulders. Morrison walked up, and I looked at him quizzically.

"What are you doing here? Aren't you supposed to be in class?"

"Call me cynical, but I have my doubts about the linguistic value of learning Spanish from a German with a lisp. I can't understand him when he speaks English. Did you know that the difference between 'I want to pay' and 'I want to jerk off' is a very confusing single consonant? Now you know."

Morrison slid in beside Sissy and began eating her lunch. Her mother had stopped making her lunch, so Sissy usually bought a sandwich or snacks from the deli across from the school in the mornings.

"What do you want?" Sissy asked.

"Your lunch."

"Seriously."

"I'm being serious. You never eat it all anyway."

She shoved half the sandwich at him. Through a mouthful, he said, "Next year is going to suck so hard when you two aren't here."

The closer we got to the end of school, the more it felt like we were being pushed towards an unknown edge.

"What if we got a place together?" Sissy asked.

"Like rented an apartment or something?" Morrison asked.

"Yeah. It could be super cool. It would be like *Three's Company*. I could be Sissy-Chrissy!" Sissy seemed overly enthusiastic about her imagined life as pseudo-Suzanne Somers. This also seemed to fit with her current look, which seemed to be preppy California girl. She had on a pink pull-over top, pleated pastel shorts, and white flats. She had ditched the perm and bleached her hair.

Obviously, Morrison was Jack, who in this case really was gay. This meant I was stuck being Janet. No one wants to be Janet.

"Where would we get the money for an apartment?" Morrison said. What he meant was there was no way we could afford one.

"I don't know. We'll figure something out." Sissy shrugged in the way I'd come to know well, the kind of indifference she always showed when it came to money. "I can ask my dad to set us up."

What they didn't know was that I had already figured something out. Mom had told me there was a letter for me when I had gotten home yesterday. It was from the University of Georgia. It was on the kitchen table, an innocent bomb waiting to go off.

"I didn't know you knew anyone who went there."

"I don't. It is probably a mistake or junk mail."

I took the envelope back to my room and started to open it. I had been waiting to find out what was going to happen, and now that it looked like I finally had, the answer I was terrified. What if I didn't get in? What if I did? My heart was racing as I finished tearing the envelope open. I was in. I had a conditional scholarship. The university was awarding me a full scholarship with room and board, but I had to make the swim team, keep a B average, and work on campus fifteen hours a week to receive a stipend. There was an SASE and form I needed to complete to accept the offer. I had to follow up with the head of the swim program about training over the summer.

I was excited. I was terrified. I wanted to tell everyone. I was scared to tell anyone. My excitement and terror paralyzed me. So, I let Sissy and Morrison make decoration plans for our fantasy apartment.

I considered telling them at school the next day. I knew I had handled things badly with the application. I was determined to do a better job this time. Keeping this a secret was eating away at me. I knew Sissy would be mad, but she always seemed to get over it, so it was a matter of managing how mad she got.

There was a small voice at the back of my head asking why my best friend would be mad at me for getting a scholarship to go to college. That voice was telling me to be careful. That voice struggled to be heard for a long time. It tried to warn me.

I saw Sissy by her locker before first period. I realized she was wearing the belt she had accused me of stealing from her.

"Oh, good, you found the belt."

Sissy glanced down at her waist. "What?"

"You thought I took it."

"I never said any such thing."

"But you said . . ."

"Don't be so paranoid. I would never say anything like that to you." I knew she didn't mean to do it, but she unbalanced me all the time.

Maybe I was paranoid. It wasn't the time to tell her about the letter. I decided to wait until there was a better time.

CHAPTER 42

It rained for days that April. We were used to rain, but this was relentless. Everything was wet or damp to the touch. My feet hadn't been dry in days. Water was rising in the cattle pastures and along the creeks and canals. Everything smelled like mildew.

Then it abruptly stopped, and the sun came out, and it made it so humid that we missed the rain. Somehow, it was less humid in the pouring rain.

I got on the bus, and Morrison looked overly excited for 7:00 a.m.

"Remember about Lake Istokpoga's name?" he said.

"About people dying there?

"Yes, but specifically about the whirlpools. I always assumed the name was to warn people away, and something was lost in translation. Or maybe an alligator grabbing and spinning someone under the water was the whirlpool."

"Yeah, so . . . ?"

"After the rain stopped yesterday, I had to get out of the trailer. Travis was over. He's decided to start calling me Moron instead of Morrison. My mom insists he is just kidding. Stupid fucker. He threw a beer bottle at me when I called him Travesty. Anyhow, I went to the tree. I saw a group of birds take off and looked over. Near shore, I saw the water moving funny. As I watched it, the trees near there started leaning. The ground started opening up, and the small trees fell over. For a brief moment, it looked like a small whirlpool as the water disappeared, and then it filled the hole.

It just looks like part of the lake again. I would never have seen if
I wasn't up in the tree."

"What was it?"

"I think it was a sinkhole. It must have given way from all the rain."

"So, what you're telling me is that the ground around the tree
could swallow us up at any time?"

"No, I'm telling you I think I figured out the legend, and it's fucking awesome."

"If you say so. Is the tree safe?"

"Totally. It looked like the hole was only a few feet deep."

I had exciting news too. My news wasn't fucking awesome. My
news was that I was leaving. I'd formally accepted UGA's offer. I
so wanted to tell Morrison. I was afraid that if I told him first and
Sissy found out, she might not get over being mad at me this time.
Could I trust him not to tell her? I didn't know anymore. Would
they try and stop me?

CHAPTER 43
PAST - MAY 1986

I rehearsed what I wanted to say to Sissy and Morrison and my mother and brother over and over in my head. I felt like I had all the words, but they jumbled up in my mouth until they clogged my throat. They choked me into silence. Sissy didn't notice. She was more concerned about the prom.

Morrison and I didn't want to go, but Sissy had been insistent we were all going together. She expected Morrison and me to continue our dating charade, and she would go with Derek Colding, all of us crammed into rented clothes and a rented limousine. She wanted all of us to color coordinate with matching accessories. I dreaded the thought of the poofy dress she was going to force me into. Why couldn't I wear pants? I was curious what Morrison would look like in a tux. I was curious what I would look like in a tux.

Morrison and I brought up the expense, and she threw her credit card at us. Literally, she threw it at us and shouted, "Problem solved."

The only problem was Derek didn't ask her. Worse yet, she had heard he was taking Kandy. Kandy hadn't been the one giving him hand jobs between classes.

We were walking out to Sissy's car after school and saw a tow truck in the school parking lot. Sissy started smiling.

"Such a shame," she said as she walked by Derek, who was talking to the tow truck driver. All four of his tires were flat.

He broke off his conversation and stormed over to us. "Did you fucking do this, you fucking psycho bitch?"

"Derek, I can't be the only person you screwed over?"

He came at her, and Morrison, who stood several inches taller than Derek, got in between them and placed his hand on his chest. "Derek, back the fuck off. You probably ran over some nails."

In the car that evening, Sissy seemed ebullient. She no longer wanted to go to prom. She wanted to go back to the bar in West Palm Beach and make our own prom. She railed on and on about not wanting to watch a bunch of rednecks dry-humping to "Smokin' in the Boys Room" and that half the girls would be prom pregnant at graduation.

Morrison was giddy when we got into the car to drive to West Palm. He sat up front, and he and Sissy sang along to mixtapes for most of the two-hour ride. Sissy hated punk, and Morrison hated Top 40, but they found common ground in Duran Duran and Depeche Mode.

The street was more crowded this time, and we had to park a few blocks away. Sissy was already getting loud when we walked into the bar. She was all shoulders and sparkle in her planned prom dress. The shaggy blond bartender with the mustache was behind the bar. Sissy headed straight for the back bar, and he called after her. She didn't listen, and he waved me over.

"It's Celebration Saturday. Tell your friend to tone it down."

I nodded like I understood and went after her.

Instead of flashing lights and performers, there was a guy in a button-up shirt and khakis on stage. Madonna was playing quietly in the background. The guy was reading from a legal pad with his arm around a girl. She looked younger than us. He was crying. I looked around the room, and it was mostly middle-aged men and a few women. Everyone looked somber.

Thankfully, Sissy caught the vibe and settled down. We found a quiet spot near the bar. The man on stage was talking about someone named Frank. The girl leaned into him. It sounded like Frank had died. I felt like an intruder.

Sissy waved the bartender over and asked what this was all about, asked when the drag queens would go on, and ordered three gin and tonics, all in the same breath.

"Drag night is only once a month. You missed it last week. This is Celebration Saturday." He saw the incomprehension in her eyes and continued as he made the drinks.

"Once a month, we get together to remember those who died. We never used to have to do this, but AIDS is killing a lot of people. There aren't always funerals, and when there are, we aren't always invited. There are also occasional suicides. Dying from cancer or a heart attack is almost quaint these days. So once a month, we get together to celebrate a person's life instead of mourning their death."

I wondered if my mother had ever written any of the obits. I wondered how filled with lies they were, depending on who was paying for the write-up. How many people might she have unknowingly erased?

He looked up and nodded towards the stage as he handed over our drinks. "Usually, it's a bit more upbeat than this. That's Frank's daughter on stage. We've all known her since she was a little girl."

Sissy responded with a face that looked like she knew Frank and was mourning him, too. We moved away from the bar.

"That poor girl," she said. "Did he die of AIDS, do you think? Do you think she has it?"

"Jesus, Sissy, stop," Morrison said as he sipped his drink. I was back to eating ice cubes and refilling Morrison's glass with my drink.

I watched them come off the stage. I realized that the guy who had been speaking was Willy Wonky. He looked so ordinary that I hadn't recognized him at first. He walked straight to the bar at the back with his hand outstretched, and the bartender wordlessly handed him a beer. He buckled onto a stool, and they exchanged a few words I couldn't hear.

The girl, who I now saw looked about fourteen, was being comforted by a group of people on the far side of the room. I could barely remember my own father's funeral. I didn't remember being comforted by people. Michael and my mother were also devastated. We each had our own grief, and we didn't do a very good job comforting one another. I wondered if something like this would have helped me.

Someone else went up on stage and said, "Frank knew he was sick. He knew you would all be here tonight. He wanted you to remember him how he lived, not how he died. He wanted you to feel his presence, so he asked that I sing something tonight."

He looked up and said, "Frank, I will get you for this." He looked down at the girl and said, "I'm sorry, Sarah."

At that, he bowed his head, and somewhere unseen, music began playing the opening notes to "We are the World."

"Philip, you asshole!" he screamed to his right.

There was a laugh offstage, and the music stopped. It started again with a different song. He looked at the audience and earnestly began singing,

When I was a little bitty boy
My grandmother bought me a cute little toy
Silver bells hanging on a string
She told me it was my ding-a-ling-a-ling, oh

The room was silent and respectful until the recognition began to ripple around the room. By the time he started the second verse, people had caught onto what was happening, and the solemn atmosphere was destroyed by laughter. Even his daughter was laughing. I didn't know who Frank was, but now I missed him, too.

I wanted to talk to his daughter, to offer my condolences, to tell her I understood. I imagined her to be lonely and fatherless like I was. I looked for her and found her surrounded by a group of men. She was far from fatherless. She had a family, and they were rallying around her. I watched her that night and she was never left alone. Someone was always holding her, talking to her, hugging her. I never wanted to intrude, to take a moment of that away from her. I had brief flashes of my father's funeral. I didn't remember Michael or my mother holding me. I remembered getting into a strange car. I remembered waiting for my mother for hours. I remembered feeling so scared and alone.

We were back near the bar again, and a guy came up to order a drink. He looked kind of preppy, but I saw a Siouxsie Sioux button on a satchel thrown across this shoulder. He looked a few years older than us.

He glanced over at Morrison and nodded. Morrison nodded back. "Can I get a Sam Adams?" he asked the bartender and then turned to Morrison and asked, "You want another one?"

"Yes. I mean no. I—I'm good, thanks. Thank you. Um . . . I have a drinks. I mean, I have my drink and her drink," pointing at me.

Sissy had just ordered a second round, and Morrison was drinking for both of us.

Morrison looked like he wanted to say something more to the guy, but all he managed to do was stare. It started to get embarrassing. I decided to intervene.

"Hi, I'm Michelle, and this is Morrison."

"Morrison, like Toni Morrison?"

Morrison began nodding like a bobblehead.

"Hey, I'm Russ."

Russ went to shake Morrison's hand, but he was holding both our drinks, and they started laughing at the increasing awkwardness.

I stuck around until Morrison could speak semi-normally and left him to get to know Russ.

I drifted to a quiet spot. Bill (aka Willy Wonky) saw me and asked if I had figured my life out yet. I shrugged. He shrugged back.

"Take what you can get out of life. You have no idea how short it really is. For you, for anyone."

I stood there and thought about what he said. I thought about what would happen if I stayed in Lorida and got an apartment with Sissy and Morrison. I thought about the scholarship. A part of me that I didn't fully understand needed to leave. I knew that and I was having trouble making peace with it. I worried about what leaving would mean. Sensibly, I told myself that I could leave and come back. I could go to school and come home on breaks and even come back and live with them over the summer or after I graduated. I wasn't sure what I wanted to go to school for, but I thought maybe I could choose a major that would enable me to get a decent job in Sebring, Okeechobee, or even Tampa. I could help my mom. The fantasy felt real for the first time. I wondered what my father would think. Would he be proud of me?

Sissy, who had been talking to one of the Jupiter hairdressers, looked over and saw Morrison talking to Russ. Her expression changed instantly. She walked over to Morrison, almost protectively. I could see her introducing herself.

Other than going to the bathroom a few times, Sissy didn't leave Morrison's side for the rest of the night. When we got in the car later, Morrison leaned over the front seat and excitedly showed me his arm. On it, written in blue ink, was Russ's phone number.

There was no singalong for the ride home.

CHAPTER 44
PAST - MAY 1986

I was nervous, but I finally told my mother and brother about the scholarship at dinner that week. I thought it would be easier to start with them and work up to telling Sissy and Morrison. It didn't work out like that.

"Is this what that letter was about?" Mom said. She sounded hurt and angry but not surprised. I nodded.

"You are *seriously* going through with this?" Michael said incredulously.

"Why did you lie to me about the letter? Why didn't you tell us what you were planning?" Mom asked.

"You've been planning this for months and never said anything! What the fuck, Michelle?" Michael cut in.

"I didn't think I would get in. None of it seemed real. I won't be gone forever, just for school."

"When are you leaving?" Michael asked. Was that all he cared about?

"In July."

"Is there a reason you didn't tell us?" Mom asked, her anger already dissolving into a look of sorrow. I had seen my mother sad for years, but this was different. I had done this to her. I felt horrible.

"Is there anything else you need to say to us?" Michael asked accusingly. I didn't understand why he was so furious with me. I knew they might be upset, but I hoped maybe they would be pleased for me.

I shook my head no.

Michael grabbed his keys and left. My mother got up from the couch and said, "I'm going to go lay down for a while."

In the morning, there was an impenetrable wall up surrounding my mother. She wasn't going to let me see how hurt she was. Looking down at her coffee cup, she said, "Michelle, I should have told you last night that I am proud of you." She turned and looked at me and said, "I'm sorry for whatever I did that made you feel like you couldn't talk to me."

That had been my opportunity. I should have talked to her, told her it wasn't her fault. I should have told her I was scared. I should have asked how she felt. I should have said a lot of things I didn't say. I should have realized she had been reaching out to me all year. She had been trying to celebrate milestones and victories—Michael's promotion, the swim meet, even my eighteenth birthday—finally ready to overcome some of the grief that had inhabited our lives for so long, but each time she had tried, I had ruined it. I had told her not to bother about the swim meet, that it wasn't a big deal—but it was. When she had asked about having a party for my eighteenth birthday, I had told her I wasn't a baby anymore. I hadn't told her that Sissy and Morrison had made fun of me when I had said my mother wanted to throw a party. There was so much I didn't understand.

I dreaded telling Sissy and Morrison. I knew I was going to hurt them too. My hand was forced by Coach Roberts and the school. The school knew about the scholarship and planned on announcing it at the senior breakfast.

The irony was that I was partly leaving thanks to Sissy. She had shown me a world beyond Lorida. She had shown me lives different than the one I knew. She had shown me what freedom felt like. She had made me both more afraid and less afraid. I was now more afraid of staying than of leaving. I owed her so much, even if she didn't know it.

I fumbled through telling them at lunch.

"It really sucks to find out our friendship means so little to you," Sissy said. "You know what you are? You're a selfish fucking liar."

Morrison looked sad. He started to say something, but Sissy grabbed his arm, and they walked away from me. I saw them head to the parking lot instead of back to class.

They left me on my own to take the bus home. I knew not to expect a call. I didn't bother going to the tree. I knew Morrison would be with Sissy. I was alone now.

CHAPTER 45
PRESENT - JUNE 2001

I was right: the storm only lasts a few minutes. The road is wet, and steam rises from the scorching pavement to meet back up with the clouds. Driving into Sebring, I'm startled to see how much has changed in fifteen years. Former landmarks are now parking lots. Former parking lots now have a drive-thru lane. I see a gas station I remember stopping at with my mother has become a quaint antique store. The fancy car dealer building is now a grocery store. The Tastee Freez is now a Target. Businesses are hermit crabs taking over new shells when they become empty.

There are places that I think must have once been trees and scrubland, but there is a building there now, and I can't remember what the land should look like.

I think I should feel nostalgic or maybe be upset by all the changes, but I'm not. I don't care what has happened to Sebring. In a way, the changes mean I don't need to remember what was because it's no longer there. I wish I could bulldoze my past and let kudzu and Virginia creeper cover all my memories until they are hazy green blobs. The closer I get, the harder it is to avoid everything that happened.

I see the street that leads to the high school and continue straight past it but get stuck at the train crossing. Freight and passenger trains pass through Lorida and Sebring. The tracks run alongside US-98, and when I was a kid, I could see them through the trees if I walked to the head of our road. There was a crossing at Cowhouse Road, and occasionally I would hear the conductors sounding horns, warning cars. The stretch of road right before the crossing was almost black with skid marks from cars surprised by the sudden appearance of a train in the middle of nowhere. The train cars chugged along in front of the school, each with its own distinctive rumble. Some sounded like they were in a hurry, while others sounded like they were taking their time. Whenever I heard an urgent horn and knew it wasn't near a road crossing, I always worried it was because of a stray dog, and I didn't even like dogs, but it still unsettled me. I knew it was likely some jackasses playing around on the tracks. I listened, waiting to hear the horn grow frantic. There wasn't much to do in Lorida, so little, in fact, that playing chicken with a train started to sound like a sensible way to spend an afternoon.

When I was little, my favorites were the Amtrak trains. The Silver Star and Silver Meteor soared north to New York and south to Miami. Sometimes I'd cross the road and stand near the tracks so I could see the people in the train cars. I would wave, and sometimes people waved back. Those trains had sleeper cars, and I always wondered what it would feel like to sleep on the train. I would be too excited to sleep. I would be going somewhere new. I could tell from the blurred expressions this was a boring part of the trip for most people. I tried to guess from their faces if they were coming or going. I wondered if they were happy or sad. The trains didn't stop in Lorida, but that didn't keep me from imagining what it would feel like to leave. I know what that feels like now, and as the last car passes and the barrier lifts, it hits me that I am almost home.

CHAPTER 46
PAST - JUNE 1986

Florida doesn't have seasons as northerners understand them. There is a wet season, dry season, snowbird season, lovebug season, and hurricane season. These are not distinct seasons, more comings and goings. By late spring, the migratory birds have long departed, and the local birds are busy mating and nesting; so are the alligators. We were in lovebug and hurricane season.

I was waiting for the bus on one of the last days of the school year. It was early, but there had already been a thunderstorm. It refilled the muddy puddle by the bus stop. I had been watching tadpoles grow over the last two weeks. They had stubby legs now. Days were hot and sunny, and the puddle was often dangerously low by afternoon, but most days, the rains came and refilled it. I hoped the frogs would grow big enough to leave before the puddle shrank to nothing but cracked mud.

I didn't see Morrison after school or at the tree anymore. His problems at home were bad, and he slept over at Sissy's whenever possible. At least, I assumed that was where he was. I didn't fault him for that, but I missed him. I missed Sissy too. At least, I missed how I was already starting to remember her, somehow forgetting the last several months. I felt like everything was my fault. I was trying to repair things with Mom and Michael, but I didn't know how. It mostly consisted of me doing the dishes and staying out of their way.

I rode the bus home alone, listening to the mix-tapes Sissy and

Morrison had made me. One afternoon, I got off the bus, and as I walked up to the trailer, I heard my mother and brother arguing inside. I stopped to listen before I opened the door.

"Michael, I know she's awful. What can we do?"

"Mom, you have no idea. I just want her out of our lives forever."

It was a punch in the gut. When I opened the door, they abruptly stopped talking. It would be years before I realized they hadn't been talking about me.

School was nothing more than habit in the final days. We showed up and went through the motions. Fewer than half the seniors were going to college, and most of them were going in-state. I was one of a handful of kids with scholarships, mostly athletic, so the school made a big deal out of us. We ran, tackled, and swam our way out.

On a still, cloudless day, I stood on a football field with Sissy and almost two hundred of our classmates and graduated. It was stifling, and most of us were wearing T-shirts and shorts under the polyester gowns. Sissy hadn't gotten over being mad this time. Michael had just started a new job and couldn't get the day off, but Mom and Morrison were there. Mom didn't seem angry with me, but she had been keeping her distance. Even so, I could hear her and Morrison clapping when I walked across the field.

I should have been excited. Instead I felt tired and empty. School was over. That was it—it was over. Everything built to this, then, nothing. My yearbook was filled with meaningless sentiments from people who already felt like strangers.

Morrison and I resumed working at Sweetwater Shores. They had agreed to hire me full-time for the month between graduation and when I left to start the summer swim program. After about a week, things started to feel okay again between us. We started to slide back into our old routines. The routines from last summer, when Sissy had been away. When everything had been okay. He seemed to be back home again. I assumed as much because he appeared at our house ready for work one morning. My mother drove us to work, and we'd catch a ride home with a new groundskeeper who lived out past Lorida.

I wanted Morrison to be okay with me leaving for college. I was long past hoping anyone would be proud of me. He avoided talking about it, so I didn't bring it up.

Sissy showed up at work one day. Morrison was on his lunch break, hanging out near my lifeguard perch.

"Let's go to the movies. *Ferris Bueller's Day Off* is playing. Skipping work to see the movie would be *so perfect.*"

"Right now?" I asked. I whistled at a kid to stop running.

"Of course, it will be fun!" She was acting like everything was fine between us. "Come on, Michelle, don't be a spoilsport."

"Come on, Chelle, let's go."

"I—I can't miss work. There aren't any other lifeguards." I couldn't afford to miss work.

"Well, they will just have to live without me," Morrison said, and he disappeared behind one of the tall hedges.

He reappeared a few minutes later, pretending to have been hit by a golf ball. They left together. The tired emptiness returned. I should have gone with them. It was all slipping away.

At work the next day, Morrison tried to explain how hard it was for Sissy. He told me she said she missed me and how sad she was I was leaving. He told me she was having trouble finding a job. He said she was talking about Amway. He said that I had college, and he had another year left of school, but Sissy didn't have anything. She didn't know what to do. This wasn't how I had imagined Sissy was feeling. I found myself in a familiar loop—confused by what she said and what she did.

Morrison convinced me to go to the movies with him after work on Friday. I bitterly thought that Sissy must be busy. The Circle Theater was playing *Top Gun*.

It was twilight when we left the theater.

"That was quite the propaganda film," I said.

"*For homosexuality* . . . almost makes me want to enlist," Morrison replied.

My mother was going to pick us up at 8:30 p.m. in front of the theater, so we had a few minutes to kill. We decided to walk around the circle until she got there.

"Are you going to be alright going up there by yourself?"

"To Athens? I don't know."

"I know I have been a bit of a shit to you about this. I'm sorry. I want to be happy for you, and part of me is happy for you. The other part of me doesn't want my best friend to leave. I never told you this, but you really helped me last year. I was planning to drop out, but then we got to be friends, and then I had a reason to go to school."

"I'm sorry . . ."

He cut me off. "No, don't be sorry. I'm sorry. I'm going to quit being a selfish asshole. I need to sort my own shit out. Who knows, maybe if I graduate, I can join you next year."

I wanted to tell him how much this meant to me, how much he meant to me. I still didn't know how. Punching him in the arm seemed wrong this time. We saw my mother pull up in front of the theater and ran across the circle to her.

I never got the chance to tell him how much what he said meant to me. How much he helped me that night.

CHAPTER 47

Morrison must have talked to Sissy because she was there one day after work saying we needed one last adventure. She hugged me fiercely when she saw me. I was wary of her this time. Part of me wanted to believe this was real. I knew there was something wrong, but I couldn't stop chasing that feeling she provoked in me when we were first friends. She had a present for me—a box of Sanrio papers, smelly erasers, and pencils. She even included a book of stamps and a note with her address on it.

Morrison wanted to go to Roman's Place, Sissy wanted to go to Disney World, and I just wanted to sit in the backseat and listen to the radio and hear them argue about nothing. Sissy offered to pay for our Disney tickets. It looked like she was going to get her way when it occurred to her that the park would be overrun with sunburnt tourists and their screaming kids. It was that magical time of year. We considered Six Flags Atlantis, the beaches near Sarasota, and even Miami Beach before we decided we were lethargically hot. Morrison and I spent all day working in the sun, so spending the day outside wasn't the treat it once was. Doing something at night made the most sense, so Morrison won, and we went to Roman's.

Unlike the last two times, it was a regular night. The back bar was now a dance floor, and people were dancing and having a good time. Before long, Sissy was snorting coke in the bathroom, Morrison was talking to the guy he had met last time, and I was once again fake-drinking a G&T. The biggest difference this time was that I felt content. I looked for Bill/Willy Wonky, but I didn't see him. I wanted to tell him I was going to college.

Sissy and Morrison spent most of the time dancing, and I was happy to hang back and watch them. They saw me and forced me out on the dance floor with them. We were together again. I was free and alive. I started to feel the emptiness lift. I was happy for the first time in months. I naively thought everything would work out.

Early Sunday morning, my mother drove me to Lakeland, so I could take the bus to Athens. We had to leave long before sunrise to make it there by 7:30 a.m. Route 98 blurred by in the pre-dawn hours. It was a damp, humid morning, and we drove in and out of showers.

"I wish I could drive you all the way there. I want to see where you are going to be living."

"It's okay, Mom."

"I'm just not sure the car would make it there and back, and I'm sure you don't want me living in your dorm room."

I felt like she wanted to talk, and I kept hoping she would, but the miles passed. Instead, we stuck to light topics, like obituaries. I wanted to hear what she thought about me going to college, but after what I'd overheard her and Michael saying, I was afraid to ask her. I wanted to ask if she thought Dad would be proud, but I didn't want to make her sad. I wanted to tell her I was so sorry for being selfish. I wanted to apologize for the way I had been acting. I wanted to ask if she really wanted me gone forever. I wanted to thank her. Instead, we filled the miles with the radio, speculating what Athens might be like, and discussing Michael's new truck.

The rain stopped by the time we drove into Lakeland, but the clouds were low and heavy.

We hugged and said goodbye in the small parking lot. I took my duffel bag and backpack and walked over to the idling bus. I assured her I would be back for the holidays. She looked happy and sad at the same time. I felt like there was a right thing to say, but I didn't know what it was. I waved from the bus window.

I spent the day on the bus reading and listening to tapes Morrison and Sissy had made for me. I took both the Radio Shack cassette player and Walkman with me. I had to transfer to another bus in Orlando. I looked out the window as the mountain range of sky-scrapers in Atlanta filled the horizon. I hadn't been out of Florida since before Dad died. I had only been out of the state twice, pe-riod, once to Georgia and once to South Carolina, but I had been so young I couldn't remember the details but knew that leaving the state was a big deal.

I didn't get to Athens until late that night. I had a map the school had sent me and walked in the dark from the bus station to the campus. All the buildings looked alike once I got to school, and I had to ask for directions twice. I found the dorm I was supposed to spend the rest of the summer in and checked in with the RA. He showed me my room and disappeared again. I wouldn't get a roommate until the fall semester started.

I wasn't sure what to do. I sat alone in the room, trying to get my bearings. The painted cinderblock walls were bare, but they were mine. I heard people in the hallways, and all I had to do was open the door and join them. Instead, I unpacked and found the statio-nery Sissy had given me. I wrote three letters. One to my mother and brother, letting them know I had arrived safely and how won-derful everything was. One to Sissy telling her I had arrived and how awful everything was. And one to Morrison telling him how much I missed him. I carefully wrote my new address on the letters and envelopes. I was proud I had an address all my own.

The next morning, I got up and spent hours wandering around the campus, exploring my new home. The campus was larger than all of Lorida. There were more students at the school than the whole of Sebring and Avon Park put together. I wanted a souvenir trinket, but I actually lived there now and didn't think it counted as a place I visited. I might still get salt and pepper shakers or a back scratcher to add to my collection. I found the swim complex and looked around. I couldn't wait to get into the pool. I was scheduled to meet the coach and other freshmen on Friday. We were expected to train three to four hours a day and work at the swim camp during

the week. Between working at the camp and a small stipend, I'd
have a little pocket money. My mom had bought the bus ticket to
get me to college, but I wanted to be able to afford the fare to go
home during break. I missed her and Michael already.

Morrison was the first to write me back.

Dear Chelle,

*You won't fucking believe this—I got fucking fired! Somehow that fuck-
wad Covington found out I was the one who peed in his bag. How did he
even find out? He went to the board and demanded I be arrested. I denied
it, mainly because I wondered if I could be arrested for doing something
like that. I mean, it seems like the kind of thing you should get arrested
for. Maybe not in Florida, but like a sane place would (and should) arrest
you for something like that. Anyhow, they called me in and said that "Mr.
Covington is a gold star member and upstanding wanker . . . blah blah
blah . . . and you are just a little shit."*

*So, I got fucking fired. I'm not sure where else to get a job around here.
Do you think they will give me a reference? hahahahahaha. I needed this
job. I was going to save all my money this summer in case I needed an
exit plan. Travesty is back again, and I think he is here to stay this time.
I mean, I miss being at work just to have some place to go. I can't be at
Sissy's all the time. I sleep at the tree some nights. I should probably get a
tent. Oh, wait, I don't have a fucking job to be able to afford a tent.*

What am I going to do?

I miss you.

M.

CHAPTER 48
PAST - AUGUST 1986

I received a few more letters from him, but this one made me ache inside.

Dear Chelle,

Sorry I haven't written more. I think about you all the time. Things aren't going great here. I'm trying to figure everything out, but I'm not sure what to do.

First the good thing going on—I think I really really like Russ—his real name is Russell Dearborn. Isn't that the coolest name?! I'm not sure how serious he is. We've only seen each other a few times when he's been able to drive up for the day. He sometimes sneaks and calls me from work. I can't call from Sissy's—it is long distance, and she was mad when her mother asked her about a $20 call to Juno Beach (that's where he lives). Sissy said we could drive down to see him, but then she spazzed on me. She keeps promising we'll go to Roman's and then something always comes up.

The not so good news is that my mom is moving in with Travesty. He's made it clear that I'm not part of the deal. My mom thinks I want to be free and "enjoy my wild oats," whatever the fuck that means. I don't want to be free. I want my mom, as fucked up as she is, and I feel like a wuss for saying that. So, I'm not sure what I'm going to do once she moves in with him. Do you think your mom would let me crash there? I'm sorry to have to ask. I will get a job and pay my own way.

I'm scared. Everything felt better when you were here. I miss you so much.

Enough about my bullshit drama. How is school? What is college like?
That is awesome you're doing so well with the swim program. What is
your roommate like? What is Athens like? What movies have you seen?
I miss you! Write back soon!
Sunshine

I read his tight scrawl over and over. At that moment, I wanted to
be in the tree, this time me holding him while he slept.

I planned to call and talk to my mom about him staying there.
But first, I needed to get a bunch of quarters, and before I knew
what happened, the week flew by with the start of classes. I had
registered for six classes and had two hours of daily swim practice
during the week. The classes were harder than I expected. I knew I
had to maintain a B average and found myself working until midnight every night to keep up. By the time I looked up each night, it
was too late to call home. The weekends meant working out and
drills in the pool. I had been a good swimmer in Lorida. Now I was
barely average. I was training and swimming alongside people who
were probably going to go to the 1988 Olympics. The only way I
could keep up was to put in extra time.

Every day I wrote to Morrison in my head while I did laps. I
wanted to tell him about the history teacher who refused to look
at anyone directly and talked in the third person. I wanted to tell
him that three guys and one girl had asked me out. That none were
Harry Anderson, but I might give one of them a chance. I wanted
to tell him that my roommate slept with orthodontic headgear, and
the first night she put it on, I almost screamed.

Before I had a chance to call my mom to see if he could stay with
her, I received a postcard from Morrison.

M,
    Don't worry about asking your mom. I don't need a place to stay any-
more. I got it figured out. I know what I am going to do. I wanted to call
and tell you, but don't know how to reach you there.
    Thank you for everything.
    Love,
    M

CHAPTER 49
PAST - SEPTEMBER 1986

Over Labor Day weekend, I sat down and wrote him a long letter. I told him about all of my classes and professors. I told him about my orthodontically challenged roommate, who wasn't that bad. I told him how I sat through the wrong class because I was too embarrassed to get up and leave. I told him about the campus and the areas around campus. I told him about the movie theaters that were within walking distance. I told him he would love all the small clubs that played live music. I told him how a guy said I looked like Pat Benatar as a compliment instead of an insult. I told him about swimming. I begged him to visit. I told him I would be back for winter break and maybe Thanksgiving, too, if I could earn a little extra cash. I told him about my shiny new life because I wanted to share it, and I wanted him to be part of it. I told him how much I missed him. I mailed the thick wad of notebook paper to the trailer. I wasn't certain if it would reach him there, but I didn't know where else to send the letter. I hoped his mom would give it to him. I didn't want to send it to Sissy's house. I was afraid she would see how much more I wrote to him.

I had written to Sissy, too, but the letters weren't as long (or as honest). The letters I got back from her felt like the ones she had written when she was at the camp. She told me how perfect everything was for her. I knew from Morrison that wasn't true. The friendship between us—if that was what it was—was still damaged. I hoped we could patch things for real up when I went home for break. That she would be able to see I wasn't abandoning her.

I didn't hear back from Morrison all that week. On Saturday, I mailed him another letter, this one shorter, as classes and swim practice started taking over more and more of my time. I didn't mention it in my letter, but I had started making some new friends. I wanted him to visit so he could meet them. When I hadn't heard from him by Wednesday, I used my laundry money to call the only number I had for him, the phone at the trailer. Each dorm had a bank of payphones near the mailboxes. I slipped inside and shut the door.

As soon as the call connected, the automated voice said the number was no longer in service. I was worried and decided to call Sissy. I used to call her every night, but we hadn't spoken in well over a month.

She sounded happy when she heard my voice. She acted like everything was normal. She started telling me about a guy she had met at the country club who was going to get her a job at his real estate company. It took a few minutes and a couple dollars in change to get a word in edgewise.

"Do you know where Morrison is? Is he okay? I tried to call him, and the line is disconnected."

"Oh, is *that* why you finally called me?"

"No, no. That's not it at all. I've missed you, too."

Too. That tiny word. I knew I fucked up. I knew better. Here was everything I had left behind. Here was the old bad feeling back again. I felt my stomach drop.

"*Too?* Really? You are *too* fucking much."

"I'm sorry, Sissy, that wasn't how I meant it."

"Isn't it?"

The automated voice demanded more money, and I fed quarters into the phone.

"Sissy, I don't want to fight with you." I felt bolder and more in control now that I had been away from her for a while.

"You are the one calling me out of the blue wanting something, as usual. Where were you when I needed you? You've always been so fucking selfish."

"Please, I am running out of change."

She barked a laugh and said, "Typical."

"Please, I am worried about Morrison. Is he okay?"

"Now, all of a sudden, you remember he exists? You left. You don't give a shit about either of us. And no, I haven't seen him. I have no idea where he is. Is that what you wanted to know? If you were here, you would know he hasn't been okay all summer. Fuck you, Michelle."

She slammed the phone down.

I thought of the fish out in Lake Istokpoga, swimming freely and then finding themselves yanked backward. Pulling against an invisible enemy. Straining against the pain until there is no fight left. I spent a long week trying to focus on swimming and my classes. I avoided my new friends. I felt like I was being disloyal to Morrison and Sissy. What she said ate away at me. I did care about both of them. I wrote Sissy a letter apologizing, trying to explain that I was worried about Morrison and how much I missed her. I checked my mailbox twice a day. My most recent letter to Morrison was returned.

Finally, the following week there was an envelope with Sissy's handwriting and her return address. I opened it standing in front of the mailboxes. As I did, a newspaper clipping fluttered out. I picked it up off the floor and started to read her letter. .

Dear 'Hell,

I hope you are fucking happy with yourself, you fucking bitch. Morrison is dead because of you. You let him down. You might as well have killed him. He needed you and all you cared about was yourself. Fuck you, bitch. You are dead to me, just like Morrison is dead. I never want to see you again. You destroy everything you touch. You should kill yourself too. Everyone would be better off without you.

S

My face was burning hot. I was too stunned to cry. I slid down the wall, unable to bear my weight.

SUSPECTED HOMICIDE NEAR LORIDA RULED A SUICIDE

Sebring, Fla. (AP) — Police detectives have determined that the body found dead east of Lorida died by suicide.

The body was found Wednesday morning near the railroad crossing at Cowhouse Road, east of Lorida. Investigators initially thought the death suspicious.

Sebring police Chief Bob Seafert said Friday that further investigation and an examination of the body determined the injuries were sustained when the victim was struck by a train. The person's identity hasn't been released pending notification of the next of kin.

CHAPTER 50

Mom is at the regional hospital on the other side of Lake Jackson. Once I'm through Sebring, it only takes me a few minutes to get there and park my exhausted car. I rush inside and ask a bored-looking young woman at the information desk how to get to intensive care. She asks what room I'm looking for, and I repeat what Michael told me on the phone. She points me to a bank of elevators and tells me to go to the third floor, turn right, and follow the signs. She also tells me that visiting hours are almost over. *Shit. Shit. Shit.*

I know I have spent over thirteen hours trying to get here, but waiting for the elevator may be what finally pushes me over the edge. What if I'm too late? What if she wakes up and doesn't want me there? The elevator pings and I step inside.

On the third floor, I step off the elevator and turn right, passing a small waiting room. I don't see Michael, just a woman with dark hair reading a magazine. I find room 320 and open the door.

Michael is holding mom's hand, talking to her quietly. She is unconscious, covered in wires and tubes. She looks so frail. Her once mousy brown bob is now short layers of messy gray hair. Machines beep, monitoring her heart rate, and there is an oxygen mask on her face. Her skin is slack and papery.

I work in a hospital, but this all feels foreign to me. My mother should be sitting at her table with lukewarm instant coffee, yellow legal tablets, and a half-finished crossword puzzle, not here.

Michael gets up and comes over to me. I take him in. I'm startled by how grown-up he seems. I don't feel grown-up at all. He is
wearing a polo shirt with an embroidered logo of a car and navy
blue pants. He wears glasses now. He hugs me quickly, patting me
on the back and pulling away.

"I'm sorry it took me so long to get here."

My words have broken the silence. He nods, seemingly unable to
speak. He pulls me toward the bed, and we stand there holding our
mother's hands until the hospital intercom announces that visiting
hours will end in five minutes and will resume tomorrow morning
at 9:00 a.m.

We each kiss her lightly, and Michael goes to the nurse's station.
He seems to know the nurses by name. I hear him confirming that
they have his home, pager, and cell phone numbers. They promise
to take care of her and will call him if anything changes.

We walk toward the elevators, and Michael veers into the waiting
room. The woman reading the magazine looks up at him.

"This is my sister, Michelle," he says as he introduces me to the
woman I saw when I got off the elevator. It is only now that I
wonder what I look like. Wonder what I must smell like. My short,
messy curls, finally saved from the ravages of chlorine by coconut
oil and a decent swim cap, are disheveled from the drive and heat.

She stands up, and neither one of us is sure what to do. Is this his
girlfriend? Do we hug? Shake hands? Instead, we say hello. What is
her name? Should I ask?

She seems to sense my anxiety and confusion and introduces herself as Rosalita but adds that everyone calls her Rose or Rosie. She
reaches for Michael's hand and gives it a quick squeeze, answering
the question as to why she is here.

The intercom tells us we need to leave. Exiting the automatic
doors, the heat radiates from the pavement. The sun is down, but
cars and surfaces are warm to the touch. We walk out to the parking
lot together and stop at my car to talk.

"The neurologist came in about an hour before you got here. The
swelling in her brain hasn't gotten any worse. She made it past the

first twenty-four hours. They are 'cautiously optimistic,' whatever that means," Michael says as he reaches for Rosie. "They are going to do another scan in the morning, and if she shows continued improvement, they will begin taking her out of the coma. They won't know if there is brain damage until she is out of the coma."

Now that I am here, I don't know what I am supposed to do, but Michael answers that question.

"Can you stay at Mom's?"

"Yes, of course."

"She has a dog, and we can't bring him home—Rosie is allergic. Can you take care of him?"

"Sure." It just gets better and better. I can barely take care of myself.

"Okay, thanks. I'll see you back here tomorrow."

"I—I don't know where she lives."

A shadow crosses his face, and I can see that he is annoyed.

"Go through Lorida and make a left on Arbuckle Creek Road. Then make the first right and turn left at the second Charming Lane. There are two streets with the same name parallel to one another. Mom's house is on the left, just past the green house with the big cement manatee in the yard."

His words are whirling together. I can't take in what he is saying. My brain is too jumbled.

"Please, can you show me how to get there?" He sighs. I know I should be able to find it, but it's dark, and I'm not okay. He looks exhausted but agrees. I realize I'm not even sure where he lives now. Do they live together? I should know this.

He and Rosalita get into a Honda SUV, and I follow them out of the lot. We follow Route 27 and turn at Route 98 towards Lorida. It's pitch black, and I can see small red eyes catching my headlights along the road. We turn left at Arbuckle Creek Road, and from there, I focus on Michael's taillights to navigate in the dark. The road is unpaved, and nothing is marked. I would never have found my way here. He slows, and we turn down a gravel driveway erratically lined with palm trees. I park next to what I assume is Mom's car.

There is frantic, shrill barking behind the door as we move to the porch. By the weak light of a yellow light bulb, Michael lifts a ceramic pot and pulls out a key. There isn't anything in the pot, not even dirt. It seems to exist to "hide" a spare key. Maybe they could paint "key here" on the pot to save a burglar a few extra seconds. He hands me the key and unlocks the door with his own.

Michael opens the door, and a small furry thing hurtles itself outside, spinning in circles around Michael's legs as Rosalita backs away.

It's a trivial beige and white dog. He pees mightily on a jungle bush growing under the front window and resumes his greetings. He sniffs me but is mostly interested in Michael.

"Hey, Hairy," he says to the dog.

"His name is Harry?"

"Hairy, with an I. After Pufnstuf died, Mom decided she wanted another cat and went to the humane society. She was waiting to be taken back to the cat room when she saw the staff chasing Hairy. He ran and hid under her chair. He growled at them but licked her hand. They were taking him to put him to sleep. She took him home instead of a cat. She says he showed good sense trying to bite people who planned to kill him. She called him Hairy Houdini because he figured out how to escape." I could tell he loved this story. How long had it been since I called? How long had Hairy been here?

"You going to be okay?" he asks.

"Yes," I lie.

He says he will call in the morning so we can make plans to go back to the hospital. Then he is gone. I am alone in a strange dark place with this intense small creature staring at me as if I can explain what is going on.

I grab my purse and the grocery bag with a change of clothes and toothbrush from the car and go inside. Hairy follows me. I wander from room to room. Mom's bedroom has a double bed and furniture I've never seen before. There is a dog bed next to the nightstand. There is a second bedroom with an unmade bed and boxes. For a split second, it reminds me of Sissy's sister's room. The dining room is Mom's workspace in the trailer, transposed to this new space. She has notepads, photos of old people, and an electric typewriter. There is a half-filled cup of coffee with scum forming on the top. I pick it up, take it to the small kitchen, and put it in the sink. I walk back to the living room and stand there trying to figure out what to do. It seems intrusive to sleep in Mom's bed. The spare bedroom doesn't have a TV, and I sleep better with one on for background noise. I find a sheet and settle onto the couch for the night.

I feel disgusting. I'm covered in highway, snack foods, sweat, and possibly lovebugs. I take a quick shower and realize that I forgot pajamas—well, that's not exactly true. I didn't think I would make it all the way here, and I certainly didn't think through staying the night. I brush my teeth, find a clean T-shirt and underwear in the grocery bag, and put them on.

The windows are open, and there is a ceiling fan rotating above the couch. I sit down and turn on the TV. Hairy joins me as I mindlessly flick through the channels.

I'm home, but I'm not home. Was the trailer home? How is it that this house that I've never been to smells like home?

I think back to what it was like after dad died. I didn't appreciate how happy we were until we were unhappy. Until my mother went from making us big Sunday dinners to forgetting it was dinnertime. She disappeared into her bedroom a lot. I knew she was crying, but I didn't understand why she hid from us. Didn't she know we were sad, too? I remember wondering if it was something I did to make her sad.

We had no savings, and the life insurance policy dad's work offered barely covered the funeral expenses. Then, two months after dad died, mom announced we were moving. We had been living in a small house with a backyard and a swing set. I didn't understand what was happening but knew I didn't want to leave my home. I was eight and Michael twelve.

Mom had gotten the job with the newspaper by then, but it didn't pay much. We moved into the mobile home in Paradise Acres. At the old house, Michael and I had our own rooms. Mom said it would be such fun to have a bunk bed and share a room.

Michael seemed sad but pretended everything was okay. So did mom. So, I did the same. I pretended I wasn't sad. I learned not to cry. I learned to push my feelings deep inside me. To close myself off.

We had to say goodbye to our friends and our old schools. When you are eight, switching schools is switching universes. Everything felt wrong, and I missed my dad. Home wasn't home anymore.

Michael and I retreated further into our own worlds, as did my mother. Michael had lost two fathers, but one was still alive and didn't bother to see him, which meant that he missed the father who had loved him twice as much. Maybe even more than me. My mother tried to hold it all together. She didn't want us to see her pain, but we felt it all the same. We tried to be good. To go to school and not tell her when we were sad or scared. She felt it all the same. Everyone was in pain, and none of us knew how to express it. We hid from the pain and from each other. So, we went on with life, and grief became a pebble in our shoes, creating a constant blister. We grew accustomed to it and expected it to be there. Eventually, the pain became a comfort. We made a new home but never forgot the one we lost.

CHAPTER 51

I scream before I know why I'm screaming.

I'm not sure where I am. I'm scared and confused. The TV is on. Then the fog clears, and I remember. Hairy is barking furiously. I jump up, and Hairy seems excited when I join him at the door. I peer outside. My heart feels like it is slamming against my rib cage. I expect to see something terrible.

Evidently, we are about to attack the garbage men. It isn't quite light out, but they are already collecting, trying to avoid the heat.

They go up the street, and Hairy seems quite pleased we vanquished them. I go back to the couch and turn on the local news, trying to get my bearings.

A Florida man caught smuggling rare fish in his pants was arrested today at Tampa International Airport. The Fish and Wildlife Service reports that they were being transported in opaque pill bottles. He was caught when one of the bottles started leaking. Sounds kinda fishy to me. Ashley, over to you. Thanks, Howard, that is quite the fish story. The weather today will be a high of 94 with scattered thunderstorms . . .

I get dressed. I'm still wearing the T-shirt I slept in, but I've put my bra back on. I put on the shorts from the grocery bag. Hairy and I patrol the yard. I'm hit by a combination of smells I forgot existed. Atlanta smells like hot concrete and exhaust fumes. The air here smells of flowers and cattle, of stagnant water and fresh rain. Even the bad smells smell good. There are cobwebs covered in dew and dragonflies alighting on plants. I can hear an osprey in the distance.

In the light of day, I see that Hairy is kind of homely. His fur is wiry and clumps together. His eyes bulge and are a bit crusty. He has a bald patch near his tail, and he smells funny. His teeth jut out at angles. He looks like a hodgepodge of about ten different kinds of dogs. He is also rather bossy.

Once back inside, Hairy goes to the kitchen and starts barking. It dawns on me he's hungry. I'm hungry, too, and eat some toast while he eats the glop I found in the cupboard. He paws at his empty water bowl, which I fill at his request. Afterward, he informs me it is time to go outside again. He runs around, sniffs things, pees, poops, barks at a cane toad, pees again, and then asks to be let back inside. He settles down for a nap. This dog has his life more together than I do.

I go back outside and walk to the end of the driveway. Most of the houses on Mom's road are newer, prefab homes. Her place is a simple cinderblock house with a small Florida room. It's older and could withstand hurricane-force winds, but it's built lower to the ground and could flood. The other houses are situated higher, but they are little more than cardboard boxes on stilts. As I surmised the night before, the driveway is erratically lined with palm trees. Some are short and stubby, and others are tall and skinny. The jungle bushes are blooming against the house, and there are a few caladiums. It's a nice little place. In the daylight, I can now see that I am parked next to a maroon Buick sedan.

To the west, thunderheads are forming. It's going to rain again. I go back inside.

I'm not sure what to do with myself. I feel like an interloper. Michael said he might have to work for a few hours this morning, and either he would meet me here or join me at the hospital. He wants to get there right at 9:00 a.m., so we can hear any news from the doctors when they make the morning rounds. It is 6:30 a.m., and he said he would call by 7:00 a.m.

I get up from the couch and pace from room to room. Every-thing is tidy aside from the dining room table. I want to clean up for her, to do something, but everything is her version of orderly.

I only recognize a few things from the trailer, mostly knickknacks. Across from the dining table is a sideboard covered in framed pho-tos. I see one of my dad I don't remember. She put photos of him away after he died, and we moved. There are photos of Michael and me at Disney World and Tarpon Springs. There is a photo of Mom, Dad, and Michael before I was born. I can see the lump of me under her shirt. There is a recent photo of Michael and Rosalita. Next to that is a photo of a pretty girl I don't recognize. The skin prickles on my neck when I realize it's me. I don't remember Mom taking it. I look like I am about fourteen or fifteen. Mom also has the 8x10 of my terrible senior portrait. It hurts to look at it. I pick it up. On the back, she has written, "1986, my beautiful daughter." A wave of conflicting emotions washes over me.

She loved me. The photo is still out, despite everything I've done. Maybe she still loves me.

I am so confused.

I ache for the girl in that photo and for my mother. Both seem so lost right now.

Morrison saw me. He saw all of me. And I saw him. It was all we each needed, two hurting, vulnerable kids trying to figure out who they were.

I wonder if Sissy saw this in me too. If she saw that confused girl and wanted to help her or if she saw her and hated her for being weak. I still don't know what she saw in me that caused her to want to be my friend. *Was she my friend?* It felt like it, but why did she do and say what she did? I was drawn to Sissy because of how she made me feel, at least at first, and spent the rest of our friendship chasing that feeling. *Was our friendship ever real?*

Some of what I dredged up on the drive has been flickering at the edges of my subconscious. I feel like I need answers to questions I have long avoided asking. I want to know more about what drove Morrison to kill himself. The phone rings, startling me. It's Michael calling to tell me he will meet me at the hospital. Visiting hours don't start for almost two hours.

I resume my pacing. I wash Hairy's bowl. I turn the TV off and then turn it back on. I walk back to the sideboard and look at the photos. I keep coming back to look at the photos of me. I feel like I am waking from a bad dream.

Who was I? Who am I? I never meant to hurt anyone. Looking at the photos, I can see that I was just a kid, a stupid kid. This realization is unsettling. Morrison was just a stupid kid too.

I can't sit here any longer. On impulse, I grab my purse. It seems like a long shot, but I don't know what else to do. I know the way to Sissy's house by heart, even though I've never driven there myself. It is on the way to the hospital. I know that she and her family might be long gone, but it seems like a place to start. I want to deal with the grief I've carried for so long, before the grief that I could soon face with my mother.

CHAPTER 52

The rain starts on the way to Sissy's house. It might be over in a few minutes, but I don't have time to waste. I park in front of her house. I don't have an umbrella and run for the door.

I feel idiotic and exposed as I push the doorbell. I realize after I've done it that it is far too early to show up unannounced on someone's doorstep. The door swings open, and Sissy's mother looks at me.

Without changing expression, she says, "Oh, it's you. You aren't dead." She lets me in without further explanation.

Sissy's house hasn't changed much. I am shocked that it isn't as big or fancy as I remembered. Mrs. Davis looks like a ghost of a person. Like she is haunting her own house. Her clothes hang on a brittle frame, and she has the bearing of a much older woman. She walks into the living room, and I assume she wants me to follow her.

My chest is getting tight, and I cough. I try and pull it together inside. Why did I come here? Why am I doing this? I have a sudden, desperate urge to run to my car and drive back to Georgia as fast as I can. I remind myself that I am there for answers. I tell myself I'm no longer a stupid eighteen-year-old girl. But what if I am an equally stupid thirty-three-year-old woman? I take a deep breath. As deep as I am capable of, because I can't seem to get enough air.

I sound like I have run up a flight of stairs when I say, "Mrs. Davis, I'm very sorry to bother you. I was hoping to speak with Sissy and . . ."

She stops me and curtly says, "Please don't call her that. Her name is Cecilia." The blank expression wavers for just a moment as we both register the harshness in her voice. The emptiness returns and, in a monotone, she says, "That's what Jessica called her because she couldn't pronounce Cecilia when she was little."

"I'm sorry, Mrs. Davis, I didn't know that. Sissy . . . Cecilia, told me it was her nickname."

"You always reminded me of Jessica."

I'm not sure what to say to this. I knew she always stared at me, but I never knew why. I had always assumed she disapproved of me. Was judging me. I thought I was doing or saying something wrong. Oh, God, the clothes. I had forgotten about the clothes.

"Jessica was so pretty. Everyone loved her." She gets up, leaves the room, and returns with a framed photo.

I had never seen a photo of Sissy's sister. It strikes me how odd that is. I never realized photos were missing from the house. Maybe she put them away like Mom put the photos of Dad away. The photo looks like it was taken at a pageant or something like that. Jessica was indeed very pretty.

Mrs. Davis pulls the photo back to her and stares at it silently. I wait for her to explain, but she doesn't. The pause morphs into an uncomfortable silence.

"I'm sorry, Mrs. Davis, I was hoping to speak with Sis—Cecilia. Do you know where I can find her?"

"You got away. My beautiful Jessica didn't get away."

I replay this in my head a few times, trying to make sense of what she is saying. But I can't. So, I blurt out, "Mrs. Davis, what happened to Jessica?"

She seems unperturbed by my abruptness. "I had hoped your friendship with Cecilia meant she was sorry, even if she didn't show it." She is stroking the frame and pulls the photo to her chest. She looks up at me and says, "I'm glad you got away."

"What happened to Jessica?"

I hear the front door opening and a metallic clang as something heavy drops to the floor.

Sissy's mother looks toward the door and says, "Don?"

"I got rained out. I'm just dropping my clubs off and . . ." He stops when he sees me. He says hello and starts to introduce himself to me.

Sissy's mother interrupts him, "Don, this is Michelle, Cecilia's friend from school. She says she wants to talk to her, but I don't think that is a good idea."

Something shifts between them, and they stare at each other. He avoids looking in my direction. He wants no part of this and walks into the kitchen.

"Excuse me, Michelle, I'll be back in a sec." She follows him, and I wonder if I should leave. I can hear their voices starting to get louder. It sounds like an old fight. There is no warm-up. It gets vicious fast. The older the fight, the more brutal it sounds to an outsider.

I hear Sissy's mother say, "You don't care what happened. You always believed her."

"Gigi, stop. I don't want to do this today."

"You lived with her lies because they were easier than the truth."

"Just tell her where she lives. Don't get involved."

"You were never here. You were always working."

"What does that have to do with anything?"

"I lost my daughter."

"*Our* daughter, you don't get to claim all the pain for yourself!"

"Our daughter," she says mockingly. "You don't know what it is like for me. I have to live with what happened every day. It's like it doesn't even matter to you."

"Why won't you stop this? It was an accident. She was a child!"

"She was never a child!"

"You've got to stop this. Take your fucking pills."

I hear the door to the garage slam, and Sissy's mother returns, alert and intense. I have never seen this version of her before. Had her composure been an act earlier? Maybe they are more alike than I ever realized.

"I'm sorry about that," she says, now focusing on me. "Do you know how Cecilia's sister died?"

"She told me it was an accident."

"Jessica had a severe allergy to bees. We had a couple of close calls when she was little. We had bottles of epinephrine and needles in the bathroom. We had bee sting drills like fire drills.

"She and Cecilia were outside playing. Jessica stepped on something that hurt her foot. It wasn't clear right away what had happened. I heard Jessica yell, and I thought they were playing at first. When I saw Jessica lying on the ground, I knew something was wrong. Cecilia was standing there, watching her. I told Cecilia to run and get the epinephrine kit and call 911. We had practiced this. I didn't want to leave Jessica alone . . . with Cecilia. I waited and waited for her to come back outside. She eventually came out with the epinephrine but no needle. She said she couldn't find them. The ambulance arrived, but Jessica never regained consciousness. She was in a coma for a month before she died."

A chill begins to settle over me. I had believed Sissy when she told me her sister had an accident and died. I felt sorry for her when Morrison told me she saw it happen, but she had watched it happen—maybe even let it.

Mrs. Davis continues softly, "I found the needles when I was cleaning Cecilia's room. All the needles were bent. Cecilia made up some absurd story. It was deliberate. Don tried to convince me I had imagined what had happened. I know what happened—Cecilia killed her sister."

I feel sick. I believed Sissy when she told me it was my fault Morrison died. What *really* happened to Morrison? What did she do to him? What if he didn't commit suicide? The newspaper article said they suspected homicide at first. Why? Could she have killed him, too?

"Cecilia was so needy, so demanding. She cried all the time. Not like Jessica. Jessica was . . . so perfect. She was such a beautiful, happy child. Cecilia was always difficult. Even the pregnancy was difficult. It was like she somehow knew I never wanted her. She should have been the one to die, not Jessica."

I have no idea how to respond. I had all of these ideas about

Sissy's home life. It was yet one more thing I got wrong. I am horrified to think that I was once jealous of her life. Part of me starts to feel sorry for Sissy. What if she didn't let her sister die? What if it was just a horrible accident? Sissy wasn't the easiest person—but she was only ten when her sister died. Could a child really do that? Could Sissy? What if it was all in Mrs. Davis's head?

What if what happened to Morrison was somehow an accident? What if it wasn't my fault?

I realize I'm trying to fix the past again. Rewrite it. Trying to step on the snake egg and change the ending. None of the self-deception in the world will bring back Sissy's sister or Morrison.

Mrs. Davis continues, "When I confronted Sissy about the needles, she lied about not being able to find them, and then she told me she had been playing with them. When she was older, she asked me what I thought would have happened if I had gone for the epinephrine instead of her. She wondered if Jessica would still be alive. She made sure I felt responsible for her death. I should have known what Cecilia was capable of, but she was only ten. I knew enough not to want to leave Jessica alone with her." She stops and looks directly at me. "Cecilia knew that using 'Sissy' hurt me every time it was said. She knew we liked Jessica better, so she took her away. She wanted all our love. All our attention. She would get so angry. She thought that we loved her because we gave her things. We gave her things because we couldn't stand her. The TV, cable, phone, car, money, all of it was so that she would leave us alone. It was a relief when you came along. We knew something was wrong with her. We sent her to that camp. She came back worse."

"Mrs. Davis, where can I find Cecilia?" I press. I want to get out of that house. Away from Sissy's mother. I now understand more about Sissy than I wanted to. Her home life was as bad as Morrison's, worse when I thought about it. But was she a victim or a murderer? Both?

"I'm telling you all of this, so you understand. You got away. Jessica didn't. I didn't. Morrison didn't. She's poison."

"I really do need to speak with her."

She stares at me. I'm not sure why she told me what she did or what she wants from me, but I recognize that stare. Those are Sissy's dead eyes staring at me.

"Fine. She lives by Lake Lotela. I'll write down the address."

Whatever questions I had had when I arrived are forgotten. Everything I remembered is turning out to be lies. Is this why Sissy always made me feel afraid? What really happened to Morrison? Did I cause Sissy to kill him when I called looking for him? Did she know I loved him more, like with her parents and her sister? Is it still my fault, regardless?

CHAPTER 53

It's still raining when I leave. Driving to the hospital, I go over and over what Sissy's mother told me.

Shit. I'm late. Visiting hours have already started. Michael is already there and looks at me with a mixture of irritation and disgust.

"Where were you? I called the house an hour ago, and there was no answer."

"Sorry." I don't want to tell him I went to Sissy's house.

"I got here just in time to talk with the doctor. He says there is no change, and it is a matter of wait and see."

We sit there in silence, machines beeping ceaselessly in the background. I feel like he regrets asking me to come. My anxiety is overwhelming. The machines' beeping fills the room. Should I leave? Yes, I should leave. I'm trying to figure out the words to say that will enable me to leave without making Michael hate me even more.

"I need to go back to work soon, just for a few hours. Will you stay with her? At least until I can get back this afternoon. *Please*, Michelle."

"Yes, yes, I will be here." Will I?

I can't stop thinking about what Mrs. Davis told me and what I overheard. I can't stop thinking about Sissy and what she did to her sister, and maybe to Morrison. I am angry with myself because Sissy is the center of attention when I should be focusing on my mother. I should be here for her. Instead, I am sitting in this chair anxious and uncomfortable, as far away from my mother as she is from me.

I fidget and pace the room for almost two hours. I promised Michael, but my heart won't quit racing. I need to get out of there. I convince myself it will be okay if I leave for an hour. I convince myself Michael won't mind. That Mom is in good hands. That I am useless anyway. I'll tell him I ran home to check on Hairy if he catches me. *Liar. Liar. Liar.*

I have to talk to Sissy. I have to know what happened to Morrison.

CHAPTER 54

When you are young, you accept things as they are. You don't know enough to be truly afraid. Things that should scare you are part of daily life. Sometimes, you don't know how to name what scares you. You are told your fears are silly. The words dismiss you, but the feelings remain. When you are an adult, fear is often based on experience and a rational response to danger. In many ways, the vague shapes of childhood fears grow into unnamed anxiety that is even more convincing. The shadow creature in the closet transforms into a scarier beast that lives in your mind. Turning the light on no longer banishes it. You know it's there, and it knows you are there, and no one can protect you from it. It consumes you from the inside. I'm surprised there is anything left of me.

That is what I think as I approach Sissy's house. I am mad at myself that she still has this effect on me. I should have questioned more. I was so stupid. But I'm starting to realize I'm not as stupid as I was, and that is all that keeps me moving. I'm finally ready to confront her.

The rain has stopped, and everything glistens as the sun reappears. This is a neighborhood without sidewalks. Nothing and no one is out of place. It looks like suburban utopia. The lawns are so perfect that they look fake. In the driveway are a new Lexus and a small pickup truck. I assume from the cars that Sissy is home.

I want this to be over. At the same time, I want to run away, back to my safe, repressed oblivion. Could I go back there now if I wanted to? Blood is pounding in my ears, and my chest is getting tight again. I want to leave, but I stop myself and take a deep breath.

I need to know what happened to Morrison. It's hot, but it's anxiety sweat seeping along my back and under my arms. I can smell my body odor as I walk across the thick, wet grass to the front door. I brace myself as I ring the doorbell.

A few seconds later, the door opens. I'm prepared to deal with Sissy's rage and accusations. Will she scream at me like she did at her mother about going to the camp? Should I avoid going inside? In this idyllic development, there are certain to be nosy witnesses peering from behind tailored curtains. I'm trying to imagine what she will look like now and I'm not prepared for what I see.

I am so startled that I stumble backward and slip off the porch step. I fall onto the grass, scrambling like a crab. My heart is pounding so hard that I get tunnel vision for a second. I feel like I am going to pass out. I dig my hands into the wet grass and feel the sandy soil underneath. I feel something start crawling on my hand and shake it off without thinking.

Morrison is standing in the doorway. "What the fuck do you want?" he asks.

Everything is disconnecting inside of me. I'm on the ground, but I feel like I am falling. I feel like I am hallucinating. The pressure in my head and chest is overwhelming. Morrison is alive. He is alive.

Morrison walks over, looming above me. *"What are you doing here?"*

I hear myself say, "I . . . I wanted to speak to Sissy."

He towers over me, looking at me with disgust on his face. The face I have spent the last fifteen years grieving is gone. I have no idea who this man is.

"You are unbelievable. I'll be sure to tell Sissy you stopped by." He turns and walks back to the house but doesn't go inside.

I scramble to my feet, searching the grass for where I dropped my keys, and run towards my car. I reach the door and yank it open, throwing myself behind the wheel. I crank the ignition, my foot already on the gas pedal. It turns and splutters—flooded it. *Damn it!* I know I have to wait for the gas to drain out before I can try again.

Morrison is standing on the porch, staring at me coldly.

I beg and plead with the car to start. It tries and almost catches and dies.

I need to get away from here. I feel like my head is a balloon that is either about to burst or float away. I should never have come home.

My hand tries to start the car again, and this time, it catches. I can't get my heart rate and breathing under control. I am sweating uncontrollably. Black spots dance in front of my eyes. I shouldn't be driving. I put the car into gear and pull out of the development. Back on the highway, I consider heading north and never coming back here again. I stop myself and go to the hospital to sit with my mother. I promised Michael. I can at least do the one thing he asked of me.

Aside from nurses coming and going, checking instruments and testing for reactions, it is quiet. My chest aches, and I can still feel the adrenaline coursing through my system. I have spent fifteen years blaming myself for Morrison's death. He was never dead. Why did Sissy do this to me? Why did Morrison do this to me? They both lied to me. Why? My heart is breaking for that stupid, stupid eighteen-year-old girl who believed them.

I sit with my mother, mostly holding her hand or stroking it. I don't mean to, but I finally crash and fall asleep sitting next to her. When I wake up, Michael is there. The first thing I think when I see him is how much I have missed him. Then I see the look on his face.

"Michelle, Morrison called the dealership looking for you. He asked you to call him."

He reaches into his pocket and hands me a folded piece of paper. "How did he know where to find you?" I ask in confusion.

"Um, because I've worked on his truck for years. He said you came by his house today. How did you do that if you were here? You promised."

I'm slammed in the gut again. Michael and Morrison know each other. He knew he was alive the whole time. If I had just come home. If I had just said why I was avoiding coming home. If I had just . . . I want to throw up.

"I'm sorry, Michael. I'm so sorry. I was only gone for a little while, I swear. I didn't understand. I don't understand. I'm all mixed up."

He looks at me with irritation.

I keep repeating that I am sorry. I start crying, something I never do. I can't remember the last time I cried. I feel broken, like I am grieving all over again, but I don't know who for or why. It certainly isn't Morrison.

"Michelle, what is going on with you?"

He sits down, watching me and watching Mom. I want to explain that I thought Morrison was dead.

I'm about to try and explain something I don't yet understand myself when the machines start making different noises. Michael jumps up and calls the nurses.

Mom is starting to regain consciousness. Her eyes flutter open twice. I'm not sure if she knows I am here. We stay until visiting hours are over, hoping she will fully wake up. I want to tell Michael what is going on, but it doesn't feel right talking about everything with Mom starting to wake up. I don't want her to wake up and hear the mess I've made of my life.

I return to Mom's house and begin to berate myself, yet again. To call myself names that are almost comforting slaps. They return me to the dark place I have inhabited my whole life.

Wait, not my whole life.

I go stand in front of the framed photos and find the one of Michael and me at Disney World. There I am with messy, frizzy hair and a big toothy smile, leaning into my big brother, hugging his hip. I look for the one of me as a teenager, posing unselfconscious for the camera. I also find the one my mother took when I won the state championships. That girl doesn't look like the others. There is something wrong with her.

I start looking for photo albums and find a stack in a cabinet. There are a bunch of photos from when we were younger, when my father was alive. There is a gap after he died, and then it picks up again as I enter high school. I see that I start to disappear in eleventh grade—after Sissy and I became friends. I find the rest of the photos from the swim meet. Michael is smiling wide enough that I can see the gap in his teeth, Morrison has his arm around me, holding me close, and Sissy—Sissy looks angry. I've never seen these photos before.

For a fleeting second, I hear a voice deep inside, and I know something isn't right.

My inner diatribe begins to resume, only for the first time in more than fifteen years it dawns on me that the voice isn't mine. Slowly, I realize it's hers. It's Sissy telling me I am a terrible friend. It's Sissy telling me I am ugly. It's Sissy telling me I smell bad. It's Sissy telling me my family is embarrassed by me. It's Sissy telling me I don't belong. It's Sissy telling me that being poor is bad. It's Sissy telling me I am a murderer. It's Sissy telling me that my mother and brother don't want me. It's Sissy telling me I am lucky to have a friend like her. It's Sissy telling me that no one else could or should love me. It's Sissy telling me I am worthless.

Had she actually said these things, I would have realized it was her voice. She hadn't. She had whispered around the edges and let me figure out the words. Sissy took away who I was, planted poisonous seeds, and let my unsure, adolescent mind nurture the fears and doubts. Once they flowered, she came to my aid, offering her "friendship," when in fact, she was working to reinforce my every fear. She cultivated my isolation and self-loathing. She took Morrison away from me. He saw me for who I was and loved me. At least, I thought he did. I knew she lied. I learned to lie by watching her. She destroyed that strong little girl with the frizzy hair, crooked teeth, and a family who loved her. Or she thought she did. I can still feel that girl deep inside of me, and she is far braver than the woman I have become.

Of course, it had been easy to manipulate me. I realize now that I agreed with her insinuation there was something wrong with me. That she was right. She made me ashamed of my life. She convinced me to devalue myself and my family. It is crushing to realize how dumb I was. I let her hurt all of us. Never again. Whatever part of me that felt sorry for her earlier is gone. Whatever her mother did to her doesn't excuse what she did to me. I want to hurt her, physically hurt her, and the realness of those thoughts scares me.

All of my self-hatred has been misdirected. I hate her now. I hate everything she did to me. Everything she took from me. From my mother. From Michael. I hate her.

Is this why I've never known who I am? Just as I started to become me, I met Sissy. Even though I haven't spoken to her in fifteen years, the mirror I've been looking in for fifteen years is a lie. It was Sissy in the mirror. I've been arguing with her in my head all these years. She is the loathsome voice that scares me at 3:00 a.m.

Hairy and I hear a knock at the door. Is it Sissy? Morrison? Do they know I am here? What did Michael tell them? Hairy's insistent barking convinces me that the threat is real. Am I in danger this time? I look for a chain, so I can crack the door and peek out.

From behind the door, I hear, "Michelle, it's Michael's girlfriend, Rosie. I have some dinner for you."

I open the door, and she steps inside bearing a plate covered in clingwrap. Hairy is delighted she brought him food. She walks into the kitchen and sets the plate down. Hairy remains in the kitchen, watching the plate.

She looks at me and asks, "Are you okay?"

No. I am *so* not okay right now. My whole life has been a hateful lie, and I feel like I might never sleep again.

"Yes, just a bit tired." Do I look as crazy as I feel?

Rosie is about to leave but stops and turns to me.

"Michael was upset when he came home. I assumed it was about your mother. It was about you. He was hurt that you left your mother alone today. He was so happy when you agreed to come home. It might be good if you could leave as soon as your mother is out of the woods. Let them be to get on with things. He understands how you feel about them and won't bother you again." She straightens herself as if getting that off her chest was a physical act.

"What? How I feel about them? What does that mean?" My heart won't stop racing.

"Michael told me why you left."

"What does that mean?" My voice sounds shrill.

"He told me your friend from school talked to him."

"What friend?" I ask, knowing the answer.

"Sissy. He told me that Sissy talked to him a few times. He said that Sissy told him she felt sorry for your family and wanted to help. That she didn't understand why you were so embarrassed by them. She told him how you talked about moving out all the time. Sissy acted like she cared and wanted to help."

"*No, no . . .*" is all I can manage to say.

I am gripping the door for support. Why hadn't he told me what she said? Rosie looks at me and continues.

"I met Sissy when she came by the car dealership to look at a car. Michael and I work together. She acted like I was invisible. I heard how she spoke to him. I didn't find out who she was until later, and I thought it was odd that she never mentioned you. When Michael told me what Sissy had said, something didn't feel right. There was nothing caring or helpful about her. Michael didn't like her, but for some reason, he believed her. That is why I am here. I know Michael, and I know your mother. If there is any truth in what Sissy said, I think it would be best for you to leave. If there isn't . . ."

"Please, Rosie, none of what she said is true. It never was. Sissy lies. Please, I have to talk to Michael. I have to explain. Please."

"He was asleep on the couch when I left. Let him get some rest. Talk to him tomorrow. But talk for real, okay? I know Michael, and he doesn't talk. He keeps it all inside. I'm guessing that maybe you do, too."

Rosie leaves, and I can't stop shaking. I have to explain to Michael about Sissy. I have to tell him why I never came back and hope he will understand. Even as I work to explain it to myself, it sounds idiotic. How could I have been so stupid? How could I have let her do this? Then I remind myself, she didn't do this. I did. I am responsible for all of this.

Hairy and I stay up late watching TV. I'm not sure if he is allowed on the couch, but he assures me he is. We share the plate Rosie brought over for dinner. Hairy eats most of it. I feel sick inside.

I watch heat lightning flickering outside. My brain keeps flashing on what I thought I knew and what I now know. The pieces keep moving and reforming. It's like trying to solve a jigsaw puzzle by strobe light.

I'm not sure of anything now. Nothing seems real. Everything was a lie.

CHAPTER 55
PRESENT - JUNE 23, 2001

The phone rings in darkness. I stagger around, feeling my way towards the noise. I had only been asleep for a few hours. I find the phone on the wall in the kitchen.

"Chelle, Mom is awake! She is talking! They think she's going to be okay."

I'm suddenly wide awake.

"Oh, my god, Michael. Thank you, thank you." For a few seconds, I forget everything else and am genuinely happy. Relieved.

"Betsy, the one nurse, called me a few minutes ago. She said mom is a bit out of it, but she knows her name and where she is."

"Can we go see her now?"

"No, I asked. She said they needed to examine her further and do morning rounds. Her doctor wants to meet with us at 8:00 a.m. You will be there, won't you?"

"Yes, of course. But Michael, before we go to the hospital, can we talk?"

"Yes. We need to talk. Can I pick you up in a little while?"

"I'll be ready."

I'm not ready when he gets there. The shorts I wore on the drive down smell funny and are stained from the boiled peanuts. Everything I had on yesterday is rank from anxious sweat. Mom has a washing machine, and I threw my clothes in with a bit of dish soap when I couldn't find any laundry detergent. I started the dryer ten minutes ago, and everything is still wet.

Michael is antsy to leave. He suggests I wear some of mom's clothes. He goes to her bedroom and is handing me a blouse and a pair of pants when he remembers something. He takes me to the other bedroom and begins rummaging in the closet. He pulls out boxes marked "Christmas stuff" and an old suitcase. From the back of the closet, he yanks out a few large cardboard boxes with my name on them.

He says he remembered moving this stuff into the house. He tells me that Mom had been saving up for a long time. She had wanted to make a proper home for us again. It took her longer than she expected.

"After you left, she took on more work at the paper and was finally able to buy this place. She left the second bedroom ready in case you ever came home to visit." He starts to say something else and trails off.

I flip the lid open, and inside is stuff I left behind when I went to college. I find the treasured possessions of my childhood self wrapped in my old T-shirts, shorts, jeans, and more. I am still about the same size. The clothes smell stale, but it's an improvement over sweat and boiled peanuts. At the bottom of the box are the clothes Sissy gave me. They cause the hair on the back of my neck and arms to stand up. I avoid even touching them. I find a few pairs of shorts and T-shirts and shove the box back in the closet.

In the car, I have fifteen minutes to explain why I never came back. Fifteen minutes to explain a life that hurt me every day. That hurt him and mom. A lonely life based on lies.

I tell him what Sissy wrote me and how I thought I was responsible for Morrison's death. It rushes out in disjunct fragments. I haven't had enough time to make it all make sense in my own head.

"Michelle, why didn't you just ask about Morrison?"

"I did." I explain how I called the Sebring Police Department. I had called and asked about the person who was killed in the train accident. I asked if the person had been identified, making up a story about looking for a missing person. The desk sergeant asked me to hold, only he didn't place me on hold. I could hear voices in the background. I heard snippets: ". . . train accident . . . ID . . . kid . . . homo . . . haven't found . . . next of kin . . ." I hung up before the sergeant came back to the line.

"Why didn't you ask us?"

"I did. Well, I asked Mom. I called her before I called the police. I asked if she had seen him. She told me he usually stopped by once or twice a week, but he hadn't been by in a while. She asked me if he was okay. I couldn't bring myself to tell her that I thought he was dead."

"He did disappear for a while. I didn't see him for at least six months." I can see he is thinking about all of this, putting the pieces together. "Michelle, he told me you two weren't friends anymore. You were a dead subject as far as he was concerned. We never mentioned you when we talked. I told Mom. That's why she never mentioned him either. And you never brought him up, so we assumed the feeling was mutual. We didn't know what had happened, but we knew you two had been close."

Everything was beginning to make more sense.

"Sissy would sometimes wait for me late at night, at the turn off to our road. I should have told you about that. It was when I was working second shift. She made a pass at me one night, and I turned her down. She was just a kid. I was uncomfortable telling you. I was worried you'd think I was lying, or Sissy would say I did something I didn't do. She only did it the once. But it wasn't the only time she stopped me on the road. She would tell me how she was worried about you. How you didn't seem happy. We could see that easily enough. Then she said you wanted to move away, implying you were ashamed of us. She told us how you had applied to college out of state long before you told us you got in. Then right after you told us, she came by the trailer when you weren't home. She started yelling at Mom, mad we were letting you leave. She blamed Mom and said you were only leaving to get away from us. I didn't like her, but it was like she got inside my head. A lot of what she said was true."

I can tell that he believed her and how much it hurt him. He is also having trouble shaking what he believed, reconfiguring the last fifteen years without all the lies.

"I'm sorry, Chelle, I believed her. I shouldn't have. I should've known better. She never actually said what you had said. She mostly implied and let us make up the rest on our own. We didn't know why you never came back. Why you were so distant with us. Why you lied and hid stuff from us. We were close, and then you started acting differently. You talked differently. You spent all your time at her house. It felt like you wanted no part of us. It was easy to think the worst."

"I'm sorry, too. I should've explained or tried. She got inside my head too. I didn't see how she had affected me until I came home. I don't know what I was thinking after Morrison died . . . after I thought he died. I thought it was my fault. I thought I just hurt people. I thought you would be better off without me. I was certain you didn't want me around."

"But why did you leave in the first place? You could have gone to college around here."

This is it. This is where I know my explanation will fall apart in Michael's eyes. I know he won't understand. Even when we were young, I knew Michael wanted a safe, quiet life. That was what he had always wanted. And I wanted to know what was out there, to explore. I had hidden my desire to leave from them, but that was because I didn't want to hurt them. I didn't think they would un-derstand that I wanted—needed—more. And wanting more meant leaving them.

I lean my head against the window. "Because I needed to do it for me. I had only ever lived in Lorida, and I didn't feel like I belonged here. I thought maybe I would somewhere else."

"But you belonged with us."

"I needed to know what else was out there."

"So, we weren't enough?"

"It was about me, not you."

I feel like the conversation ends in a bad place as we pull into the hospital parking lot. Did I actually think one conversation would fix everything? Could I ever make things okay again with Michael? Or was damage done, no matter who was at fault? Would things have turned out okay if Sissy hadn't manipulated everyone? What if I had never met her? Would I have left? Would I have come back? Would we have stayed close?

I hadn't deliberately hurt him and Mom, but I hurt them all the same. Sissy's lie about Morrison's death could have been as harmless as a baby snake. I was the one who made it dangerous. Her lie wasn't what destroyed everything. My believing it was. I crashed us into the tree.

We meet with Mom's doctor, who tells us she is in remarkably good shape, all things considered. The CAT scan showed the swelling had come down, and she should continue to recover over the next few weeks. Her long-term memory seemed unaffected. They were managing the headache with pain medication.

"Can we see her?" Michael asks.

"Yes, of course."

We silently walk to her room.

"Can I go in first? I'd like to talk to Mom. Let her know you're here." Michael says.

I walk to the waiting room. He comes back for me a few minutes later.

"Hi, Mom."

"Michelle, look at you." She looks tired and weak, but she smiles when she sees me.

We want to hug, but she's still wired to the machines. I come around to the side of the bed, and we hug as best we can.

"Baby, I'm so glad you're here."

"Me, too," I say hoarsely.

"I couldn't believe it when Michael told me."

She sounds better than I expected. She tries to shift, and Michael goes over to adjust the bed for her.

"Your brother told me we shouldn't believe what that girl told us. That we should listen to you. What happened? I never understood."

"Neither did I, but I am starting to." I'm not ready to jump back into this again, but I know I owe them both an explanation.

"She told Michael you were embarrassed by us. She said that was why you stayed away. Why you went so far away to college. Why you didn't come back. She said you two still talked all the time and made Michael feel real bad about that. She said that you came home to see her, and she couldn't get you to come by and see us.

"Right after you told us you were going to college, she came by the trailer and started ranting and raving that it was all my fault and I had to stop you from leaving. Whatever your reasons were for going, and as bad as it hurt, I knew you needed to go. I was proud of you. We both were," she says, looking at Michael. "I wasn't going to stop you, and I hated that awful girl for trying to. I hoped she would leave you alone once you went to college."

At first, I think I want to cry, but rage starts taking over, stopping the tears.

"Mom, I never came home. I felt like I couldn't come back because I was responsible for Morrison's death. That was what Sissy told me. I didn't know he was alive until yesterday. Sissy lies. I haven't spoken to her since I left. Please don't believe anything she ever said. I was ashamed of myself, not you. I hated myself. I thought you wanted me to leave. That is why I didn't come home."

It suddenly dawns on me. The argument between Michael and Mom was about Sissy, not me. They wanted *her* out of our lives.

Michael seems to be waiting to see how mom is going to take everything. I have so much more I want to say.

"Mom, I'm sorry. I'm so sorry. I will try and make everything right again, I promise."

"I'm sorry, too, baby. I should have believed who I knew you to be, not that horrible girl."

Who I knew you to be. Who was that? Who is that?

"You changed after you met that girl. You seemed so happy at first. Then you started changing, and I didn't know why. I didn't know why you were unhappy. She made it sound like it was our fault."

She reaches for my hand, and, despite her condition, she tries to make me feel better. It's almost more than I can bear. I should be the one comforting her.

I try and explain what happened, as much as I understand it. The pieces are clicking together. We are starting to click back together.

Mom falls asleep, and Michael says he needs to go to the dealership for a few hours. He drops me back at Mom's house so I can come back to the hospital in my car.

CHAPTER 56

I let Hairy out to pee. I am exhausted from the morning's revelations. I stare at the scrap of paper Michael has given me with Morrison's phone number. Why does he want me to call him? So, he and Sissy can gloat? Why did they do this to me? It should be enough that Mom, Michael, and I have a chance to be a family again. Why can't I leave it at that?

For the first time in fifteen years, I hear my own voice loud and clear. It's like I was asleep in my own body. Sissy's voice in my head has finally been overpowered. I am starting to feel strong again. I had forgotten what that even felt like.

I want answers. I'm done avoiding everything. I pick up the phone and call him.

He seems to know it's me.

"Michelle?"

"Yeah, it's me."

"I just have one question."

Just one? I have a million fucking questions. "What?" I respond. All my bravado has faltered hearing his voice again.

"Why did you keep it? The keychain."

I remember my keys landing in the grass after I'd fallen. He must have seen them. I still use the keychain he made for me with Harry Anderson's initials. It is worn, but the HA is still visible.

"Because it was all I had left of you. I always had you with me, wherever I went." It's the truth. I'm done lying.

"What? That makes no sense. Why would you fucking want that

if you hated me so much? You're sick."

"I . . . I never hated you."

"Well, you never gave a shit about me. You didn't care what I was going through. You were too busy with your new life. Sissy told me how you wrote and told her how glad you were to be rid of me. That I was a loser. That you had 'college friends' now."

Here it is again. I'm hearing variations of the same thing over and over again. Sissy was rather thorough in her destruction of my life.

"No, that's not what happened at all. It isn't. I swear. You never responded to my letters. One was returned. I tried to find you. Then Sissy told me I was responsible for what happened." The words tumble out in a rush to explain.

He challenges me, like he doesn't believe me, and says, "Okay, so what happened to me?"

"I thought you died. I thought you committed suicide. The train."

"Fuck," is all he says.

"Morrison, I swear I thought you were dead. You're why I never came back. I couldn't face being here. I couldn't face that you needed me, and I wasn't there. I thought I was a selfish monster who deserved nothing. That I didn't even deserve my family. Oh, God. I believed her."

"*Fuck. Fuck. Fuck.*"

"I know."

"No, you don't know."

"What?"

"Somebody did die, but it wasn't me. I believed her, too." I hear someone in the background. "I gotta go. Can we talk later?"

"I don't know this number. Can I call you?"

"Yes. Call me at about five. I should be done with work by then."

CHAPTER 57

What did he mean someone died? *Who* died? The thought gnaws at me.

I pull my clean clothes out of the dryer and rummage in the boxes for a few more things to wear, including pajamas, and throw them in the washer. I take Hairy out again. I give him a snack and go back to the hospital.

Mom dozes on and off all afternoon. She is awake for a while after the nurse takes her vitals and gives her more pain medication. She tentatively asks me about my life in Atlanta.

"I'm probably going to be fired when I get home—back to Atlanta, I mean."

I tell her what happened with Gladys Anderson. She tells me I did the right thing. Even if it doesn't change the situation, it is a relief to hear her say that. I wish the hospital could see that I was lying to do the right thing.

Eventually, we turn the TV on to fill the silence we aren't yet sure how to bridge.

At a few minutes to five, I quietly slide out of the room and find a payphone in the waiting area. I call Morrison. He picks up on the first ring.

I wasn't sure where he was, but I could hear engine noises in the background.

"Morrison, what did you mean someone died? Who died?"

"Russ. I wrote you about him. We started seeing each other right after you left."

"What happened to him?"

"The train. He was the one who was killed by the train, not me. It wasn't me. It was him."

"The last I heard from you, you said you knew what you were going to do. Then nothing. After I got Sissy's letter, I thought what you wrote me was a goodbye."

"I had sorted out a place to stay—with Russ. We were figuring all that out. I was going to meet up with him over the weekend. He never called. Then the cops showed up and started questioning me. Russ hadn't come home, and his roommate got worried. I hadn't heard from him, either. I convinced myself he had had second thoughts about everything and dumped me. His roommate report-ed him missing. He also told them about us. I didn't know anything about the body they found by the train tracks. Not until later.

"It was really bad, Chelle. They started accusing me of killing him. They were talking about the 'gay stuff' as they called it, saying we had had a lover's quarrel. They were threatening to arrest me. Sissy said that we had been together all night. She pretended like we were a couple. She said that Russ had been obsessed with me and wouldn't take no for an answer. They decided they liked her story and said it was suicide."

I look at my hand. I am gripping the phone booth frame so hard that pins and needles are shooting down my arm.

"She convinced me it was an accident. She said we had to lie, or they would arrest me. Now I realize the lie went both ways."

"What do you mean?"

"The lie covered Sissy too."

"Where was she when Russell died?"

"I don't know. I never asked her. I didn't know what had hap-pened to Russ, but I knew I was scared of the cops. I thought she was protecting me. She never asked me where I had been. That didn't occur to me until you showed up—that I don't know where she had been either."

"I went by Sissy's old house today. I wanted to talk to her about what happened to you. Her mother was home—that was how I found you. Her mother told me Sissy had killed her sister. I mean, I don't know if she did, but her mother seemed certain of it."

"Like actually killed her?"

"If what Sissy's mother said was true, it was more like she let her die. Or it could have been an accident. Her mother isn't how I remembered. She's awful."

"You have no idea."

"Do you think Sissy killed Russ?"

"I don't know what to think anymore. I feel so fucking stupid. . . . I was so grateful to her. I thought she was protecting me from the cops. She held me while I cried and told me she would take care of me. That it was an accident. I didn't know what had happened, but I wanted to believe her. I had to believe her. I didn't have anywhere else to go. I also knew Russ wouldn't have been in Lorida if it wasn't for me. I didn't even know he was coming to see me. I convinced myself his car broke down. I felt responsible all these years."

I feel sick at all the pain Sissy invented. "I get that."

We make plans to meet early the next morning before Morrison goes to work. We need time to think and decide what to do next. I go back in to sit with Mom.

When Michael arrives a little while later, we watch TV and find small, safe stories to tell. "Do you remember . . ." is uncomfortable at first, but slowly I find myself warming to memories I had boxed away. He only stays a little while, and Mom and I are on our own again.

Mom pats the bed, and I sit next to her.

"Baby, I need to tell you something I should have told you a long time ago. I never expected you to stay in Lorida. I didn't want to stay in Lorida. I never wanted to come to Lorida. I got stuck here." She looks at the surprise on my face and continues. "Despite everything I believed about why you left, I was so proud of you for earning that scholarship and taking those chances.

"Your daddy and I got together when I was living in a little town near Charleston. He drove a truck for a good while, and Charleston was along his regular route. He was originally from Georgia but was living near Jacksonville when we met. We tried living in Charleston, but he had trouble finding work. He got a job in Fort Myers, and we moved down there.

"Fort Myers was nice—that was where you learned to love the water. You were just a little baby, but you loved the ocean. Then he was transferred to Lake Wales. You and your brother were settled there, but your dad and I weren't. We wanted more." Her eyes begin filling with tears. "I never told you or your brother this because I couldn't bear to think about it. Everything was going to be okay, and then it was all gone. He was gone, and so was our future."

"What are you talking about?"

"Your daddy had worked for a man in Fort Myers. He knew someone who managed a trucking company in Delaware. The man wanted to talk to your daddy about being a dispatch manager. It was a good job. He would be off the road and could spend more time with all of us. He was so happy. Your daddy was on his way to meet with people from the company when the accident happened."

I had no idea how much had been ripped away that day.

"Honey, I was just starting to figure out my own life when your dad died. I was so excited about a new start for all of us. I was thinking maybe I could go to school once we got to Delaware. After he died, I had no idea what to do. Sometimes I was so angry at the world, sometimes I was even angry at your father.

"I brought you and your brother to Lorida because I knew the man who owned the trailer, and he let me rent it without a security deposit. We could have ended up anywhere that didn't require a security deposit. I stayed in Lorida because I didn't have anywhere else to go. I felt like part of me died when your dad died. You did have somewhere to go, and I knew that. I should have told you that. I didn't know how to tell you to go without you thinking I didn't want you here. I felt unwanted in my own family, and I was more afraid you would think I didn't care, when I cared more than anything.

"I don't have a good relationship with my family, and I was trying so hard to avoid those mistakes that I made all new ones of my own. I wanted you to do all the things I could only dream of. The things I gave up on when your father died. I should have told you that. Maybe things would have turned out different.

"I should have said more about a lot of things. I spent a lot of years feeling so lost, just putting one foot in front of the other. Getting through days. I've spent a lot of time thinking about that. I'm still figuring out what to do about the life I had, the life I wanted, and the one I have."

I know it isn't a good time to ask, but I also know there will never be a good time. The last three days have made me realize that I can't wait any longer. That I've already missed years of opportunities. I want to know all about the things we never talked about. I want something real in place of all of my confusing memories. I don't trust any of my memories anymore.

"Can you tell me more about Daddy and his family?"

"What do you want to know?"

"I don't know. Just tell me about them. I don't know anything."

"Well, your dad's father, your grandfather, was a farmer and a painter. He sold his produce and paintings side-by-side at a roadside cart. I think he was originally from Mississippi, but I'm not certain. He lived most of his life in Georgia. He was a real nice man. Your grandmother, well, she was a piece of work."

"How so?"

"We all stopped talking when you were a baby because your grandmother got religion and said you and Michael were going to hell because you weren't properly baptized. She said she couldn't have anything to do with us if we didn't join her church and get baptized. You know how your father was. He didn't believe in all that."

"No, I don't know how he was. Not really," I say quietly.

"No, maybe you don't, and that is my fault. I thought maybe if we didn't talk about him, I could keep the pain of missing him off of you. You didn't get much of a chance to know him. He was a good man. He was a good father."

I want her to keep going. I want to hear more. I want to get to know both of them. I want to understand. I want to ask all the questions I've held inside for so long.

"Go on," I say.

"Anyhow, your father told your grandmother she wasn't acting like a true Christian. That was how he got that scar on his hairline. He spent the rest of his life waiting for an apology that never came. It hurt him dearly, his mother acting like that with him. I think your grandfather had long been the peacemaker, but after he died, she had no one to tell her to stop. They never spoke again. Your daddy was so hurt by what she did. That's why he never talked about it, and I guess I got in that habit, too. Then after he died, what was there to say? I was already in the habit of not talking about it."

"Is that why we never went to church?"

"Pretty much. Your daddy said he would rather pray to God on his own terms because he didn't trust how people used religion to hurt one another."

"And his mother didn't even come to Dad's funeral?"

"Oh, she came alright. I guess you don't remember that. She came and brought her own preacher man. He started trying to take over the service from Pastor Williams. As I said, we didn't go to church, but your father believed in God, and Pastor Williams and your dad were good friends. She started a big fuss. Eventually, a bunch of your dad's friends tried to remove them, not realizing it was his mother. She called them devils. She punched Pastor Williams's wife. It was by accident. She was swinging for me."

"All of my memories of that day are confusing." When I try and remember that day, it feels like a TV show I once watched, not like something I experienced.

"We got you out of there as fast as we could. I had one of our neighbors take you home until I could come get you. You didn't need to see all of that. It was bad enough you lost your daddy."

"I remember I kept asking what happened, and no one would tell me. I remember being taken away. I assumed it had something to do with me, that I had done something wrong. I kept crying, and I thought if I cried hard enough, you and Michael would know and would come back for me."

"Oh, baby." She reaches out, takes my hand, and starts crying. I squeeze back.

"Will you tell me more?"

We talk until visiting hours are over. We talk about her family and more about dad's family. We talk about my memories, and she confirms or corrects many of them. I didn't know daddy had a brother who died in the Korean War. Mom said that could have been what changed my grandmother, but she figured she had always been mean.

I also find out why she didn't like to talk about her family.

"My family never liked your father. They had some stupid idea that I would get back together with Michael's father. They might have learned to accept your dad if we had stayed, but I didn't want to stay. My sister had the nerve to tell me that Michael wouldn't get to know his father because of me. The bastard lived around there and had yet to meet him."

"So, we left. And started our life together. I thought I had all the time in the world. I thought that they would come around in time. If they could see what a good father he was to Michael, maybe they would see what I saw." She stops and asks me to hand her the water the nurse had left on the meal tray. She continues sadly, "Only I didn't have all the time in the world. Your grandmother died when I was eight months pregnant with you. We didn't think our car would survive the trip, and we couldn't risk breaking down. The doctor said I shouldn't fly or take the train. I was scared to take the bus by myself in my condition, and going all together would have meant taking your three-year-old brother on a trip that would take fourteen hours and two transfers. I didn't go to the funeral. I couldn't go."

"They never forgave me. They blamed your father for 'stealing me away,' but I was the one who had wanted to leave. I've tried to patch things up over the years, but there is too much anger, and no one wants to listen or forgive."

"Oh, Mom, why didn't you tell me all of this?"

"It hurt too much to talk about. When you left, I thought maybe it was something I was doing. Causing. I remember talking to your grandad, your dad's dad, about my family. He told me there were some painful branches in his own family tree. He said he finally grew to an age where he accepted his kinfolk as part of his past, but they weren't part of his present. That was his making, and he welcomed me as his daughter. I wish you had gotten a chance to know him."

We also talked about grief. She told me that she thought if she made her life small enough, she could hold onto what she had. She became overly cautious. She was afraid of being too close to anyone. She didn't want to lose anyone again. She had lost my father. And then she all but lost me. I had reinforced her fears instead of allaying them.

Mom found and released so much of the pain and resentment I had held for so long. I hoped I did the same for her. I could never admit it, but I resented my father for dying. I had resented my mother for not sharing her grief. For leaving me alone to figure out my own grief and never talking about Dad. I realize now she did the very best she could. I realize now she was only thirty-six when he died, only a few years older than I am now.

On the drive back to Mom's house, it dawns on me that I did the same thing after Morrison died. After I thought he died. I am still having trouble getting my head around him being alive. I also made my life small. Yes, I thought I was responsible, but like Mom, I didn't want to hurt anymore. I didn't want to get close to anyone again because to do that would be to lose them. I lost my dad. I lost Morrison. I had lost everyone I was ever close to. I had so much hurt and loss inside me. I thought if I lost anyone else I loved that it might finally break me for good. But Mom isn't broken, and neither am I. We both spent a long time hurting. I want that to be over for both of us.

I go home to Hairy and am drawn back to the cabinet with the photo albums. I pull out the shoebox I saw yesterday but avoided. Inside is the program for Dad's funeral, cards and letters, photos, and the obituary she wrote for him.

"Walker Frances Miller left us far too soon on Wednesday, September 22, 1976. Walker was born in Valdosta, GA, and graduated from Valdosta High School. He did not consider this a highlight of his life. He considered waking early and going out fishing with friends a highlight. He was proud of knowing every service center along the Florida Turnpike and would often stop to call home from the Okahumpka Service Plaza because the name made his wife laugh. He cherished letting his son pretend to drive sitting in his lap. He loved watching Gilligan's Island *with his beloved daughter and always rooted for the castaways to get off the island.*

He would want everyone to know that he hated avocados and loved a cold Jax beer on a hot day. He also had strong opinions about the placement of raisins in food (in cereal = good, cookies = disappointment, and potato salad = you're in league with the devil).

He is loved and missed by his wife, Penny Dean Miller, and his children Michael (12) and Michelle (8). He was just 41 years old."

I fall asleep in my clothes, the TV droning in the background. It's the first real sleep I've had since Michael called me in Atlanta.

CHAPTER 58

Morrison wants to meet at the park by City Pier in Sebring at 7:00 a.m. Hairy is confused when I jump up at 6:00 and start getting ready. I am about to walk out the door when I see his leash and decide to take him with me. He sticks his head out the window and barks at trees as we drive down Route 98 towards Sebring.

We park and walk down to the picnic benches by the small beach area. Hairy barks at a small flock of ibises, scattering them. Morrison is already there, sitting on top of one of the tables. He is wearing a baseball hat, a Pansy Division T-shirt, and lightweight pants with pockets everywhere. He is wearing a hearing aid in his left ear. He is a grown man, the skinny kid that has haunted my memories is long gone. His tan is deep, like he works outside. His still-young face looks prematurely worn and creased.

He gets up and walks over to us. He bends down and says, "Hello, Hairy."

Apparently, everyone knew Morrison was alive but me.

The sun is barely up, but it is already hard and bright. We duck back under one of the pavilions and sit on one of the picnic tables. Hairy settles at my feet, like he investigates suspicious deaths all the time.

Neither one of us is sure where to start.

"What do you think happened to Russ?" I ask.

"I don't know, but I think Sissy had something to do with it. I brought him up last night, and she got mad. She wanted to know why I was asking. Then the next thing I knew, she was consoling me, telling me it wasn't my fault. I wanted to talk to you before I confronted her directly. I wanted to know what she told you about what happened."

I tell him about the letters I wrote him and how one was returned. About calling the trailer. About the letter, Sissy wrote me with the newspaper clipping. About calling the police.

"Do you think she knows you suspect she had something to do with it?" I ask.

"I don't know. I got out of there before she was up this morning, so I didn't have to talk to her. She always knows when I am upset, and I didn't think I could hide this from her."

"I'm so sorry I wasn't here."

"I thought about that, too. You thought I was dead, so why would you write or call a dead man? I knew where you were and how to find you. I was grieving for Russ, and when I heard what you supposedly said, I was too ready to believe it. I should have trusted you. I should have written to you or talked to Michael. I believed it because that was how I felt about myself. I don't think I realized how much I hated myself. Sissy convinced me my fears were real, and I hated you for that. I should have contacted you, and everything would have been different. That is my fault, not yours."

I hadn't thought of it like that. I had accepted all the blame. At that moment, it hits me. Much of Sissy's power came from what we thought of ourselves. What she convinced us to hate about ourselves. We believed her because she voiced our worst fears. None of them were real. Worst of all, she knew exactly what she was doing.

"Can I ask you something? It has bothered me all these years. Last night brought a lot of things to the surface."

I nod.

"Did you tell on me about peeing in the golf bag?"

His question is so absurd and unexpected that I almost laugh. "No, of course not."

"Fuck. I'm so fucking stupid." Morrison gets up and starts pacing, causing the ibises to scatter again and Hairy to bark. "After I got fired, Sissy was right there for me. She asked me who else knew. I had only told you, and later, when we were hanging out, I had told her. She never said you told. She said other stuff that let me make that conclusion all on my own. Then after Russ died, I was sure of it. I thought you hated me that much. Oh, Sissy and I fucking hated you. It was this thing that bonded us. I should have seen it before. She was the one who told, then she fucking came to my rescue after I got fired. She set me up. Oh, god, Chelle, I'm so sorry."

He pulls off his baseball hat and runs his hands through his hair. It is shorter and a bit thinner, but it's still floppy.

He resettles on the bench, and I cautiously put my arm around his shoulder. We lean into each other. We still fit together in our adult bodies.

"What are we going to do?"

"I don't know. The cops were assholes last time. If they didn't care then, why would they care now? And they will know I lied when I said I was with Sissy. Who knows what she will tell them. They will believe her."

He glances down at his watch.

"Do you need to go?"

"Not just yet. I should leave by eight at the latest to get ready for this morning's trip."

"Where do you work?" It seems like such a mundane question, but I want something normal to cling to for a moment.

"I work for a place that does kayak rentals and tours and boat charters. I take people out on the lake or up the creeks. We do mid-week specials for retirees and schools. Normally, I don't get started until later on Sundays, but a group of Norwegian birdwatchers wants to go out this morning. There are a couple pairs of roseate spoonbills nesting on Arbuckle Creek."

There he is, the Morrison I have missed all these years. I want him to tell me all about the spoonbills. He catches me smiling at him and smiles back.

"How did you end up living with Sissy?"

"I was supposed to move in with Russ. I was going to quit school, get my GED, and get a job. I thought I could figure things out from there. I couldn't stay with my mom and fucking Travis. I had nowhere to go. Sissy took me in after Russ died. I was a wreck. I dropped out of school. There were weeks I didn't even leave the house. She made me think she was the only person in the world who cared about me. Eventually, we got our own place, and she got to live out her *Three's Company* fantasy, only there were only ever two of us because none of her relationships lasted. Most of the guys I met were weirded out by the situation. Or maybe it was Sissy they were weirded out by. How did I not see all of this before? I was so stupid."

"You and me both."

"She's a real estate agent, by the way. She specializes in timeshares and retiree coffin condos, as she calls them. She's good at it."

This makes perfect sense.

"How's your mom?" I ask.

"She died several years ago."

"I'm sorry. What happened?"

"Travis happened."

"Your mother's boyfriend?"

"Yeah. He was a heroin addict. He OD'd in 1990, but not before he gave her HIV. She died from pneumonia in 1996."

"I'm so sorry."

"It is what it is. What about you?"

"I live an exciting life as a medical records clerk. Oh, wait, maybe I don't anymore. I'm probably being fired as we speak. And before you ask, I didn't pee on anything." I can see how far I've come from my life in Atlanta in the last few days, though I'm still coming to terms with that. Atlanta now feels like a place I've been visiting for years.

"You seeing anyone?" he asks.

"Nah. I don't want to be with anyone. Romantically I mean. But I have moved on from Harry Anderson. I'm now in a threesome with Mulder and Scully."

"Seriously? No one? Why?"

"There is no why. This has always been me. It just took a little while for me to understand what I had always known."

"That makes sense."

We shift, and he moves his arm around my shoulder. I explain about Gladys Anderson and how she led me home.

We have been avoiding talking about Sissy. It's like old times. "Morrison, what are we going to do about Sissy?"

"I don't know. I mean, I can't see confronting her about Russ. What's she going to do, suddenly confess?"

"But we have to do something. . . ."

"I know."

He looks down at his watch again and says, "I'm sorry, Chelle, I need to get to work."

"It's okay. I need to get back to the hospital."

We walk to the parking lot and start going our separate ways.

"Please give your mom my best and tell her I will be by to see her soon."

He smiles at me, and I see the boy I once knew. I have no idea what to do with everything he told me, but I know I have to do something. He might not be ready to confront Sissy, but I am.

CHAPTER 59

Parked under a ficus tree in the hospital parking lot, I try and explain to Hairy that what we are about to do is probably illegal. He lets me wrap him in the thin blanket I brought from the house. I nestle him against my shoulder, and we dart across the parking lot and into the hospital.

The nurses don't think twice about a mother and her blanket-swaddled child entering the hospital. My mother, on the other hand, seems to think this is one revelation too many.

"Michelle?!"

I quietly close the door and flip back the blanket, revealing Hairy's toothy, happy face. Her smile is worth getting arrested for.

"How's my Hairy? Do you miss me?" He wriggles in my arms until he is free and kissing her face. She laughs and coos at him.

"Don't worry, Mom, I'm taking good care of him for you."

"He does tricks, you know. He knows how to tell you he is hungry."

"I don't think that is actually a trick."

"I think it is. He seems so proud of himself when he asks, and I give him a treat." His ears prick up at the word treat.

Michael and Rosalita arrive with lunch for everyone. We almost get caught when the nurse comes in to check on Mom, but I manage to throw Hairy and the blanket over my shoulder and pretend I am shushing him to sleep.

Michael, Rosie, Mom, and I are still laughing about baby Hairy when Sissy walks through the door. There is stunned silence. She is holding a cheap grocery store bouquet of flowers and goes over to my mother's bedside and air-kisses her. Hairy starts growling from underneath the sheet at Mom's feet.

"Michelle, why didn't you tell me your mom was in the hospital?" she says, zeroing in on me. It is hard to tell which is more fake—the smile or the teeth. Morrison, Mom, and Michael all look older, older than they should, but it looks like time stood still for Sissy.

I feel blood rushing to my face. Here she is, finally. This is my chance. I want to scream at her. I want to pummel her. I want to hurt her like she has hurt all of us. Instead, I am mute and immobile. She's still robbing me of my voice. I thought I could face her. I felt so strong last night.

Sissy places the flowers on the bedside table, knocking my mother's reading glasses to the floor. She is taking all of the air out of the room. I start to see spots in front of my eyes. I can hear her talking, but I am going under water. I feel like I am drowning.

And then Michael is standing next to me, and I feel him slip his arm around my shoulders. I think of that photo of us as kids and slip my arm around his waist and squeeze back. It brings me back to the surface. I gasp for air.

"What are you doing here?" Michael asks, stepping forward, so he is between Sissy and me.

"Mike, that's a ridiculous question. We're old friends. I was devastated to hear about your mother's health scare."

Michael tightens his grasp on my shoulder. I didn't realize what seeing her would do to me. I feel like I am seventeen again, weak and pathetic. Mom looks at me, and I feel ashamed.

"Sissy, it's good of you to visit, but now isn't a good time," Mom says, as she struggles to sit up. "I think it would be best if you go." She is trying to protect me. They both are. That, more than anything, snaps me out of Sissy's grip.

"Of course. Mrs. Miller, you just tell me if you need anything. I'm always here to help."

As Sissy walks toward the door, I say, "Please, give Morrison my best."

The shot lands. She turns. There *she* is. The real Sissy, the mask fallen. The stare. The eyes that hurt. My smile is as dead as hers.

I can hear the firecracker pop of her heels against the tile floor as she storms down the corridor toward the elevator.

"What a piece of work," Rosie says, breaking the stunned silence.

"I should have protected you from her. I never liked that girl," Mom says from the bed.

"It's all my fault," I say.

"I'm so sorry I listened to her," Michael says.

We are tripping over each other to try and dress the old wounds Sissy inflicted on each of us.

"*¡Ay, Dios mío!* Would you listen to yourselves?" We all turn to Rosie.

"Yes, yes, you need to fix things with one another, but your real problem just walked in here. Why?" she says. "Why did she come here? How did she even *know* to come here?"

Rosie is right. How *did* Sissy know I was here? Morrison was the only other person who knew where I was, but I can't imagine Morrison telling her. But what if he did? What if I am wrong about him? I've been wrong about everything else. How do I know he was telling me the truth this morning? Maybe he was just trying to find out what I knew so he could tell Sissy. I need to know why she showed up and what she wants.

I search my purse for change. Michael asks what I am doing, then he reaches into his pocket and hands me several quarters.

I walk out to the payphone in the waiting room and dial Morrison's number. It rings a few times.

"Hello?"

"Morrison, we need to talk."

"Yeah, we do. I just canceled my afternoon charter. I was going to come to the hospital to try and find you. Let's meet somewhere more private."

"Where?" I'm not sure I like the sounds of this.

"Can you meet me at the tree?"

I hesitate.

"Michelle?"

"Yes, yes, I will meet you there."

"Okay, give me thirty minutes."

I want to believe Morrison. And yet, something doesn't feel right. "Morrison, did you tell Sissy I was at the hospital?" I don't hear anything, and then there is a click, and the dial tone returns.

I sit down in one of the chairs near the phones, trying to collect my thoughts. What is going on? Sissy isn't what I remembered. She was electric and dynamic in my memories. The woman in the hospital room was petty and spiteful. That magnetism from our youth is gone. I hate this woman. My memories and new reality collide and ricochet off one another.

Of course, she is different than I remember. I am different than I remember. Why wouldn't she be? None of my memories from those years are right or true. The Sissy I remembered was larger than life. She was powerful, and I was weak. Just as she had made me into less than I was, I had made her into more than she was.

She's also far more dangerous than I realized. But enough is enough.

I'm back in control when I walk into Mom's hospital room. "Mom, I'm sorry about that. She won't ever bother you again."

I turn to Michael and say, "I need to leave. I need to talk to Morrison. I need to figure out how to deal with this—with her. Can you take Hairy home? I'm not sure when I'll be back."

He nods. This time he isn't angry with me for leaving. He's angry with Sissy. He now fully believes me about what happened.

"What are you going to do?" he asks.

I say I want to deal with Sissy, but I have no idea what that means. I have no idea how I am going to protect my family from her. Naively, I also want an apology. I want her to recognize and admit what she did. I don't know what I expect Morrison to do, but this all has to do with him, too, and I need to talk to him. The police didn't question Russ's death the first time, so why would they now? It is up to me to stop her from hurting anyone else.

"I don't know, but I now know what Sissy is capable of. I'm not going to let her hurt us anymore."

Michael hugs me, the first real hug I've had from him in years.

I am trying to stay calm, but there is real rage building. I'm trying not to listen to the susurrations of doubt saying that Morrison told Sissy I was at the hospital. As I drive out to Lorida, towards the tree, my fury grows. All of what I believed about myself had been Sissy's lies. I had spent my life unsure of who I was because I had believed her. I was never that person. That person doesn't even exist. I want that scared, confused teenage girl from the hospital to finally find some peace.

I thought I had let my best friend kill himself. I spent my life thinking I hurt people. That I was inherently bad and wrong. I second-guessed everything. I avoided being close to anyone, including my family. I didn't want to hurt anyone else.

There was *never* anything wrong with me. It was always Sissy who was wrong. She was always the monster. She is still the monster.

CHAPTER 60

I desperately want the air to move so I can breathe. The heat is smothering. It's claustrophobic. It makes it hard to think. It needs to rain. I know it will make everything more humid, but I want that brief moment when the rain starts and the heat stops. Maybe it will clear my head of the chaos I feel inside. Instead, the clouds keep building, adding to the sky's burden. I can see a dark curtain of rain to the west, well away from Lorida.

I park along the road and start walking down to the tree. I slap and kill flies, gnats, and mosquitoes with a vengeance. They are a substitute for Sissy. Slapping the Sissy-mosquitoes also means slapping myself. *Slap!* My skin burns as my palm hits sweaty flesh over and over again. I've completely lost the calm I had at the hospital. *Slap!* I don't know if I have ever been this angry before. *Slap!*

It's too hot to be this enraged.

I get to the tree ahead of Morrison. I look at what is left of the "stairs" on the tree and think about the tetanus shot question on the medical intake form. I walk towards the lake until the ground gets soft and mucky. I pace. I need to talk to him. We need to do something. What? Why did he want to meet here? This is no time for nostalgia.

I hear branches breaking underfoot and turn to look for Morrison. The woods are thick and green this time of year. Ferns grow high in spots, and the tree canopy is dense, creating deep shade, even at the height of day.

It isn't Morrison who appears in the clearing by the tree. It's Sissy. "What the hell are you doing here?" I demand.

"A better question would be, what the fuck are *you* doing here? You left, remember? You should have stayed gone."

Oh god, Morrison set me up. He sent her here. No one will see what is about to happen. I know in my gut something bad is coming. She isn't here to talk.

It doesn't matter. I need to do this on my own. I'm not frozen this time. I am still angry, but I am finally regaining some sense of control. I look at Sissy for the first time in fifteen years. I'm sizing her up for the first time since eleventh grade, and this time, I truly see her.

Sissy's wearing the pastel skirted suit and matching pumps she had on at the hospital. She looks utterly absurd in the woods. Her face is unnaturally tan. It looks too tight and is slightly off-kilter. The perm is gone, replaced by what looks to be a discarded wig from *Friends*. Her makeup is too heavy for this weather. Her French manicure is free of the hassles of housework. Fake boobs, new cheekbones. Staring at her now, I can see the façade. I can see how much of her is a manufactured persona. And I was wrong. Time hasn't stood still for her. She's spent fifteen years chasing it, trying to beat it into submission, but time has gotten in a few hits in too. Everything is a pretense. Nothing is real.

As if she can read my mind, she looks me up and down and says, "Wow, you haven't changed a bit. Poor thing, you haven't even gotten any new clothes."

"Why did you do all this?" I scream.

"Do what?"

"Hurt me. Ruin my life. We were supposed to be best friends."

"We were! That's what you don't get. Everything was perfect. We *were* best friends. I did everything for you. Nothing was ever enough for you. *You* were the one who hurt *me!* I never did anything but try and help you."

"What are you talking about? You undermined me constantly. You turned everyone against me!"

"How? That's ridiculous."

"No, it isn't."

"You were going to sneak away and leave. You ruined everything. You ruin everything you touch."

"You destroyed my life!"

"You did that, not me. Don't go blaming me for what you did."

"I thought I was a monster because of you."

"Aren't you? Maybe I just told you the truth you knew all along. Maybe everyone was better off without you. Nothing was ever enough for you. I wasn't enough. Morrison wasn't enough. Your family wasn't enough. You were a selfish bitch. You got what you deserved."

"What I wanted was perfectly normal. I was eighteen years old!" Why am I defending myself to her? I am being sucked into a fight that can't be won. I can feel her worming her way inside my head again, causing me to doubt myself. Was this all really because she didn't want me to leave her?

"You were so fucking selfish. Whatever you had, you threw away when you left." She smugly adds, "I never threw Morrison away like you did."

"I never threw him away. I never threw anyone away!"

The last few days have been revelatory for me, but she's known what she's done all along. She's not sorry in the slightest. She's never going to apologize. She truly sees herself as the victim.

I start lashing back. "You made me think I was worthless. I thought I deserved nothing, all because of you." I don't know why I want her to hear this. I know she isn't going to apologize. "But I was wrong. I was wrong about everything. I was wrong about myself, but more importantly, I was wrong about you."

"You don't know anything about me," Sissy growls.

"I know more than you think. I know about Jessica."

"What do you *think* you know?"

"Your mother told me what you did to her."

"Oh, you mean how I called 911 and tried to save her?"

"I know you hid the needles, and that is why she died."

"You know what my mother wants to believe. The truth, the actual truth, is that Jessica died for no good reason. For the stupidest of all fucking reasons. I was a little kid, and I did something stupid, and Jessica died. She was the only person who ever gave a fuck about me." For once, Sissy's emotions seem genuine.

"Do you want to know what happened? *What really happened?* I had seen an episode of *Scooby-Doo* where they had voodoo dolls. Imagine being scared by *Scooby-Doo* and taking it seriously! Oh, but I did. There was a girl in school who had been teasing me relentlessly. No one listened. No one cared. My mother told me I was making unnecessary drama, and the girl just wanted to be friends. So, I made a fucking voodoo doll of the girl. I couldn't find any pins, but I knew where we kept the syringes. They just sat there. We had never had to use them. I was going to put them back. Only the needles all bent when I stuck them in the doll. I hid them. I assumed my mother would notice and replace them. I didn't want to get in trouble.

"After Jessica died, I told my mother what really happened. She couldn't accept that Jessica died for such a stupid reason, so she blamed me. She told me it was all my fault." Sissy's voice begins to waver, "She never let me forget that Jessica died because of me. I wished she had gone in the house for the needles because she would have known what to do. Instead, she insisted it was deliberate that I had killed her. It was just a stupid accident." For all of Sissy's lies, this feels like the truth. I can't believe I am starting to feel sorry for her.

"You could have told me all that," I say sadly, "when we were friends. I would have believed you."

"You honestly think I would've trusted you?!" Sissy scoffs. "All you do is lie and hide."

"Not anymore."

I start to feel doubts creeping in. Maybe this isn't all Sissy's fault. What if I got it wrong yet again? What she did to my family and me was heinous, but what about Russ? Maybe I was too ready to believe what Morrison told me. What if that was an accident too? Or worse, what if he was lying? What if Morrison had something to do with Russ's death? Morrison isn't here, and Sissy is. Why? Is he intentionally pitting Sissy and me against each other? To what end?

That's when I catch a glimpse of Morrison running toward us through the woods. I pray he is on my side. What if he isn't? Two against one. I'll never make it out of here.

Morrison jogs into the clearing. He looks at both of us, and I can't read his face. I spot a small gun tucked into the side of his pants as he approaches. I realize I am holding my breath, waiting to see what he is going to do. Sissy is also waiting.

I start backing up as he walks towards me.

"I'm sorry I'm late, Chelle."

He turns and stands beside me and faces Sissy.

I am so relieved. He didn't set me up. Sissy is furious when she sees him with me. She is starting to lose control. Morrison and I are finally in control. "Sissy, what did you do to Russ? I have to know," he demands.

She starts laughing at him—until he draws the gun from his waistband and points it at her.

"You fucker!" she screams. "I tore the house apart looking for that."

I don't know what I had expected to happen, but this has gotten dangerous fast.

"Sissy, tell us what happened to Russ," I say.

She looks back and forth between Morrison and the gun and turns to me.

"Morrison lied to me about Russ, just like you lied about college. He was also going to leave. This is all your fault. If you'd stayed, Morrison would have stayed, and Russ would never have died. Morrison, she is responsible for all of this, you see that right?"

"No, I don't see that," Morrison says. There is such sorrow in his face. I'm here confronting a mental boogieman, one of my own making, but Morrison is confronting his best friend. His best friend who killed his first love. His best friend who destroyed our friendship. His best friend who has controlled his whole adult life.

"You two were so fucking stupid. You know that letter you sent Morrison about how wonderful your life at school was? Morrison's slut of a mother dropped it off, and I read it. I burned most of the pages, aside from the ones I needed to for my letters. Your hand-writing was so easy to fake. I put the new letter back in the envelope and gave it to him. Morrison was so pissed when you told him, almost as an afterthought, that it was too bad Russ was dead, but you were having too much fun at school with all your new friends to come home. Oh, how did you know about Russ dying? Morrison was too pathetic to leave the house, so I graciously offered to mail his letter to you. He poured his little broken heart out to you. *Such a drama queen.*"

Sissy is smiling. She is proud of what she did. The horror of it all is washing over us.

"He never questioned what you wrote, or rather what you didn't write. He must never have trusted you, or he wouldn't have believed me when I told him all the awful things you said about him when he wasn't around."

"You did that, not Michelle!" he yells at her, shooting me a pained look.

But Sissy isn't stopping.

"And you, you stupid bitch? You totally believed he was dead. So much for that college education. Didn't you even have a quarter for a phone call? You're both so fucking stupid. The best part is that it was going to be a practical joke. You two assholes were the ones who managed to keep it going all this time. All you had to do was make a phone call or come home or show up for Christmas, and this would've all been over. *Fucking losers.*"

I realize with disgust that she is right. All I had to do was come home and see my family. All I had to do was mention Morrison to my brother and how much I'd missed him since he died. I never talked about Morrison. He was the pain I carried that I wouldn't let anyone see. My mother never talked about my father, and I never talked about Morrison. Carrying that pain alone had only made it grow. I had imprisoned myself. So had Morrison.

"Your brother turned me down one night. I made him pay for that. It was so easy to get him to hate you. I insinuated a few things, and you did the rest. He was so ready to believe me. When I needed a car, I would call him. I told him I wanted to help him out since he was here, *all alone with your mother*. I could see the disgust on his face, and it was all directed at you. It took so very little to get him to hate you.

"You didn't deserve what you had, so I took it away. No more mother, no more brother, no more best friend, no more home. I would have taken that ridiculous scholarship away if I could have. Seriously, what was it about flailing around in the water that made you so fucking special?"

In a flash, I remember the fight we had right after we met when she demeaned me for swimming. Now, like then, it triggers something. That had been my chance to get away from her. That should have been the fight that ended our friendship. For a split second, I had seen her for who she was that day, but she had confused me with that story about her sister dying.

I wasn't an easily confused teenager anymore. I was going to get away this time.

"If you're so clever and special, what are you doing here? Why are you still chasing after us? Don't you have any other friends? You don't, do you? You never did. Sissy, no one wants you, not us, not even your own parents."

I know I've gone too far.

Sissy looks savage. She scans the ground. She spots a broken branch from a live oak and grabs it. I can tell from how she is holding it that the wood is dense and heavy.

Morrison laughs, thinking she can't be serious. He's pointing the gun at her, but he still sees his friend. He has spent too many years with her. He doesn't see what I see. I can see the look on her face. This isn't a game.

She comes toward us, and I flinch and back away, assuming she's coming for me. She isn't. She is going for Morrison. She's going for the gun.

That catches us both off guard. The first swing knocks the gun from his hand. The second one catches him at his temple, and he crumples. She scrambles through the mud and ferns, looking for the gun. I know if she finds it, we're done. I rush over and tackle her as she gets her hand around the grip.

"Fucking bitch," she screams as we wrestle.

"Stop, Sissy! Don't do this!"

We're fighting for the gun, rolling into the dense underbrush, thorns pricking my back and arms as we tumble. I know it is over when she shoves the barrel against my side and pulls the trigger. I expect noise and pain, but all I hear are soft clicks. Frustration causes her to jab the gun into my ribs harder and harder with every ineffective click.

I roll away and jump up, adrenaline taking over. I have nothing to defend myself with, but I remember the woods. I begin to run, dodging tree limbs, crushing ferns underfoot. Thunder rumbles in the distance.

She drops the gun in frustration, grabs the tree branch she used on Morrison, and begins chasing after me. She only looks like she is in good shape. It is all plastic surgery and no muscle tone. I'm easily able to outrun her. Should I try and get to the car and go for help? What will she do to Morrison if I leave?

I turn back to look for her and trip over some cypress knees, landing on top of them. The air is knocked out of me. Did I break my ribs? I am gasping for air, but it hurts to breathe.

I'm close to the water's edge. Sissy is upon me in seconds, and I scramble up, clumsily jumping over a log. Sissy chases after me, swinging the branch at me, and the log moves.

Sissy stops when the log raises its head and slams her with its tail. It's an alligator. Sissy goes flying and lands with a thud. The alligator slides into the dark water.

The gator could have easily grabbed Sissy and pulled her under the water. I wish real life was like the movies. If this were *Lake Placid* or *Frogs*, she'd be dead already. But the alligator wants no part of our drama. It's far less dangerous than Sissy right now.

Sissy is still on the ground. I look around for something to defend myself with, but the branches I find are too large or rotten. I see a broken stick at the water's edge. My hands slide in the fetid mud, and I can't get a tight grip. My chest hurts so bad. I get up and start moving, angling to get back to Morrison so I can check on him. I tell myself she can't have killed him. That she didn't hit him that hard. That everything will be okay.

Sissy is up again and coming for me. Neither of us is moving as fast as we were. I dodge around and back down to the water, hoping there might be another alligator, one a bit more willing to eat her. She hesitates but follows. The sun is getting low, making long shadows dance in the trees.

I catch sight of Morrison. He is leaning against the tree, throwing up. There is blood streaming down the side of his face. I know this can't go on forever. Maybe I can tire her out, and Morrison will be able to help me fight her off.

I lead her away from him and back near the edge of the lake. She's covered in muck and has lost both of her shoes, but that isn't stopping her. I see a muddy patch free of cypress trees and roots and head towards that. Sissy isn't tiring. She is gaining on me. I run across the muck as fast as I can. I feel my feet sliding under me, and for a moment, I feel like I am falling backward. I propel myself forward, trying to get out of the sludge before I fall. But I can feel myself starting to sink as I tumble forward onto a dry patch of ground. Sissy is right behind me. I can't get up fast enough. I throw my arms up and brace myself for the blow.

Then I hear a wet sucking noise, and she is gone. So is the patch of mud. A sinkhole is opening up along the water's edge, pulling dirt and small plants into its maw.

I feel the ground around me starting to give way and scramble back towards the clearing. I can hear water beginning to fill the hole. I can't hear Sissy.

I go back to Morrison and find him unconscious again. I shake him, and he opens his eyes. He looks confused.

"Come on, we gotta get out of here."

Somewhere beneath us, in the dark, is Sissy. For once, I don't hear her voice. There is only the usual frog, bird, and insect song at dusk and the sound of Morrison and me leaving the woods.

EPILOGUE

I could say that a giant alligator killed my best friend. Or a sinkhole. But, like the train, neither of those would be true.

Morrison and I limped out of the woods. It had started drizzling, but the storm missed us. He called 911 on his cell phone. By the time we reached our cars, there was a state trooper pulling up.

I started to explain but kept stopping to hold my side and catch my breath. The officer looked at us and called for an ambulance. Morrison eventually filled in the pieces I had missed.

Sissy had sensed something was wrong the night before. When he left early for work, she followed him. She saw us meet at the park and then followed me to the hospital. He didn't know all of this until Sissy called him, screaming at him from the hospital parking lot. I called him a few minutes later, asking to meet. Sissy had been waiting outside and followed me. She didn't know for certain but suspected we would want to meet after her performance in the hospital room. Morrison suggested the tree because only he and I knew where it was. Sissy had never been there. He wanted somewhere we could talk privately. He didn't expect her to follow me.

Morrison saw her car when he pulled up and got down to the tree as fast as he could. After their conversation the night before, he had found her gun and had put it in his truck. He hadn't trusted her. When he saw her car, he thought it might be useful. He didn't like guns and had thought it would be safer without the bullets. They were still in his cup holder.

I had two cracked ribs from my fall, and Morrison had a concussion. He was admitted for observation overnight. He was on the floor above my mother's room. With any luck, the doctor said, they would both be discharged the following day.

Later we were told that the recent rains and weight of us running across the thin layer of dirt and limestone must have caused the sinkhole to open. It took a little while, but they got Sissy out of the pit. It was a relatively small sinkhole, but enough to trap her. It was only about four feet deep, and water filled the hole as she struggled and screamed. Sissy was alive and raging like she had rabies. She was covered in filth and more than a few leeches, screaming at anyone who would listen that everything was our fault and that we had tried to kill her. She had broken her arm and twisted her ankle in the fall.

Morrison and I accused her of attempted murder, and she said the same about us. It was looking like the cops were going to charge all of us when they found a stash of cocaine in Sissy's car. That was enough to hold her and start to tip things in our favor.

Cecilia—I can't call her Sissy anymore—was in jail.

By Florida standards, her attack on us was barely enough to get her charged, let alone sent to prison. But then Morrison told the police that he suspected Cecilia of killing Russ. There was a new chief of police, and when she reviewed the original file, she saw how the original detectives had mishandled the investigation. She made a point to reopen the case. Bill Collins, a well-regarded Palm Beach attorney, saw an article about the case and contacted the Sebring police. It turned out that Willy Wonky led a secret double life as a lawyer.

Bill had always wondered about what had happened to Russ. Something hadn't sat right with him at the time. He said a woman had called Roman's a few times looking for Russ. She had called the day before he was killed. He said he now believed it had been Cecilia. Bill helped arrange a more thorough review of the autopsy files, which revealed defensive injuries on Russ's hands. The train had covered whatever she had done to kill him. It had probably been blunt force trauma, which was why it had been easy to blame the train and close the case.

Sissy was held on two charges of assault in the first degree and possession of a controlled substance while they gathered evidence to bring to the grand jury regarding Russ's death. The prosecutor also wanted to charge her with attempted murder. The judge denied bail. The grand jury agreed there was enough evidence to bring a charge of first-degree murder, attempted murder, and first-degree assault.

She'll go to trial in five weeks. Morrison and I will be testifying against her. I think about Jessica's accident and wonder if Cecilia's mother accused her of being a killer so often that she made her into one.

Morrison moved out of Cecilia's house; it was all in her name. So was his pickup truck. For now, he's staying with Mom and me. He has the spare bedroom, and I share the couch with Hairy.

I've decided to stay in Lorida for a little while. At least until the trial is over. Mom needs some help while she recovers. I have nothing to return to in Atlanta. Here I have a chance to start over, to become the person I was supposed to be. To finally explore my place in the world now that I've realized I deserve one. I'll never get those years back, but the lost, monstrous girl I thought I was has found peace.

I realized too late, just like Dorothy, that I had the power to stop Sissy all along. Her abuse didn't end at the bottom of the sinkhole. It stopped when I quit letting her have power over me, when I saw her abuse for what it was. But I can't help myself: I still think about crushing the snake egg and saving Dad. I also imagine myself walking away from Sissy after that first fight and saving my sixteen-year-old self. Whatever her mother did to her doesn't excuse what she did to Russ, to all of us.

I've spent the last month thinking about who I was and who I am. I'm a daughter, sister, best friend, and in January, I'll be an aunt. But that is who I am to other people. I am Michelle Ann Miller. Anne is gone. She never really existed. I am that beautiful girl in the photos.

I like to swim. I am a reformed liar. I have a degree in English, with honors, that I once didn't feel like I deserved to have or use. I want to see the Grand Canyon and buy my own souvenir spoon. I belong here, with my family, but I also belong to other places, places I haven't yet discovered.

I now know what it is like to swim out past the horizon and what it takes to get back to shore. I'm done living in the void.

This is my second chance at everything. It's Morrison's second chance, too. He says he wants to become a park ranger. He wants to go to school for environmental science. He wants to move past what happened, whatever that means for him. Still, I wonder how much damage Sissy has done to him beyond what I already know. I hear him at night. I know he has nightmares, too.

"Hey, Chelle," Morrison says as he comes in the door from work. Michael was able to get Morrison a cheap car at an auction, so he didn't lose his job, as well. They've been working on it together to get it past inspection.

"I was thinking," I say as I get up and head to the fridge.

"Yeah?"

"Let's go to the tree."

"Seriously? You want to go back there?"

"Yeah. She's ruined enough. She's not ruining that, too."

We get into Morrison's car and park along the highway and walk down through the woods. Stoner Couch is nothing but rusty springs and a few pieces of wood.

We cautiously climb into the tree, some of the boards little more than nails and dust now, and look out at the lake. It is hot, but there is a breeze pushing the air around.

"Are you ever going to tell me what the F stands for in your middle name?" I ask.

Morrison looks at me and says, "You met Joy. What do you think it stands for?"

For a minute, the only F word that springs to mind is, well, the F word. Then I remember Joy. Joy, who loved Morrison, but who never grew up. Joy, who was forever stuck in 1969.

"Oh god, it's Flower, isn't it?"

"Yep."

We sit a second, and the giggle in my chest fights its way out. Then Morrison starts laughing. It is everything I have yearned for and missed for the last fifteen years.

"Do you remember how I showed you that owl was a dove?" he asks then.

"Yeah."

"Doves don't pretend to be owls, but they can sound like them. Looking at a dove as it coos and still insisting it is an owl is the problem. I think I always knew something was wrong. I'd get glimpses, but I couldn't see things clearly. I trusted what she said, not what she did. Not what I felt. I was never sure what to believe."

I know what he means.

I reach into my purse and hand Morrison a warm Sprite. "Do you remember Celebration Saturday?"

"What?"

"When we went to the bar in West Palm. It was the night you first met Russ, right?"

"Of course."

"I've spent the last fifteen years grieving for Russ, even if I didn't know it. I thought it might be nice to recognize him tonight. To celebrate him, and maybe you could tell me about him since I never got to know him." I lean over and clink bottles with him. I'm learning to talk again.

We talk about little stuff at first, but eventually, he tells me about Russell Dearborn, who died on Friday, September 26, 1986. About how much he loved him and how much it still hurts. Russell was in school for business, but he wanted to be involved in music or film. He mixed Tang and Mountain Dew and called it rocket fuel. He loved the Fine Young Cannibals. He wanted to travel. He had a pet lizard. He was just twenty-one when he died.

We remember Russ and all that was lost, all that Sissy took away, until the breeze drops with the sun and the mosquitoes chase us back home.

ACKNOWLEDGMENTS

To start, I want to thank you, dear reader. I genuinely appreciate you even just perusing *Sinkhole*. You should know that there were a lot of people who made this book possible. First, I want to thank the whole University of New Orleans staff. I couldn't have dreamed of a better home for *Sinkhole*. Thanks to GK Darby, who heard the worst pitch in the history of pitches and, despite that, asked to see the manuscript. Abram Himelstein, who saw something in the first draft, which was undeniably rough. Huge thanks to editor Chelsey Shannon who provided expert guidance and helped bring these characters to life. Thanks to Alex Dimeff for a fantastic cover and fixing my grammatical missteps. Thanks to Christian Stenico for finding even more missteps and for determining that the plural of Sleestak is, in fact, Sleestak.

Thanks to Kaye Publicity, Dana Kaye, Jordan Brown, and Julia Borcherts, for taking a chance on a debut novel.

Thanks to Airboat Wildlife Adventures for enabling me to see, feel, and smell Lake Istokpoga (that's it on the cover). And to The Sebring Historical Society, especially Ingrid D. Utech, for allowing me access to newspapers, yearbooks, and local history, providing details, I may have otherwise missed.

Huge thank-yous to Aj Michel, Alicia Catlos, Ali Seay, Barbara Taylor, Billy McKay, Cyndy Twoys, Julie Dorn, Marianne Bohr, and who read various drafts. Special thanks to Donny Smith, who sent his reactions in real-time, allowing me to get a sense of the pacing, and Meredith Babb, who told me to quit rushing. And to Brad Bertelli, who said I needed more lovebugs. Thanks to DB Pedlar, who has been encouraging me (and many other writers) for decades. A huge thanks to John Mutter for our Samovar writers' group (RIP BEA).

Thanks to my zine friends for cheering me on over the last few years. Special thanks to Aj Michel for being a sounding board and good friend throughout this process. Thanks to Jeff Somers, Ayun Halliday, Liz Mason, Kathy Moseley, and Gavin Grant for their early support.

Thanks to Marianne Bohr for being a publishing mentor and writing friend. Thanks to Jeanne Kramer for being a publishing mentor. Thanks to Christine Taylor for being the first person to pre-order a copy. Jan Buckner for always knowing the right things to say.

Thank you to my JHUP family. Thanks to Barbara Kline Pope for always being supportive. Thanks to Kelly Rogers for offering to help with rights, Kathryn Marguy for the publicity advice, Heidi Vincent for the marketing advice, Alicia Catlos for the dependable absurdity, and Erik Smist, who has supported my eccentricities from the start. Thanks to the HFS team for making sure books get where they need to be. Thanks to Paul Peroutka and Malcolm Wallace for helping with all the packages.

Thanks to Richard Montgomery for the author photos. He refused payment and instead allowed me to donate to Wide Angle Youth Media (www.wideanglemedia.org).

I want to thank my canine companions, Alex George and Vera, who were with me for just about every page. It is also fair to thank Writers' Tears (a fine Irish whiskey), Café Bustelo, my bathrobe, and all sorts of potato chips, each of which was integral to the process.

Finally, thank you to Jan, Earl, Patrick, and Garnet. I don't have the words to thank them enough for their support and encouragement. I am also grateful to Jan for teaching me to never leave the house without at least one book and introducing me to bookselling. I am especially thankful to Patrick for his patience, brainstorming, and advice. He helped me work through some difficult scenes on our pandemic walks. His unwavering support makes everything possible.